APPLE ANNIE
& THE DUDE

PETER S. FISCHER

www.petersfischer.com

Also By Peter S. Fischer
Me and Murder, She Wrote
Expendable: A Tale of Love and War
The Blood of Tyrants
The Terror of Tyrants

The Hollywood Murder Mystery Series
Jezebel in Blue Satin
We Don't Need No Stinking Badges
Love Has Nothing to Do With It
Everybody Wants an Oscar
The Unkindness of Strangers
Nice Guys Finish Dead
Pray For Us Sinners
Has Anybody Here Seen Wyckham
Eyewitness to Murder
A Deadly Shoot in Texas
Everybody Lets Rock
A Touch of Homicide
Some Like 'Em Dead
Dead Men Pay No Debts
Apple Annie and the Dude
...and coming soon!
Dead and Buried
Cue The Crows
Murder Aboard The Highland Rose
Ashes to Ashes
The Case of the Shaggy Stalker

Apple Annie and the Dude Copyright © 2017 by Peter S. Fischer

All rights reserved. Except as permitted under the U.S. Copyright Act of 1976, no part of this publication may be reproduced, distributed or transmitted in any form or by any means, or stored in a database or retrieval system, without prior written permission of the publisher. The characters and events in this book are fictitious. Any similarity to persons living or dead is coincidental and not intended by the author. However, certain events and passages, including dialogue, may involve or refer to celebrities well known to the public in the year 1961. All of these are fictional as well.

ISBN 978-1974268290

To my wife, Lucille...
Ever cheerful, ever faithful, ever supportive
and ever loving.

PROLOGUE

Jillian Marx is dead.

The woman who bore my only child died three days ago of heart failure. It was a blessing. Stricken three years ago with an incurable form of cancer, she managed to keep her condition from us until almost the last moment when her body started to quit on her. Unable to stand she retreated to her favorite easy chair. When that became a burden, she took to her bed. On Monday evening my daughter Yvette and I had joined her in her bedroom where Jill read aloud from Yvette's favorite book. Sometime in the early hours of January 10, 1961, Jill left us. When we found her the next morning her face was calm and at peace. She was forty six years old.

The obituary in the *Los Angles Times* described her as a well-known author of much beloved children's books, unmarried yet leaving behind a daughter, Yvette, age eight. Jill was also described as a humanitarian activist and philanthropist. Yes, she was that but she was also so much more.

I met her in 1951 when my on-again off-again relationship with Bunny Lesher, now my wife, was at an all-time low. My ex-wife Lydia and her new husband Mick Clausen tried to put us together on a blind date but I wriggled out of it. Bunny and I had just split and even though she was permanently in New York and I was chained to Los Angeles, it was too soon for me to get involved even casually with another woman. I hadn't counted on Jill's doggedness. It started with lunch and progressed from there. I made it clear from the beginning that I was only interested in good times and good sex and she agreed wholeheartedly. I hadn't yet learned that this is a posture many women take while reeling in the catch ever so slightly, one romantic interlude at a time. Finally Jill realized I meant what I said and abruptly changed the rules. While I was in Canada working on Hitchcock's "I Confess" she flew into Quebec City to inform me that she was pregnant, thanked me for all I had done for her and let me know in no uncertain terms that she had no use for a husband or for a father for her child.

It took almost a year for us to come to terms with one another but in the end, I became kindly Uncle Joe with visitation rights almost any time I wished. But I was not Daddy and I was no longer a bed partner. I accepted both conditions since they afforded me unfettered access to my little girl. Twice Jill flew off to the Mayo Clinic in Rochester, Minnesota. Twice she came back telling me there was nothing wrong except for low grade anemia which was treatable. But as she continued to lose weight and her energy level dropped severely, it was obvious something else was in play. Mayo refused me any details of her condition. After all, who was I? An old boyfriend? Her condition remained secret until three months ago when she collapsed walking up the steps to her front door. Then and only then did we learn the truth. She had only weeks to live. I was heartsick and I was furious. Heartsick that we were going to lose her, furious that she had done nothing to save her own life. She had taken my hand and gripped it tightly and told me that she had no interest in spending the final days of her life, bald, frail and puking her guts out from the effects of chemotherapy. One of her closest friends had opted for aggressive treatment and the last fifteen months of her life had been a living hell. Not for me, Jill had said. Quality of life was far more important than longevity and so she'd subsisted on pain pills, active and clear-headed, awaiting the inevitable. I had always marveled at how quickly Jill had accepted Bunny into her life and now, looking back, it's obvious what she had done. Yvette was going to need a mother and Bunny had all the qualifications. Every event was a family outing whether it was a trip to the beach or a picnic in the park, we were a foursome. Unselfishly, Jill was preparing the way for the years to come in her daughter's life. Now I am standing at an open grave at the Beth Israel Cemetery, staring at the mahogany coffin which will soon be lowered permitting Jill Marx eternal rest. Yvette is standing between me and Bunny and while her brain has told her what has happened, the full import has yet to hit her. I've been told it may take months for her to come to grips with the new reality of her life. A rabbi is intoning a prayer for the dead while those of us who loved her can only look on sadly, some like Bridget O'Shaughnessy weeping openly, others like myself holding it inside as best we can. There is a basket of white lilies next to the gravesite and when the rabbi finishes his prayer, he nods to me. Stepping forward, holding Yvette by the hand, I take a single lily and place it atop the coffin. Yvette follows suit as does Bunny who is right behind us. Several minutes later the coffin is covered with flowers and then is slowly lowered into the earth. We turn and head back to our car. Soon all of us who loved her will be back at Jill's house on Franklin Avenue, drinking and eating and celebrating a very special life that had touched us all.

CHAPTER ONE

Seven weeks have passed since we laid Jill to rest. We have been living in Jill's house on Franklin Avenue so as not to disturb Yvette's routine but we can't keep it up forever. Bunny and I have a house of our own in Van Nuys, modest to be sure. I have lived there comfortably for thirteen years and I'm on a first name basis with all my neighbors but uprooting Yvette from the only home she has ever known doesn't seem to be a very bright idea. Besides, there is Bridget to consider. Bridget O'Shaugnessey has been caring for Yvette since she was brought home from the hospital eight years ago and is like a beloved grandmother to her. No question. Where we go Bridget goes. The more Bunny and I bat this around, the more likely it becomes we will either stay here or we will sell both houses and start over again in new digs, the four of us.

My partner, Bertha Bowles, has just returned from New York City and she is an unhappy lady. The temperature was in the teens and the snow in Times Square was a foot deep. Nothing paralyzes Gotham like a good snowstorm and this past week was no exception. To make matters worse she was unable to convince Piper Laurie to let us handle her career which Bertha says is about to burst forth like a rose bush in April. Hot off a brilliant performance on TV opposite Cliff Robertson in "Days of Wines and

Roses", she has been signed to play the female lead opposite Paul Newman in Robert Rossen's "The Hustler" which has just started shooting in and around the streets of New York.

"I loved her in 'Son of Ali Baba' with Tony Curtis," I say to Bertha, referencing one of the many throwaway parts she's been playing for the past eleven years in a career that was going nowhere.

"You missed the television show so keep your ignorant opinions to yourself, partner," she says.

"Okay, I misspoke," I say. "Actually I liked her better in 'Francis Goes to the Races'."

Bertha glares at me as only Bertha can glare and decides to ignore my gaucherie.

"The good news is that Rossen is interested in having us publicize the picture. I said I thought it was a wonderful idea but of course, I couldn't speak for you."

"And a good thing you didn't, Bert," I say. "New York City in the dead of winter? I'd rather undergo a root canal. In my younger years I endured enough snow in Oklahoma and Texas to claim heritage as an Eskimo. Send one of the kids."

"They don't want one of the kids, they want you," Bertha says.

The "kids" are our staff of youngsters, mostly mid to late 20's and employed by us as junior managers and assistant publicists. They will learn enough from us to strike out on their own some day. In fact one of them already has and is thriving.

"They're not getting me, Bert, and it's not just the lousy weather, it's Yvette."

She nods in understanding.

"Point taken," she says, knowing I'd rather stick around L.A. for the next several months until my personal life can sort itself out.

"Besides I'm still working on Walt Woods' picture," I say.

"Which is damned near pro bono," she growls.

"It's only part time. Anyway, they're on a strict budget."

"Doesn't mean they're penniless," Walter Wood, a good friend from the war years in Europe, is producing his first movie, a low budget true story of a priest who worked to solve the gang problem in St. Louis. It's called 'The Hoodlum Priest' and stars Don Murray and features a lot of people I've never heard of. Wood had befriended me in London when I was assigned by Stars and Stripes to do a feature interview on General Eisenhower in the spring of '44 shortly before the invasion. Wood, who was on Ike's staff, opened a lot of doors for me and helped me shake a few very important hands. I've always been grateful for his kindness and I see in this minor involvement, a chance to repay a mighty big favor.

"And how long are you going to keep up this Santa Claus routine?"

"Not long. They're going to release in about a month. After that I'm finished."

"Then how about if I get Rossen to accept Gay Summers with the caveat that you'll take over when the weather clears, say in April or May."

"Fine with me," I say.

As I head back to my office and a much needed respite from Bertha's browbeating, I suddenly remember what kind of a picture I've just signed onto. It's about pool and Paul Newman is playing a not very likable character named Fast Eddie Felson who is a loser and a double crosser. Piper Laurie's character gets raped by a first class creep named Bert and then commits suicide. Yeah, I can see that this dreary downer is going to play really big in the nabes.

I walk into my anteroom, bestowing a smile and a cheery hello on my beautiful secretary, Glenda Mae Brown. She holds up a pink telephone slip in her right hand which she waggles with a knowing smile.

"A sultry voice with a breathless quality. She left a phone number but no name. She said to remind you of a Fourth of July underneath the Malibu Pier where some of the fireworks weren't on public display."

I snatch the slip from her outstretched fingers "This one I'll dial myself, gorgeous," I say as I stride into my private office and forcefully close the door.

Three rings and then:

"Hi, good lookin'," she says when she comes on the line.

"If that's an attempt to seduce me, babe, you're out of luck. I'm married," I tell her.

"So I hear," she sighs. "The pool keeps getting smaller and smaller."

Lila James is one terrific lady and for a short time nine years ago we couldn't keep our hands off each other. I was drumbeating for Jack Warner and she was an up and coming junior copywriter for RKO's publicity department. Bunny had disappeared from my life and I was determined to see that she stayed that way. Eventually Lila saw through my futile attempt to extinguish my ten-foot tall Bunny torch and moved on to more promising husband material but it was a wild ride while it lasted.

"You can't still be looking, Lila, a classy knockout like you," I say.

"I'm done with it, Joe," she says. "I caught two of them and threw them both back. One was a lazy boozer and the other was a mama's boy. I zipped past 35 in November and decided to stop looking for the three kids and the white picket fence. For the time being I'm just a fun-loving gal about town and very choosy about who I bat my eyes at."

"As long as you're happy, Lila," I say.

"Immensely so, Joe, and I want to celebrate. How about lunch?"

"Sure. I'm free. Name it."

"The Paramount commissary."

"And why the Paramount commissary?"

"It's a surprise. Twelve-thirty. I'll leave your name at the gate."

At 12:20 I turn into the main gate of Paramount Studios on

Melrose Avenue. It's been at least a year but Benny, the security guard, gives me a smile and a long-time-no-see and tells me to park in Bing Crosby's parking spot since der Bingle is in England shooting another Road picture with Bob Hope. I thank him and pull up within twenty yards of the commissary entrance.

From what I can see, Lila hasn't changed much from that 27 year old laugh-a-minute free spirit I so well remember. Her ash blonde hair is now a lustrous auburn and when she gets up from her chair and I hug her tight I have a feeling she's had some work done in all the right places. Aside from that, her face is unlined and her smile is still worth a million bucks.

We banter for a few minutes while we're tossing back a couple of beers.

"So," she says, "what's going on with your screenplay?"

"Ouch," I wince.

"That bad? I heard MGM was looking at it."

"They passed."

With the help of a talented director named Stuartv Rosenberg I have turned my first and only novel, "A Family of Strangers", into a screenplay. A modest best seller as a novel the script has gotten a lot of compliments but no studio is willing to commit. Stu, who bought the option, is not discouraged. There are dozens of ways to get this made, he has told me. We will find the right one. I admire his optimism, Meanwhile I am happy I didn't give up my day job.

Our overworked waitress finally gets around to us and we order. I opt for a bacon cheeseburger, not really good for me but I don't care. Lila chooses a green salad with lemon juice and green tea. When I suggest she really doesn't need to diet, she arches an eyebrow and suggests that I keep my opinions to myself unless and until I become a 37 year old woman in fear of losing her hour glass figure. I raise my hands in abject apology and lean back in my chair, quickly changing the subject,

"Okay, "I say, "what's this surprise you have for me?"

She rummages in her purse, finally producing a business card which she hands me with a proud smile. I take it from her and give it the once over. It reads 'Lila James and Associates, Public Relations'. Good solid ivory stock, embossed gold lettering. Class all the way just like Lila.

"Congratulations," I say.

She just smiles.

"Thanks, but anybody can print up a business card, Joe. For two years I've taken anything I could get my hands on. Low budget sci-fis, B westerns, indies without a dime to their name. Ten days ago I finally landed a big one. 'Pocketful of Miracles.'

I perk up with a grin.

"The new Bette Davis movie?"

"Don't let Glenn Ford hear you say that," Lila says. "Officially I call it the new Frank Capra picture."

Frank Capra is a film icon with the Oscars to prove it. His forte is sentimental stories about God, country and little guys who get the best of big guys. Elitists call his films "capra-corn". Everyone else calls them wonderfully heartwarming, Norman Rockwell come to life on film. In 1933 he made a hugely popular movie named 'Lady for a Day' starring Mae Robson based on a Damon Runyon short story. Now he is remaking it with Bette Davis, one of Hollywood's all-time legends, and apparently co-starring Glenn Ford.

"What's Ford's problem?" I ask.

"The usual. Clashing egos. Jealousy. Insecurity. Paranoia."

"Sounds like just another unhappy Hollywood set."

"At the very least, " she says with a twinkle, "but I can deal with it. At least that's what I keep telling UA. So what's on your plate?"

"Basically, nothing,"I say. "I'm wrapping up a low budget for an old friend and that's it."

"You're kidding. An old workaholic like you?"

"Sad but true, Lila. You hit 40 and the engine starts to sputter."

"I hope that's not all that's starting to sputter," she says with a twinkle.

I shake my head.

"So far so good," I say.

And now I notice the twinkle fade, replaced by a frown, as she looks past me. I turn and see a very attractive young woman in the entranceway, looking around and then hurrying in our direction as soon as she spots us.

"Trouble?" I ask.

"Not for me," Lila says wryly. "You know those associates mentioned on my business card? They are her."

She arrives breathlessly at our booth. Her eyes are blue and her hair is Clairol blonde, worn long in something like Veronica Lake's peekaboo style.

"Miss James, I am so sorry to interrupt but I thought you should know immediately," she says.

"Someone died?" Lila asks with arched eyebrow.

"Dear, no," she says. "Nothing that awful but the printer called and said he couldn't have the brochures for us until tomorrow morning." All the while she is throwing glances in my direction.

"Well, then I suppose we'll have to wait until tomorrow afternoon to mail them out," Lila says.

"Exactly what I was thinking," the young lady says showing no inclination to leave. For a moment there is an awkward pause which Lila finally breaks off.

"Heather, this is Joseph Bernardi of Bowles & Bernardi. Joe, Heather Leeds."

She turns and flashes me a smile so well practiced it absolutely seems genuine. She is Harpers Bazaar beautiful but like a fashion model, there is a hint of deadness in the eyes that you can spot if you look hard enough.

Heather Leeds jabs a well manicured hand in my direction.

"Mr. Bernardi, I am so delighted to meet you. This is an honor, it really is. I mean, I'm actually talking to a legend in the business."

I am suddenly wallowing in horse excrement but still I take her hand and manage a gracious smile.

"Thank you, Heather. Very kind of you to say it."

"Not kind at all, sir. I am most sincere."

"Thanks for stopping by, Heather," Lila says icily with a look to match. Heather gets the hint.

"Sorry to have interrupted," Heather says and with one more toothsome smile flashed in my direction, she turns and hurries away. Lila watches her go.

"Ambitious little devil, my Heather. If she wasn't so damned valuable, I'd fire her in a minute."

"You mean she takes a nice meeting."

"Oh, yes," Lila says, "and a nice lunch and a nice dinner and God knows what else, especially with the male of the species. She singlehandedly got us two pictures after I had struck out, how she did it I didn't ask. When she heard you and I were lunching she could hardly contain herself. For over an hour she fished around for an invitation to join us until I told her it was personal and private. As you can see even that didn't stop her."

"Well, dear friend," I say, "you and I both know that personal ambition is not a commodity in short supply in this business."

"In other words, stop whining and keep my mouth shut."

"You said it, not me. How about another beer?"

She smiles.

"How about a double martini on the rocks? " she says as she signals to our waitress.

Heather Leeds aside, we have a wonderful lunch, spending a good part of it chatting about a mutual friend, Peter Falk, who has been signed to a pretty hefty role as one of Ford's cohorts. Peter's also been nominated for an Academy Award at the ceremony upcoming in April. In an otherwise forgettable picture entitled "Murder, Inc." Peter was a standout and the Academy members noticed him. A pretty big honor for a young actor in his first major film role.

"Mr. Capra and he are as chummy as long lost cousins," Lila tells me. "In fact, Peter may be the only one on the set who isn't fighting with somebody."

Over the rest of lunch, we swap Peter stories and laugh a lot because he is genuinely one of a kind. By the time I've put away a pie a la mode I've forgotten my ill thought out promise to pitch in on "The Hustler". Three beers have fogged my brain and I'm looking forward to a 45 minute catnap on my office sofa. I give Lila one more big hug goodbye and then I'm out the door and heading for my car.

"Joe! Wait up!"

I turn at the sound of my name and see a familiar figure hurrying toward me. During the last two years that I toiled for Warner Bros., Dexter Craven was my trusted right hand and when I left to go into business with Bertha, Dexter was promoted to my job. He lasted a matter of weeks, unable to deal with the autocratic whims of Jack Warner. Dexter is bright as hell but he's a lover, not a fighter. He and J.L. were like vampires and sunshine.

Dexter hurries to my side and we shake hands and clap each other on the shoulder as guys are wont to do and as for me, it really is nice to see him again.

"I saw you lunching with Lila but I didn't want to interrupt," he says.

"That was silly, Dex," I say. "Glad to see you anytime. So what's up? You working here for Paramount?"

"No, I'm out of the publicity business, Joe. Cissy and I have been working together for a couple of years writing celebrity bios."

"That's terrific," I say. "How is Cissy?"

I know her well. Cute as a button but with the tenacity of a bulldog, she's almost anal in her doggedness. She and Dexter are an anomaly on the Hollywood scene, college sweethearts, and married almost ten years when I walked away from Warners.

"Still as gorgeous as ever," Dexter says."We've been commissioned to do a book on Mack Sennett and she's hip deep into research."

Sennett, a legend from the silent era, was an industry pioneer who created the Keystone Kops, discovered Mabel Normand and turned an English music hall comic named Charlie Chaplin into one of movieland's brightest stars. Sennett died about three months ago and while many old timers remember him with affection, the newer crowd give him only a passing thought if they think about him at all. This book may rectify that.

"You can't believe what a dynamo she is, Joe," Dex says. "I get the easy part. I write. She digs. Newspaper morgues, out of print books, friends thought long dead. She's found stuff on Sennett nobody knew existed."

"Can't wait to read it, Dex. So what are you doing here at the studio?"

"Gotta pay the bills, Joe, so Vogue's hired me to do a cover story on Bette Davis for their July issue."

"Lucky you. All these years and I've never met the lady."

"Well, she's a pip," Dexter says. "Bawdy, brilliant and a helluva lot of fun. We've got two or three more sessions left and to tell you the truth, Joe, I'll be sorry to see them end. And by the way, belated congratulations. You and Bunny finally got it together."

"It took a while," I say. Dex knows all about my Bunny troubles. He was on hand for most of them.

A few minutes later we swap business cards and make a mutual pledge to get together soon for dinner with our wives. We may.

We may not. Hollywood is like that. Friendships are made on movie sets and often forgotten the day after the wrap party. In a business populated by ambitious sharks, Dexter Craven is a fun, self-effacing man who makes good company and I make a mental note not to lose track of him and Cissy again.

CHAPTER TWO

Tuesday morning.

As soon as I walk through the door I know something's afoot. Glenda Mae gives me that look that says no coffee for you and don't get settled down behind your desk.

"What?" I ask.

"The breathless babe with the sultry voice, she just called you from the hospital. She needs to talk chop-chop."

Not good news.

"She say why?"

"Left a number. Room 233. Shall I get her?"

"Please," I say.

I go into my office, check out the return address on a couple of personal looking letters that are probably from insurance salesmen and then reach for the phone as Glenda Mae buzzes the intercom. I pick up.

"What happened? Are you all right?" I ask.

"Aside from being in traction, I'm fine," Lila says. "As for what happened, it's a short but embarrassing story. Are you busy?"

"Not overly."

"Good. Come see me. It's important."

"Can I ask what—"

"No. 10:30. Hollywood Presbyterian. Room 233. Don't be late." With that she hangs up. Traction? What the hell has she done to herself?

At quarter past I park my car in the visitor's lot. I'd considered bringing flowers but instead I dropped by a liquor store and picked up a pint of Smirnoff's, knowing how stiff-necked hospitals can be about self-medication. I'm about to walk in the front entrance when my newest buddy from New York hurries out as if he has a bus to catch. The last time I saw him he was wearing a battered fedora and a worn out blue overcoat, his wardrobe in 'Murder Inc." Now he's wearing the same hat but today the coat is brown.

"Peter!" Falk looks at me, his face lights up and then he scowls.

"Hey, Joe, what's with you? Yesterday you come on the lot, you don't even bother to drop by the set to say hello."

"I was going to call you," I say.

"Yeah? You know how many dames I handed that line to? Aw, forget it. How are you doing?"

"Great, and apparently so are you."

"A very fortunate man, that's me," Peter says. "I got a terrific part in a terrific movie and Mr. Capra, he is really something, Joe. A joy to work with."

"Couldn't be happier for you," I say. "What happened to your old coat?"

"The one I wore in the other picture? I gave it to Moishe Rosenberg. The guy hasn't worked in a year and it's cold in New York."

I finger the lapels of his "new" brown coat.

"And this?"

"You like it? Fourteen bucks at St. Vincent de Paul. I know, I know. Robbery. The prices out here, they're crazy."

I grin. Falk has a thing about shopping for his wardrobe in thrift shops.

"They saw you coming, Pete," I say to him.

"Who cares? It's perfect for Joy Boy. That's my character. Whatever's good for the picture.

"So how's Lila?"

He shakes his head solemnly.

"Cranky. Very cranky. She says she's going to be laid up for at least two weeks, maybe more."

"What happened?" I ask.

"Beatrice," he tells me.

"Beatrice?"

Peter suddenly checks his watch.

"I'm late," he says, "Oh, I am very late. I'll talk to you later, Joe."

With that he starts to jog toward the parking lot. Beatrice? What the hell has Beatrice got to do with anything?

"She's my cat," Lila tells me in answer to my query.

I have just entered her cramped but private hospital room. She is lying in traction, one leg raised by a chain and pulley and she looks miserable. The room is bare bones, still too early for flowers to have arrived but she doesn't care when I produce the Smirnoff's which she tucks under her pillow. I know my Lila.

"Stupid, Joe. Totally stupid," she tells me. "I'm at the top of the staircase carrying my laundry basket when I look down and a mouse scurries between my legs. I manage to suppress a scream when Beatrice bolts after the mouse just as I'm taking a step. Down the stairs I go, me, the mouse, Beatrice and the laundry basket. I try to get up. I can't. The pain in my back is excruciating. My leg is useless. It takes me almost ten minutes to crawl over to the phone and a half an hour before the ambulance shows up. The doctor is quick to tell me how lucky I am, that I could have been paralyzed. Do I look lucky, Joe? Do I sound lucky?"

"Not particularly," I say.

"You bet your ass not particularly. A broken leg, a wrenched back. I'm so lucky I could spit."

"Well, if there's anything I can do—," I start to say.

"You are such a mensch, I knew I could count on you," she says with a mile-wide grin in her face.

"What?"

"I knew if there was one person I could rely on, it would be Joe Bernardi."

A cold shiver runs up my spine. I sense I have stepped on a landmine.

"Slow down, Lila—"

"Sherman Goodwin, he had the picture before I did except that eleven days ago the IRS shut him down for some sort of hanky panky involving tax deposits. I believe the figure seven million dollars was bandied about. UA was desperate. I promised to work for nickels and dimes and that's how I swung this gig. Great. The chance of a lifetime but suddenly I'm out of action for at least two weeks." I shrug.

"There's always Heather," I say.

I can actually see the blood rising to her hairline.

"Are you out of your mind? She barely knows which end of the pencil to stick in the sharpener."

"You want me and Bertha to take over for you?"

"God, no. I want to keep this job, not lose it. I am hoping you will sort of pitch in, for old times sake."

"Pitch in?" I ask densely.

"You know, lend us your expertise. Hold the fort until I'm up and about. A favor to an old friend."

I'm beginning to get it.

"Let me see if I have this right," I say. "You want me to conduct myself as an official representative of your firm for an indeterminate amount of time so that UA doesn't terminate your involvement and hire yet another firm, say, some highly reputable outfit like Bowles & Bernardi, to replace you."

"Now you've got it," she smiles.

"And why would I do that?" I ask.

"You said it yourself, Joe. A favor to an old friend."

"I didn't say that, you did."

"Oh, stop splitting hairs. Be a pal, Joe. I really need you. Besides, didn't you say you weren't all that busy."

I start to squirm.

"Look, Lila, if it was just me, I guess I could pitch in for a week or so but Bertha—"

"Forget Bertha," she says. "You can handle her."

Oh, yeah, I think to myself. When did that start?

"And there's United Artists—"

"UA loves you, I've already talked to them. They said you did a bang-up job on 'Some Like It Hot'."

"Besides which there's Mr. Capra—"

"You and Frank are meeting in his office at one o'clock when the company breaks for lunch," she says. "It's all arranged." That winning smile has never left her lips.

"I don't suppose there's any sort of compensation involved in all this," I say.

She just laughs.

"With my medical bills?"

I nod in defeat. I am out of excuses

"Okay, I give up. Two weeks. No longer."

"Bless you, old friend."

"Does this mean I'm in charge? I mean, I really have no interest in taking orders from your Eve Harrington act-alike."

"Never actually thought of her that way but no, you call the shots, Joe. I'll deal with Heather."

I put out my hand. We shake on it. Now I have to figure out how to broach this to Bertha.

As I foresaw my partner does not take kindly to the idea.

"You've got a screw loose, Joe. We are a profit making organization, not the Salvation Army."

She's in a lousy mood and has been for over a week since Anna May Wong passed away at the age of 55. Bertha and Anna May shared the same birthday,same day, same year and suddenly Bertha has been forced to face her own mortality, something she has heretofore been unwilling to do. Personally I don't think God would have the nerve to take Bertha from us but that's just me. What she really needs is a man in her life which, at the moment, she does not have.

"It's two weeks, three at the most," I say.

"How would you like it if I suddenly took off for a month's vacation in Helsinki?" she snarls.

"Great," I say. "I'll buy your plane ticket."

"Nobody likes a wise-ass, Joe."

"What did Rossen say? About Gay Summers, I mean."

"He agreed to her reluctantly but he wants you in New York, taking over on April 1. Not a day later."

"Tell him I'll be there. That's a promise."

"And if Lila's not up and about by then?"

"The company comes first, Bert. Scout's honor."

She nods grudgingly.

"Okay, then go have your lunch with Frank and while you're at it, give him my regards."

"Will do, partner," I say as I head for the door. I'm almost out of there when I hear her voice one more time.

"Oh, and Joe, do me a favor without being too obvious about it. Find out if the old horn dog is still married to Louise or Lulubelle or whatever the hell her name is."

All I can do is smile and shake my head. There's not a lot of quit in Bertha Bowles.

A short time later I'm once again turning into the Melrose

Avenue gate at Paramount but this time, Benny the security guard waves me to a halt instead of letting me pass.

"Good afternoon, Mr. Bernardi. Captain Rhinehalter, our head of security needs to talk to you." He points. "The security office is right over there. Park wherever you like."

I thank him and pull up to a small building to the right of the gate. I have yet to meet Rhinehalter but I suspect this request involves routine paperwork.

Al Rhinehalter is a beefy guy, probably in his late thirties, with a warm smile and a no-nonsense attitude, As I thought, I need to fill out a form which gets me a studio drive-on pass good for the next thirty days. When I hand him the form, he hands me a card which I will clip onto my sun visor. I'm about to thank him when he asks, "Got a minute?"

I check my watch. I'm a few minutes early for my meeting with Frank Capra. I say sure and we go into his private office where he shuts the door before sitting.

"I'm an easy going guy, Mr. Bernardi, and I like things quiet and peaceful so I'm hoping you will help me in this regard."

"How so, Captain?"

"Start by calling me Al."

"Sure. Al. I'm Joe."

"This film is a United Artists picture, Joe, which makes you people guests on the lot, renting our facility. My job is to be as accommodating as possible and I will do my best but frankly I have had more trouble with this picture than I have had with any picture in in the last couple of years. Actors complaining about their parking spots, trucks blocking alleys by the sound stages, reports of screaming fights coming from dressing rooms, the list goes on and on. I mean, some of these babes, these queen bees who think their breath don't stink, I mean, not just actresses although they're also pretty tough to deal with."

"Some are," I say.

"I'll admit it, I've made enemies of some of these people and several have made an enemy of me. Never mind which ones but I don't take kindly to being reported to top management for trying to do my job."

"No quarrel here, Al," I say.

"I guess what I am trying to say is, please do what you can to ease tensions on the set. I'm not a babysitter and I'm not a referee. There are steps I'd like to take but I can't. This studio needs the rental fees and, like I said, I am under strict orders to be accommodating, no matter what. So anything you can do will be greatly appreciated."

"I'll do what I can," I say.

He gets up from his chair and I follow suit. He puts out his hand and we shake.

"A pleasure having you with us, Joe," he says with a smile. I tell him it's mutual and ask directions to Frank Capra's dressing room. He does better than that. He walks me over. On the way I learn he's married with two kids, ex-Shore Patrol during the Korean police action and has been with Paramount for seven years. At Capra's dressing room door we shake hands again and he starts back to his office.

I've heard a lot of things about Frank Capra, that he's either a well-mannered gentleman or an autocratic bully, a martinet with an ego the size of Mount Rainier or a loving husband and devoted family man. I wouldn't know. He could be all of these things but I've just met him and so far what I see is a gracious man who exudes Mediterranean warmth and charm. His handshake is firm and his smile seems genuine as he leads me to a table in his dressing room upon which lunch has been set up.

"I had my girl call your girl and she thought a patty melt and fries and a cold bottle of Coors would suit you just fine," Capra says.

"Perfect," I say as we sit down.

He asks for the latest on Lila's condition and I tell him what I know. He expresses great sympathy for her plight and I suspect he and Lila had become good pals in the short time they'd been working together. I learn that Capra is a devoted family man, married for more than 29 years with four kids, one of which is attending Harvard. Whatever Bertha might have been contemplating I'm pretty sure she's out of luck.

"I hear nothing but good things about you, Joe," Capra says, "not only from Lila but from just about everybody including the bean counters at UA."

"Good to hear, Mr. Capra," I say digging into my patty melt.

"Make that Frank, please," he says. "Mr. Capra makes me sound like some doddering old timer who's been around far too long."

"Not in my opinion," I say.

He shrugs.

"There are some who'll tell you I'm pretty much washed up, that I'm in a rut, rehashing old material."

"There's no sin in that, Frank, as long as the material's good. This picture has a pretty good pedigree," I say.

"So did 'Riding High'," he says, "and we know what happened to that one."

"I liked it."

"You and my cousin Rose," Capra says, wincing.

"Riding High" was a remake of an earlier Capra film titled "Broadway Bill" and the reaction was mixed, despite the presence of Bing Crosby as a happy-go-lucky horse owner. It was the start of the whispering campaign. Capra hasn't got it any more. No fresh ideas. He's mired in the simplistic movie making of the 30's and "everyman" heroes like Jefferson Smith who went to Washington and Longfellow Deeds who went to town.

He made one more film, also with Crosby, and then nothing for eight years. Now he's 64 years old and the conventional wisdom is, it's over for him, too old to handle the work despite the fact that John Ford (66) and Alfred Hitchcock (62) are still busy turning out first class films.

"Let's talk about the picture. How much did Lila tell you?" he asks.

"Not a lot," I say. "Only that it didn't seem to be a particularly happy set."

"Yes, you could say that," Capra says wryly. "The truth is, Joe, your job is not so much to beat the drum but rather to keep a lid on a lot of things better left on the sound stage and not aired in public."

"Ford and Bette Davis?"

"That's part of it."

"I think I'd better hear the rest. I hate surprises," I say.

"Father Marconi over at St. Benedict's is my confessor, Joe. I trust him completely. Can I trust you?"

"Unconditionally," I tell him making the sign of the cross.

And so he launches into a painful narrative of the events which have brought "Pocketful of Miracles" to this point. United Artists agreed to finance the picture provided Capra could obtain the rights and also sign up a superstar to play one of the two leads. The first part was easy. Columbia sold the rights for $225,000, every dollar of which came out of Capra's pocket. The second part was not so easy. For the part of Dave the Dude, the superstitious bootlegger, Capra went after Sinatra (Pass) and then Dean Martin (also Pass) and UA wouldn't even consider Steve McQueen,"a relative nobody". By chance Glenn Ford had heard of the project and made himself available and although Capra knew Ford wasn't really right for the part, he was left with no choice. UA grudgingly accepted him but only on the proviso that a major female star be signed for the co-starring part of Apple Annie, a Broadway panhandler and a hag of a woman who had somehow become Dave the Dude's good luck charm.

At this point I notice that Capra is in a lot of discomfort and having trouble concentrating. He digs in his pocket and takes out a bottle of pills.

"Frank, are you okay?" I ask.

"Damned headaches," he says. "They're driving me crazy."

He pops three pills into his mouth and washes them down with water. This is when I realize that Capra is in major pain. Three of any kind of pill is a hefty dose, even aspirin, and I'm damned sure those weren't aspirin.

"Where was I?" he asks.

"Apple Annie."

"Right. So we go for Shirley Booth who says no and then try for Helen Hayes and hit the jackpot. Miss Hayes would be delighted to play the part. She sends me a telegram letting me know how thrilled she is. I'm also thrilled. So is UA. We get a commitment from Shirley Jones to play Queenie, Dave the Dude's good hearted moll. Ford approves. Everything is a go until Ford suddenly decides he wants his real-life girlfriend Hope Lange to play Queenie, even though we have committed to Shirley with his approval. We argue. I cajole. Shirley is perfect for the part. Hope is not. It's no use. He wants Hope. He also wants a script rewrite and also other perks like a limousine at his disposal, his wardrobe tailor-made and his to keep at the end of shooting, his own still photographer, blah, blah, blah, and if he doesn't get all these things, he walks away. If he walks away I have no star and no picture so I give in and postpone the start date for a couple of months. When I do this, I lose Helen Hayes who has a prior commitment. Again the picture is hanging by a thread thanks to Mr. Glenn Ford who I really didn't want in the first place. I have no co-star and I have a 29 year old frilly little ingenue totally wrong for her part. I know I should junk the whole thing but I can't make myself do it. I'm making the wrong picture for all the wrong reasons with all the wrong people and still

I determine to stick it out. I must be crazy, Joe. Either that or senile."

"That I doubt," I say.

Capra raises his eyebrows.

"We'll see," he says, "Meanwhile somebody mentions Bette Davis and I slap myself on the forehead. Of course. Bette. Perfect, if she'll do it. We send her a script and I fly to New York. She's annoyed because she knows Helen Hayes was our first choice and furthermore she has no intention of playing an ugly hag but in the end she takes the part because she hasn't had a decent picture in years and besides she needs the money. Suddenly everyone is delighted again, even Mr. Glenn Ford, and the picture is again a go. And so six days ago we start turning the camera and my headaches have gotten worse."

"Well, Frank, you've always got Peter Falk," I say.

He grins.

"For which I will be eternally grateful. The man brightens my day whenever he walks on the set. So Joe, now that you know what you have signed on for, any second thoughts?"

"I'll survive, Frank. In fact I'm kind of looking forward to the challenge."

"And that makes you the meshuggenah at this table," Capra says. Years in Hollywood have given us Italian boys a pretty good handle on yiddish vernacular.

We finish lunch chatting about family and old movies and the joy of working for the late Harry Cohn at Columbia where Capra made most of his signature pictures. Before I leave he hands me a copy of the script which I have yet to read and then he walks me to the door.

"Oh, Joe, one other thing I failed to mention. Those perks that Mr. Glenn Ford demanded in addition to his salary? One of them was his own personal publicist so I doubt you'll have to spend much time in Mr. Ford's company."

"Maybe not," I say.

"Unless of course he wants to give you his personal input on how to publicize the picture and in particularly his girlfriend's participation in which case he will approach you with the warmest of greetings and the widest of smiles. To which I say, cobras also smile. Good luck, my friend."

I step out into the sunlight. The temperature has risen to a comfortable 62 degrees and for a brief moment I consider walking over to the sound stage and introducing myself. Quickly I change my mind. First I'll read the script. Then I will be better prepared to finally meet one of my all time idols, one I have admired ever since the days of 'Jezebel' and 'Now Voyager' and 'Dark Victory'.

CHAPTER THREE

I find myself a quiet table in the far reaches of the Paramount commissary and order coffee. It's quiet, almost deserted. At three in the afternoon the shooting companies are filming and the executives are in their cubbyholes dreaming up mischief to bedevil the rest of us. I stare at the script and I wonder why I haven't picked it up and started to read. And then it occurs to me that I am tired. Yes, tired, and maybe a little depressed. I can fake an I-don't-care with the best of them but the truth is, I do care. A lot of hours and a lot of sweat and a lot of who I am went into my screenplay and I am aching over it, hurt that nobody wants it, hurt that it is on its way to the Hollywood trash bin, the place where all unproduced screenplays eventually end up. Stu Rosenberg, who holds a two-year option on it, is doing his best. I couldn't ask for more. But we are nowhere.

I'm also starting to realize that it's more than just the script. I'm struggling to find myself. I'm good at what I do, one of the best and I have millions to prove it. But for the past year or so I find myself struggling to maintain interest. The pictures change, so do the stars, but at heart they are all the same and I am becoming bored with the whole process. I no more want to fly to New York to hawk the attributes of 'The Hustler' than I want to swim the shark-infested waters off of New Guinea. My work for Walter Wood is a labor of love and payment for an old debt. This Capra picture will be a short couple of weeks as a favor to an old friend. Beyond that, my enthusiasm for motion picture publicity is damned near nil. I keep telling myself that basically I am a writer. The world keeps telling me I'm not. I don't voice these thoughts, not even to Bunny, but I can't run from them. Am I wallowing in self-pity? Probably. Can I stop? I hope so. I decide for the sake of my friend Lila that I will push these thoughts from my brain for at least the next two weeks.

It takes me less than an hour to read the script which is more than familiar because 'Lady for a Day', the original, is a film I have seen at least three times. The sentimental hook is sure-fire. Apple Annie has a daughter, Louise, who has been attending school in Europe which costs Annie every dime she can panhandle but to Annie, it's worth it. Nothing is too good for her Louise who thinks her mother is a Park Avenue socialite. Then disaster strikes. Louise is coming to New York accompanied by her fiancee and his aristocratic father. All is lost. But Queenie comes up with the idea of staging a one night soiree at an upscale apartment with all the panhandlers of Times Square posing as the creme de la creme of New York Society. Annie will be transformed into a regal socialite and after a raft of comedic complications, Louise and her fiancé will return to Europe none the wiser.

I liked the original a lot and while this version seems a little long-winded, under Capra's guidance, there's no reason I shouldn't like this one equally as well. May Robson, the original Annie, was nominated for an Oscar but I'm positive Bette Davis can equal or surpass her superb performance. As for the contentious atmosphere on the set, I'll do my best to gloss it over, but even if I can't, that's no guarantee the picture will suffer. The filming of 'Casablanca' was far from uneventful but out of chaos came one of the best motion pictures of all time. I can also name dozens of films shot in the happiest of circumstances that turned out to be Grade D duds.

Still, as I turn the last page of the script, I feel vaguely unsettled. In my opinion as well at that of many others, Capra is a brilliant man, revered by anyone who has a sense of history about the business, and while he may wish it otherwise, maybe he's right about his style, his sense of material, and his attachment, or lack of it, to today's movie going audience. The Great Depression, where he scored his major successes, is over and done with. A major war, and also a minor one, have intervened. The nation is more worldly now. The naiviete that preceded Pearl Harbor is gone forever. It started right after WWII with films like 'Gentleman's Agreement', 'Crossfire', 'Home of the Brave', 'No Way Out', and 'Bright Victory', all adult hard-hitting realistic films about anti-Semitism or racial prejudice. Even a comedy like 'The Moon is Blue' with its freewheeling handling of sex and seduction did big business at the box office despite a 'Condemned' rating from the Catholic church and lack of a seal of approval from the industry censors. The past year has seen 'La Dolce Vida' from Fellini and 'Never on Sunday' from Jules Dassin. In America Hitchcock has just broken the mold with 'Psycho' and Richard Brooks has laid bare the seedy underbelly of evangelism in 'Elmer Gantry'. No, the movie audience has moved on. The question is, is there still room for Frank Capra?

I'm just starting to get up when I see him approaching the table. He's on the short side, skinny, with a receding hairline. He's wearing a blue pin stripe suit which is just loud enough to be considered gaudy. He stops at the edge of the table and points a well-manicured finger in my direction.

"You're Joe Bernardi," he says with a smile.

Since I'm pretty sure he's right about that, I agree with him.

"Chick MacGruder," he says, sitting without an invitation. "I'm working with Glenn."

"Dialogue coach?" I ask, knowing he isn't.

"Publicity," he says. "I understand you're replacing Lila James."

I shake my head.

"Filling in for a couple of weeks till she's back on her feet."

"Gotcha. Well, I guess you know the drill then. I stay out of your way, you stay out of mine."

"Fine by me," I say.

"Only thing is, Glenn would like to see copies of everything you come up with before they're released to the press."

"Why?"

"He's interested. He's also a co-producer of the film."

"Sure, I can do that."

"He also wants copies of any releases that concern the other cast members."

"Why? So he can rewrite them. I don't think so," I say. "You puff up Glenn, I'll handle everyone else and, Chick, to ease your mind, I see no need for me to edit anything you send out on Glenn's behalf."

His eyes narrow in obvious annoyance.

"Maybe you didn't hear me. Glenn's a co-producer on the film."

"I heard you," I say. "What's he planning to do, fire me? He can't do that. Officially I don't actually work here. But here's the deal, Chick, if this is really Ford's idea, and I'm not sure it is, why don't you have him talk to me face to face instead of having his flunky do his dirty work for him."

MacGruder looks mad enough to kill me. Instead he stands up, kicking his chair out of the way.

"You're as bad as that bitch," he says.

"Careful, Chick, Lila's a friend of mine."

"I don't mean her. I'm talking about her assistant, little Miss Cotton Candy, sweet as a Hershey bar and as dangerous as a pit viper."

"Don't be so harsh on Heather," I say. "Maybe she just has trouble making friends."

MacGruder shakes his head.

"I was hoping we could work together amicably," he says.

"Apparently that's not going to happen," I reply.

He hesitates for a moment, then says, "Fuck you", turns and strides away angrily. I watch him go. I always admire a man who can articulate his position in words of few syllables.

The company is shooting exteriors on a section of the backlot called New York Street. It's a short walk and the exercise is good for me. When I get there, everyone is milling around as the lights get adjusted for the next shot. Off to one side is a little old lady in shabby clothes, her grey hair peeping out from under a moth eaten wool hat. Only because I know the story do I realize that Bette Davis is hiding beneath all that grunge. A cigarette is dangling from her lips and she is intently studying her script. I'm about to walk over and introduce myself when I look to my left and several yards from the perimeter of the action I spot my friend Dexter Craven in a jawing match with Heather Leeds, loud enough to be overheard by several crew members. I'm too far away to hear what's being said but I doubt it's congratulations on a job well done.

Out of the corner of his eye, Dexter sees me approach and he calls out.

"Joe, thank God. Maybe you can talk some sense into this woman," he says.

Heather turns and what had been a snarl on her lips morphs ever so subtly into a welcoming smile.

"Mr. Bernardi, I've been looking all over for you," she says.

"What's going on?" I ask looking from one to the other.

Dexter speaks up first.

"This woman is trying to deny me access to Miss Davis even though it's been approved by everyone including Mr. Capra."

"Untrue," Heather says. "I was merely suggesting that he confine his interviews to non-filming hours."

"You're a liar. I told you twice my meeting with Miss Davis is scheduled in her dressing room after she has finished shooting for the day."

"That is simply not true," Heather says, "and while I may have misheard you, I certainly am not a liar." She looks at me plaintively. "I'm only trying to do what's best for the company, Mr. Bernardi."

"Yes, I'm sure," I say flatly. "Keep your appointment, Dex, and if you have any further trouble with Miss Leeds, come straight to me."

"Thanks, Joe. And if you talk to Miss Davis, tell her I'll be waiting for her in her dressing room."

"Will do," I say as he walks away. I turn my attention to Heather. "And just what the hell were you trying to pull, Miss Leeds?"

"I told you, I —"

"I know what you told me and I'm telling you, Mr. Craven is a credentialed journalist who has been given full access to Miss Davis for the purpose of this magazine story and how and when he does it is none of your business."

"I just thought—"

"None of your business, Miss Leeds," I reiterate. "Do I make myself clear?"

She tries but she can't hide the fire in her eyes. She manages a decent impression of contrition right down to a catch in her throat.

"I'm sorry, truly I am, sir. It won't happen again."

"See that it doesn't," I say.

"The last thing I want to do is displease you, sir," she says, proceeding full throttle to smooth things over, "and I know there is so much I can learn from you. Thank you for being so understanding." Gently she places her hand on my arm and looks up at me with innocent eyes that promise so much and will most certainly deliver very little.

"My wife says it's one of my more admirable traits," I say.

"Your wife is a most perceptive woman. I envy her," she says, her eyes never wavering from mine.

I've had just about enough of this comic book flirtation so I gingerly remove her hand from my arm.

"Suppose you trot back to the production office and see if there's anything going on that demands your immediate attention. If not, go home and tomorrow be in the production office at eight o'clock sharp when you and I will have a serious chat."

"Yes, sir," she says and hurries away. There is no doubt in my mind that Heather Leeds is going to be a pocketful of trouble and I am grateful that my association with her will be short-lived.

I wander back to the set and the stand-ins are still at work, taking the places of the principals as the cinematographer Robert Bronner sets the lights for the next scene. Miss Davis is now relaxing alone in her folding camp chair so I walk over to say hello.

"Miss Davis?" I say.

She looks up at me, shading her eyes from the sun.

"Don't tell me," she says. "You are the illustrious Joseph Bernardi who has come to transform this dish of broiled eel into lobster thermidor. Sir, I admire the intent while I deplore the challenge but you have my best wishes for a gallant attempt. Please sit down beside me."

I grab a nearby folding chair with "Cast Only" imprinted on the back and accept her invitation.

"Miss Davis, believe me, this is truly an honor—"

"Oh, my God, not one of those. Mr. Bernardi, I am a competent actress who has enjoyed a mildly successful career. I am not a living legend and if you insist on putting me on a pedestal, I will risk breaking every bone in my body trying to climb down from it. Do we understand one another?"

"We do." And then I wrinkle my face into a puzzled frown. "And what did you say your name was?"

Her face breaks into a grin and she shrieks with laughter and squeezes my hand.

"Hocklemeyer, laddie. Myrtle Hocklemeyer. And don't you forget it. That Davis woman wouldn't be caught dead working for an outfit like this."

"She would if the part was right," I say.

"And the pay was decent, " she says. Then she shakes her head almost apologetically. "I'm sorry. I'm being much too hard. I'm sure this is going to turn out to be a fine film. But I do know this, I've got some big shoes to fill. May Robson and I never worked together but I knew her slightly. She was a wonderful person besides being a great actress, I just hope I don't disgrace her."

"No chance of that," I say. "It's written into the contract of every living legend."

She laughs again.

"You know, Joe Bernardi, I think you and I are going to get along just fine."

"I guarantee it," I say.

"And I especially liked the way you handled the porcupine in bunny rabbit's clothing."

"You were watching."

Her demeanor turns serious.

"You will learn, Joe, that I don't miss much especially when it comes to ambitious young ladies with loose morals in tight sweaters. The Eve Harringtons of the world are with us always."

And as I look into her eyes, I can see the keen intelligence. Thirty years in front of the cameras and still going strong. She's learned a lot and forgotten little. She particularly hasn't forgotten Eve Harrington, a character in one of her signature pictures, 'All About Eve'. Eve Harrington, played by Anne Baxter, was a lying, scheming bitch who ran roughshod over anyone who got in her way to the top, all the while feigning humility and loyalty to anyone she was about to backstab.

"First team!"

The assistant director, Art Black, is on the bullhorn calling the principal performers to the set. She hefts herself easily out of her chair. At age 53 there is nothing frail or retiring about Bette Davis. She may be good for another thirty years. We promise to connect later and I head quickly toward the production office, trying to get out of the way before the camera rolls.

The production office is the nerve center of any film and ours is situated in a large building near the sound stages. The guy in charge is the Unit Production Manager upon whom all crises fall before he can shove them onto someone else and at the moment he's talking to a woman wearing a 'Visitor' badge who seems more than a little upset. He waves me over and introduces me.

"This is Miss Philby—"

"That's Mrs. Philby," she says sharply. "Mrs. Claire Philby."

"Yeah. Mrs. Philby, and she's looking for your associate."

"Heather Leeds?" I ask.

"Yeah. Her. She was here fifteen minutes ago and then left. Mrs. Philby wants her home address and I told her I couldn't do that so would you please do what you can for the lady as I have to goose the construction crew over on Stage 14 who are under the impression that a lunch hour consists of one hundred and twenty minutes."

He smiles and walks off leaving me to deal with Mrs. Claire Philby who regards me suspiciously.

"And you are?" she inquires.

"Joseph Bernardi. How do you do?"

"And do you work for Miss Leeds?"

"Not exactly," I say. "What gave you that idea?"

"The gentleman referred to her as your associate."

"I'm working with her on a temporary basis."

"Yes, I see. That would make sense. I was told Miss Leeds' partner has been laid up in the hospital as the result of a freak accident."

"Partner?" I say. This woman has been grossly misinformed.

"Perhaps you would be good enough to give me Miss Leeds' home address so that I can speak to her directly. I have come a long way, Mr. Bernardi, and spent the better part of an hour trying to get past the storm trooper guarding your front gate, I am pretty much out of patience."

I give her the once-over. I peg her at no more than 40 and if she didn't have such an imperious attitude, you might almost call her attractive.

"Tell you what, Mrs. Philby, why don't you and I sit down and you can tell me why it's so darned important that you get to see Heather."

"I don't drink coffee," she says.

"Well, sit down anyway," I say directing her to a nearby chair while I pour myself a cup of joe from the urn on the snack table. When we have settled in, I gesture to her. "The floor is yours."

She reaches in her purse and takes out an envelope and from the envelope she extracts a letter.

"This is all very straightforward, Mr. Bernardi," she says handing me the letter. "I am the personal secretary to the Dean of Northwestern University's School of Communications. This coming April we would like to bestow upon Miss Leeds our Alumna of the Year Award in recognition of her notable success in the motion picture industry."

That one catches me unawares.

"You're sure we're talking here about Heather Leeds?" I query dubiously as I look over the letter which seems genuine.

"Of course."

"And just how was Miss Leeds selected for this honor?" I ask.

"Each candidate nominates herself, submits a 500 word outline of her achievements and awards, along with the endorsements of no less than three recognizable leaders active in the industry."

"I see," I say thoughtfully. "And Miss Leeds' endorsers, all fairly young men of impeccable credentials?"

"Naturally."

Naturally, I also think.

I nod somberly as I stand up and hand back the letter.

"Well, Mrs. Philby, I certainly wouldn't want to stand in the way of Heather receiving such a prestigious honor. Come by tomorrow. I will leave a pass for you at the front gate and I will tell Heather to expect you though I will keep the subject of your visit to myself."

As she stands, the hardness disappears from her face and she smiles pleasantly, putting out her hand.

"Thank you so much, Mr. Bernardi. You are most kind and I hope that I haven't appeared overly rude."

"Rude? Of course not."

"It's just that some of my friends back in Evanston advised me to be forceful in my dealings with movie people and not be mistaken for an out-of-town hick."

I can't help but laugh.

"Is that what they think of us at your School of Communications?"

She leans in toward me, speaking quietly.

"To be truthful, I heard it from one of the professors whose short-lived career in Hollywood soured him on the whole business."

"Not exactly a new story," I say. I shake her hand. "I'll see you again tomorrow then."

"Until tomorrow," she says and walks away.

For a moment I wonder whether I should have told her the truth about Heather but no, it's none of my business. Besides given Heather's rapacious will to succeed, a dozen years from now she may own this town and the folks at Northwestern's School of Communications will look like geniuses.

CHAPTER FOUR

Bunny is agog.

The occasion of her "agogery" is my meeting with Bette Davis. Bunny has been a rabid fan ever since la belle Davis plugged David Newell to death in 'The Letter'. My guess is her admiration stems from the way Davis solves the problems in her life, decisively and permanently, a quality often missing from Bunny's modus operandi.

We're in the kitchen. Bunny is carefully washing every dinner dish before she puts it in the dishwasher for a second washing. Why she does this I have no idea. Maybe she's a germophobe. Meanwhile I am now waiting for the not-so-subtle hint that I invite her to the studio so she can meet Miss Davis and gush all over her first hand. I plan to do this, of course, but for the moment I'm going to hold off to see the clever way my beautiful wife plans to manipulate me.

I should mention that she is also agog at the thought of Heather Leeds getting a prestigious award from Northwestern University. In Bunny's eyes Heather gives new meaning to the word chutzpah. She would be laughable if she weren't so pathetic.

At that moment my daughter Yvette scampers into the kitchen holding a large sheet of art paper on which she has painted a field full of daises, all green and white and yellow. Her face and fingers are also of like coloring. We give her the run of Jill's third floor studio to paint and draw to her heart's content. It's a meaningful connection to her mother who has gone off to live with the angels. This particular fiction was related to her by our beloved housekeeper Bridget and Bunny and I do nothing to contradict it. These are not the times for reality but of faith and comfort and ever so slowly Yvette is coming to grips with a new life without Jill. With the practiced eye of a professional critic I examine her work and pronounce it brilliant. Bunny seconds my opinion. Thus encouraged, Yvette turns around and races back upstairs, promising to paint us a picture of a rowboat. Why a rowboat, I have no idea. It is moments like this when I realize how lucky I am to have a home and family waiting for me at day's end.

Wednesday morning. I arrive at the studio a few minutes before eight. It's Washington's Birthday, a national holiday in most corners of the country but Hollywood recognizes no such concession to the federal government. In this business we're lucky to get Christmas off.

I have a few well chosen words in store for Heather Leeds because even though our working relationship isn't going to last more than a couple of weeks, I don't intend to put up with any more of her self-serving bullshit. I walk into the production office at 8:05 where I find Frank Capra Jr. who is working as the second assistant director on the picture. He tells me he hasn't seen Heather but that's no surprise. She doesn't usually roll in before ten, he says. He hands me a call sheet which tells me that the company's working on Stage 9 with Glenn Ford, Peter Falk, Hope Lange and several gang member types. Bette Davis has a late call for 2:00 on New York Street along with a dozen or so panhandlers.

I'm more than a little annoyed as I check the company corkboard for messages. Heather continues to show that she is totally unprofessional and I'm starting to steam when the phone rings. I look around. Frank Jr. has left and I'm alone in the office. I walk over to a nearby desk and pick up the phone.

"Production office," I say.

"This is Benny at the main gate. I'm looking for Miss Leeds."

"She's not here, Benny. This is Joe Bernardi."

"Oh, yeah. Look, Mr. Bernardi, I got a guy here says he's her husband and he's looking for her. I told him she hasn't showed but the guy doesn't believe me. Anyway there's no pass in his name so I can't let him in but he says he's not leaving."

"Okay, Benny, let him through and direct him to the production office. On me."

"If you say so, Mr. Bernardi," Benny replies.

"I say so, Benny."

A few minutes later he walks through the door, not at all what I had expected. He's less than average height, slight build, light brown hair which is combed over to hide a balding pate, brown eyes behind horn-rimmed glasses, and wearing brown slacks, a beige sports jacket, and a sand-colored shirt open at the neck. In short, he is ordinary, everything that Heather Leeds is not.

"Mr. Leeds?" I say.

"Lovejoy," he responds.

"Heather's husband?"

"Buddy Lovejoy. Heather goes by her maiden name. Is she here?"

"Not yet. We had an eight o'clock appointment which she apparently forgot about."

"Then you must be Bernardi. She told me all about you," Lovejoy says.

"I'll bet she did."

He smiles.

"Don't worry, I've learned to take Heather's rants with a heaping teaspoon of salt."

"Good move."

"And you have no idea where she is?" Lovejoy asks.

"Wish I did."

"Then it wasn't you on the phone this morning?"

"Don't know what you're talking about," I say. "The phone woke me up around six o'clock. I was sacked out in my den. My writing partner and I are just finishing up a screenplay and I had finally packed it in around three o'clock. When it's that late, I don't disturb her, especially in the last couple of weeks. She's gotten kind of loopy. Anyway, I curled up on my sofa. Phone rings at six. Two rings. I figure she's got it so I drift back to sleep and wake up an hour later. I look around for her. She's gone but the car is still here which is odd so either she's walked somewhere, highly unlikely in our neighborhood, or she's called a cab. I phone her office. No answer. So I decide to come here."

"Not like her?"

"Not at all."

"Well, you're welcome to wait."

"Thanks."

"Coffee and doughnuts over by the wall," I tell him.

"Just ate. Thanks, anyway," he says, pulling up a chair. He's as jumpy as a grasshopper on speed. I freshen up my lukewarm coffee and then pull up a chair next to him. Maybe a little chit-chat will reveal something I ought to know about his wife.

"So, Buddy, you say you and your partner have just finished up a screenplay?"

Lovejoy nods.

"Me and Seth. Seth Donnelley. We met in grammar school in Philadelphia and went to Northwestern together. We've been writing as a team for the past fifteen years, mostly TV stuff. Maverick, Broken Arrow, Wagon Train, M Squad, a couple of Dragnets and a bunch of Zorros. This deal with 20th is our first real break. We're waiting for the final okay."

"Western?"

"Spies. George Hamilton is attached."

"Really?" I say. "George Hamilton as a spy. Isn't he a little young?" I know for a fact that George is 21 years old.

"They're going for the teen audience."

"Can't wait to see it," I manage to say. "So you and Heather, college sweethearts?"

"Actually no. We attended class together but that was about it. We bumped into each other a year ago when Seth and I were on staff at Zorro and she was a a script reader for Columbia. A few weeks later Heather and I were married. Well, you've seen her. I'm a pretty lucky guy."

"Well, Buddy, she's definitely a looker," I say.

The phone rings again. By now the room is filling up and a production assistant has grabbed the phone. After a moment she looks over in my direction and waves. I excuse myself and walk over to a nearby desk. The #1 button is blinking. I punch it and pick up.

"This is Joe Bernardi," I say.

"You know a dame named Heather Leeds?" a man asks.

I recognize his voice immediately. Aaron Kleinschmidt, LAPD Detective Lieutenant with the Homicide Bureau, is an old friend but I try to see him as little as possible. When I do people start dying all around me like acorns dropping from an oak tree.

"Don't tell me. She's dead," I venture.

"We're not that lucky. She's here at Hollywood Division screaming her lungs out at a guy who is screaming back at her. They are exes and the passage of time has healed no wounds. We're holding them both on a laundry list of charges."

"Excuse me, old friend, but I thought you were a homicide cop."

"I'm came here to interrogate a witness in a gang murder, old friend, and ended up refereeing a match between pit bulls. Especially your associate."

"And she asked to see me?"

"Hell, no," Aaron says. "We found your card in her purse."

"And you say the guy she's screaming at is her ex-husband?"

"According to him, yes. In fact he thinks they are still married. According to her, no way. Meanwhile they are threatening to kill each other and I don't think they're kidding."

I glance over at Buddy Lovejoy who is leaning back in his chair, staring up at the ceiling. This is not news he needs to digest at this moment.

"Okay, you've got them both on disturbing the peace. What do you need me for?"

Aaron raises his decibel level several notches.

"We want your ass over here to get this dame out the door."

"I'm not her keeper," I complain.

"I'll remember that next time you need something from me," Aaron says.

I pause. He's made a good point.

"Hollywood Division?"

"North Wilcox near Delongpre."

"I know where it is," I say. "I'll be there in twenty minutes."

I hang up and feed Buddy Lovejoy a line of bull about a family emergency. He mutters something that sounds sympathetic but doesn't move. He's marked out his turf and he's sticking with it no matter what. I head for my car and I am not happy. What is it about me and young females in the workplace. Two hears ago it was my wife's protege strewing trouble wherever she went. It came to a screeching halt at the Hotel Del Coronado where she got her head bashed in with a blunt object. Not that I wish the same for Heather, it just seems where I'm concerned that these babes are in the wrong place at the wrong time.

Aaron is standing at the information desk on the first floor when I walk in. He's talking either to a grungy looking perp or an undercover officer. I settle on the latter when the guy takes out his .38 police special and checks the load. Aaron approaches me.

"That dame actually works for you?" he asks.

"Not for long," I respond. "Where is she?"

"The lockup. We've got her for slugging her ex with her purse but he doesn't want to file a complaint."

"And where's he?"

"Interrogation. We're plying him with coffee and doughnuts but so far all we've gotten is his name which is Travis Wright and his address which is the Hotel Bartlett, a flophouse on the edge of Hollywood."

"And what do you expect me to do?"

"We're looking to cut them both loose but to avoid bloodshed, not simultaneously. That's where you come in. When you leave, she leaves with you."

"You're going to owe me for this," I say.

"Of course I am," Aaron grins as we head up the staircase to the second floor.

As we wend our way through the squad room, I spot a distinguished looking man with a neatly trimmed salt-and-pepper beard sitting in one of the offices being questioned by a shirt-sleeved detective.

"That's him," Aaron says.

At that moment Travis Wright turns his head in my direction. He doesn't look like a man who'd be staying at a flophouse but then I haven't had a peek at his wallet. Our eyes meet and for a fleeting moment I think I recognize him but as quickly as it came, the feeling goes. My 41 year old mind is playing tricks on me again.

The lockup is a small cage at the back of the squad room which serves as a temporary holding cell until more permanent arrangements can be made. As we approach, Heather looks up and sees me and for a brief moment her face is a blank and I can sense she is making a quick decision on how to play me. She opts for poor misunderstood victim as her eyes turn sad and her lips begin to quiver.

"Mr. Bernardi, thank God," she says, gripping the bars tightly. "Please, can you get me out of here?"

"That's what I'm here for," I say. She's dressed demurely in a white cashmere sweater, navy blue skirt and a navy kerchief around her neck. "So what's going on, Heather?" I ask.

"Not now. I'll explain it all later."

"I've cleared your release with the division commander, Miss Leeds," Aaron says. "Just keep yourself available and don't leave town without notifying us."

She readily agrees, grabs her stuff and we head for the staircase. She hesitates momentarily to throw her ex-husband a dirty look and then we are gone. A couple of minutes later, she slips into the front passenger seat of my beloved Bentley while I get behind the wheel.

"Your husband's waiting for you back at the studio." I say.

"He's worried about you."

"Buddy worries about everything. I need you to drop me off on LaCienega," she says.

"Tell me about Travis Wright," I say.

"Later," she says.

I slam on the brakes and stop.

"How about if I turn around and throw you back to the cops?" I say.

"It's none of your business."

"I'm filling in for my friend Lila which makes it my business. So which is it? La Cienega or back upstairs?"

She glares at me and then looks away in annoyance.

"We weren't married long, about two years before I left him. It was not an amicable split. We were living in San Diego. I moved up here, thinking I was done with him for good. Then from out of nowhere came a phone call this morning insisting that we meet."

"If you hated him so much, why did you agree to see him?"

"Because Buddy doesn't know about him."

"And why is that?"

"You ask a lot of goddamned questions."

"You were released in my care, remember?"

She glares at me again.

"It was not a pleasant divorce. In fact he threatened my life. There are things he would have said about me."

I'll bet, I think

"Well, that's not nice," is what I say. "So you take a phone call at six in the morning. Then what?"

"I don't want Buddy aware of him so I agree to meet him outside our apartment house, He comes by in his car and picks me up. We drive to a Howard Johnson for breakfast. He starts in about how he's sorry we broke up and it was all his fault and why can't we get back together again."

"Doesn't he know you're re-married?"

She hesitates and looks out the window.

"I don't know," she says. "Maybe not."

"Wait a minute," I say, puzzled. "Isn't the guy claiming that you two are still married?"

"He might possibly think that," Heather says.

"Well, surely he knows whether he's divorced or not," I say. "I mean, you are divorced. right?"

"Absolutely," she says. "Perhaps not in a technical sense."

I'm getting very frustrated, "What the hell is that supposed to mean?"

We're sitting stock still in the middle of the police parking lot and I'm staring at her hard. This babe who thinks she knows all the answers is suddenly very tongue-tied. Now she turns to me and there is real concern on her face.

"Legally, I can tell you that things are very confused, Mr. Bernardi. I can also tell you that Travis is a very determined and dangerous man. What he wants he usually gets. That's why you have to drop me off at La Cienega," she says. "My lawyer has an office there. I'm going to have him get a restraining order."

"If your ex is really as dangerous as you say, a restraining order isn't going to help every much."

"I know," she says, "but it's a start."

"What about Buddy? What do I tell him?"

"Tell him you couldn't find me. I'll deal with him when I get home."

By now my impression that Buddy is a doormat has been confirmed. I decide I want no further part of this domestic squabble and ask her for the lawyer's address on La Cienega. When we get there I'm puzzled. It's not an office building but a tidily kept apartment house. Maybe she does business with this guy at his home. Knowing Heather I wouldn't be surprised.

I drop her off and watch as she hurries up the walkway to the building entrance. I don't know how I got myself embroiled in this mess but I am sure as hell going to do my best to get myself out of it.

I put the car in gear and head for the studio.

CHAPTER FIVE

It's past noon when I get back to the studio. I poke my head into the production office. No sign of Buddy Lovejoy. Maybe he gave up and went home. I check the board but I have no messages. I'm about to head out to the set when Bob Bronner, the cinematographer, walks in accompanied by his camera operator. This is strange because according to the call sheet, the lunch break is scheduled for an hour from now. Right behind them comes Frank Jr. and as soon as he sees me he strides in my direction. He takes my elbow and pulls me aside, obviously upset.

"My Dad needs to see you in his dressing room right away," Frank Jr. says.

"What's the problem?"

"He'll tell you."

We hurry over to Capra's dressing room. Whatever's going on, it's not good. The company has broken for lunch an hour early and Frank Jr. is paler than I remember. Suddenly I'm thinking heart attack but why call me? The studio has a perfectly good doctor on call 24 hours a day and a hospital is close by.

We open the door without knocking and find the room empty. Frank Jr. walks over to the closed bathroom door and knocks.

"Dad?" No answer. He looks over at me. "They're out in the car. They'll be back in a minute."

I have no idea what is going on but a moment later, the rear door to the dressing room opens and Capra enters, aided by Art Black, the assistant director. Capra sits heavily in his chair and for a moment puts his head in his hands, trying to catch his breath. Another severe headache. This is not good. I also know why I was called and not a doctor. If it got around that Frank Capra was having severe and constant headaches or any kind of medical problem, the picture would be in jeopardy. If I know Capra that is the last thing he would allow to happen. He looks up at me.

"Please believe me when I say this, Joe, I am totally convinced that you are not responsible. Believe me, too, when I tell you that I want the liver of the person behind this smear fried in deep fat and served to me on a silver plate."

I have no idea what he is talking about and tell him so.

"My old friend Moe Deegan from the *Herald-Examiner* called me first thing this morning sounding the alarm," Capra says. "An anonymous tip came in to his entertainment desk very early, hand delivered, no signature, no return address, for "background only". You know what that means."

"A hatchet job," I say.

He nods. "Moe sent it over by messenger." He reaches in his shirt pocket and takes out a folded sheet of paper, unfolds it and starts to read.

"What well-known old-time director is bumbling and fumbling his way through a remake of one of his oldies? Rumor has it the old fellow is so out of touch he's suffering migraines. If I were UA I'd give serious thought to replacing the old boy with someone more in touch with today's audiences. Can anyone out there say 'Operation Petticoat'?"

Whoever wrote the letter has made reference to an up and coming young director named Blake Edwards who has a deft approach with light material.

"But it's true, about the migraines, I mean," I say.

"Yes and no. They've been happening for weeks. I've had every test in the book and the idiot doctors still can't figure out exactly what's wrong. The only thing that's keeping me sane is a daily trip to the back door of the infirmary around lunchtime. The nurse, who is sworn to secrecy, shoots me up with a giant dose of sodium phosphate which helps a lot but it's no cure." He shakes his head and manages a wan smile. "I'm telling you, Joe, it's a helluva way to direct a picture."

I smile sympathetically.

"So I guess the big question is, who's behind it?"

"Glenn Ford," Art Black says flatly.

Capra shakes his head.

"You don't know that, Art. Not for sure."

"No? A buddy of mine saw him and Edwards having lunch together last week at Chasens. They were talking about a project they wanted to do together later this year."

"Still doesn't prove anything," Capra says. He looks up at me. "Joe, I'd like you to get on this right away. If whoever's in back of this smear contacted Moe, he may have written the same note to others so we have to put a cork in it before it gets out of hand. Then I'd like you to find out who's responsible, if you can."

"I'm not a detective, Frank, but I can try."

"Good. Hire anybody you need. Private detectives, whatever. Bribery's always a good approach. Don't spare the greenbacks. Like I said, I want this bastard and I want him bad."

I nod looking from Frank Jr. to Art Black and then to Capra himself.

"And if it turns out to be Glenn Ford?"

He mulls that over.

"It won't be," he says.

"Are you so sure?"

"Glenn's a lot of things," Capra says, "but this isn't his style." I look into his eyes. He's a man conflicted. He doesn't want it to be Ford but he isn't sure. He also knows if it is, he will have to swallow his pride once again or the picture is done for.

I put out my hand.

"Give me the letter," I say.

Capra hands it over.

"Good luck," he says.

"I'll need it," I say.

I walk back to the production office. As I do a thousand thoughts swirl about my mind. Is someone out to sabotage this picture or is it just a clumsy attempt to demean Frank Capra and perhaps get him removed as the director of the film? Either choice is abhorrent to me and I am determined to find out who is behind this and why. I will also have to operate in the shadows. Hollywood is a town that feeds on misery. Someone once said of industry wannabes that it is not enough that you succeed, your best friend must also fail. The shark infested waters off the Florida Keys have nothing on Los Angeles. The slightest hint of scandal or trouble can result a feeding frenzy big enough to bring down the most powerful producer or the loftiest director. Stealth is the watchword here. Not one word of this can be allowed to leak out to the public.

As soon as I walk in the door, I see her sitting by the receptionist's desk, chatting with Mitzi, the unit's secretary-gal Friday who oversees the workings of the production office with an iron hand. At the moment, however, she and Claire Philby are giggling over something as only two women can giggle and I feel like an interloper as I approach them.

Mrs. Philby rises from her chair with a smile.

"Mr. Bernardi," she says.

"Mrs. Philby," I respond. "I hope you had no trouble getting through the gate."

"None whatsoever, thanks," she replies.

"Miss Leeds isn't here right now," I say. "Important business off the lot and I'm not sure when she's coming back."

"I can wait," she says, "if I won't be in the way."

"Up to you," I say. Out of the corner of my eye I spot Buddy Lovejoy who has just walked in the door. He glances at me, then ambles over to the coffee urn to pour himself a cup. "I'm not even sure she'll be back today. Why don't you leave me a number where you can be reached and I'll have her call you."

Mrs. Philby shakes her head.

"I prefer to talk to her in person."

"I understand. How about if you give me the number and I will call you when she shows up?"

"Yes, that would be acceptable," she says, "with your assurance that you don't give Miss Leeds the number."

"I can do that," I say, swiping a message slip and a pencil from Mitzi's desk. Mrs. Philby writes down the number and I stuff the slip into my jacket pocket. I walk her to the door.

"How long will you be in town?" I ask her.

"Until my business here is completed," she says. "Thanks so much for everything." She shakes my hand and walks out the door and starts down the corridor. An odd woman, I think to myself. Yesterday she was standoffish and imperious, today pleasant and patient. Which is the real Claire Philby, I think to myself, and which is the facade?

"I know that woman."

I turn. Buddy is standing next to me, coffee mug in hand, watching Claire Philby disappear down the hallway.

"You should, if you went to Northwestern," I say.

"Can't think of her name."

"Claire Philby," I say.

Buddy frowns.

"No," he says.

"She's the Dean's secretary at the School of Communications."

"No, she isn't. I know Claire Philby and that isn't her."

Now it's my turn to frown.

"Are you sure?"

"Many an afternoon I sat across from her desk waiting for the Dean to rip me a new one over some minor infraction. Philby is a size 50 in a frumpy black dress with hair the color of vanilla ice cream."

"Then who—?"

"I don't know," Buddy says. "Like I said, I know her face but her name escapes me. But she's definitely Northwestern." His eyes narrow. "So where's Heather?"

I hesitate. The last thing I am going to do is get in the middle of family squabble.

"I think it's time you had a long talk with your wife, Buddy," I say.

"What's that supposed to mean?"

"It means I'm not a marriage counselor but I think you're in bad need of one."

"Explain yourself," Buddy says.

"Not a prayer. Whatever's going on between you and Heather is your business, not mine. I doubt she'll be back today so go home and hash things out."

I turn away. He grabs my arm.

"Look—"

I shrug him off.

"I'm busy, Buddy. Go home."

I walk over to a desk at the far side of the room. I need to make a phone call. When I pick up the receiver, I look back toward the doorway. He's already left the room. I ask Mitzi for an outside line and I dial out.

"Ogilvy here," comes the basso profundo voice on the other end of the line.

"Bernardi here," I respond.

"Ah, Joseph," he says, "a day without a call from you is like a day without sunshine."

"Well, enjoy the rays while you can, old friend, because this call is going to be short and not so sweet."

Phineas Ogilvy is the widely read film editor for the *L.A. Times* and a close personal friend. He is brilliant and bombastic and a power to be reckoned with in the industry. To those who do not know him well, his flamboyance marks him as a powderpuff but his three ex-wives will attest to the contrary. Although he lives the good life to the hilt, alimony has forced him to the edge of penury. Undaunted he perseveres.

"What? No dinner invitation at my favorite haunt? Really, old top—"

"Did you get an anonymous poison pen note by messenger early this morning?" I interrupt.

"Concerning Mr. Capra and his newest old film? I did."

"What are you planning to do about it?" I ask.

"Why, nothing, of course. Scurrilous claptrap. Nothing more, though I am surprised at Lila James. This sort of thing is beneath her."

"Not Lila's doing, Phineas. She's in the hospital and I'm filling in for her as a favor for the next couple of weeks."

"I am delighted to hear that her hands are clean. She is a lovely lady. Thank God I needn't think ill of her. Now what's this about a hospital?"

I explain the situation briefly and then ask him about Chick MacGruder, Glenn Ford's personal publicist.

"Ah, yes. MacGruder, that sneaky little weasel who thrives on the misery of others. Quite right, Joe, it could easily have come from him."

"I don't know the man, Phineas. Is this the kind of thing Ford would condone?"

"I would think not but after the Bette Davis fiasco, I suppose anything is possible."

"What Bette Davis fiasco?"

"Good Lord, old top, where have you been for the past week? MacGruder put out a press release in which Ford takes credit for getting Davis the part in the movie which Ford said he was happy to do, rescuing her from virtual obscurity as a favor for all the help she had once given him years ago when she was at the top of her career."

"Jesus," I mutter under my breath. Talk about your insensitivity. No wonder this film is like a powder keg ready to explode. I think back to Leslie Crosbie, the femme fatale of 'The Letter', who blew away poor David Newell for having the audacity to repel her amorous advances. Given a chance, Leslie would certainly do the same to Glenn Ford without a second thought. What have I gotten myself into?

CHAPTER SIX

For a couple of minutes I sit back in my chair and consider my options. I finally realize I have none. Either Ford is responsible for the attack on Capra or he isn't and musing about it isn't going to get the job done. We need a face-to-face and the sooner the better. Mitzi checks his whereabouts and says he's in his dressing room, finished for the day. I get directions and head out. I want to get to him before he leaves for home.

As soon as I knock on his dressing room door, I hear his voice inviting me in. I step inside and see him at his vanity wearing a tee-shirt and wiping off the last remnants of his make up. He glances at me in the mirror and throws me a smile.

"Joe isn't it?" he says.

"Joe Bernardi, Mr. Ford," I reply.

"Well, come in and make yourself comfortable, Joe. I've heard wonderful things about you, mainly from Peter Falk. You have a real fan there."

"It's mutual, I assure you," I say.

He gets up from the table, wiping the cold cream from his hands with a couple of tissues, and extends his hand.

"It's nice to meet you, Joe. Can I get you something?"

"No, I'm fine," I tell him, "and meeting me may not be all

that nice, Mr. Ford. I'm here reluctantly on a matter of grave importance to the film."

Ford cocks his head curiously.

"Well, that sounds ominous. Let's sit down and you can tell me about it."

We sit and when we do I take the folded letter from my pocket and hand it to him.

"Moe Deegan at the *Herald-Examiner* received this early this morning, hand delivered anonymously."

He takes it from me and starts to read. As he does his face darkens and when he's finished he looks up at me and says, "This is vile. Who would write such a thing?"

"That's what I aim to find out," I say. I fix my eyes on his and I don't look away.

"Surely you don't think I am involved?" he says.

"I don't think anything, Mr. Ford. Not yet."

"Well, the first thing you'd better get straight is that it's not Mr. Ford, it's Glenn, and the second thing is, I know nothing about this. Nothing."

"I'm glad to hear that," I say.

"Look, Joe, I know you're just filling in for Lila James until she's on her feet so you really aren't responsible for Miss Leeds but frankly she is trouble and something needs to be done about her."

"For instance?"

"For instance she has come to me twice to get me to fire Chick MacGruder and twice I've had to tell her that Chick is none of her business. The second time we talked I was barely polite. Have you considered that maybe she's behind this?"

"Not really," I say. "May I be very frank with you, Glenn?"

"Absolutely."

"The intent of this letter seems to be to replace Capra with a newer younger director. Someone, and I'm not going to say who, spotted you and Blake Edwards at Chasens a few days ago apparently discussing a film." Again I look him in the eye. He doesn't look away.

"Blake and I are friends and we did have lunch. We've been talking for several weeks about working together on a suspense movie written by the Gordons called 'Experiment in Terror'. We think we've got Columbia interested."

"Then you have no wish to see Frank Capra replaced as the flim's director."

"Of course not," Ford says. "It's his movie, for God's sakes, and has been for the past thirty years."

"Have you any idea where this letter could have come from? Maybe something you said, a chance remark intended as a joke. Something that might have been misinterpreted."

Ford looks down the letter in his hand and his expression changes. "Wait a minute," he says. "Wait a minute." He gets up and crosses the room to his desk where he picks up the phone and dials a number. After a moment he says, "I need you in my dressing room. Now." He hangs up and looks over at me.

"I know Frank's not happy with me," Ford says. "Some of the things I've requested have irritated him. Most were for the good of the picture, others were to protect my standing in the industry. I don't have to tell you, Joe, this is a business, not a charity ball. But I did not nor would I ever do anything to hurt this film or Mr. Capra. You have my word on that."

There's a knock at the door and a moment later Chick MacGruder enters.

"What's up, boss?" he asks shutting the door behind him. He gives me a fishy look. He knows something's going on. He doesn't know what.

Ford gestures to a nearby chair.

"Sit down, Chick," he says, walking over to him. He hands him the letter. "What can you tell me about this?"

MacGruder scans it but says nothing.

"Did you send this to Moe Deegan over at the Herald-Examiner?"

"I didn't mention any names, Glenn. Certainly not yours," he whines.

"Damn it!" Ford says angrily. "What the hell were you thinking?"

"I'm sorry. I honestly thought you'd think it was a good idea."

"How in God's name would you ever think that?"

"We were talking about the picture and Edwards name came up and you said he was a hell of a good director and I just assumed, I mean, I thought—"

"You just assumed." Ford says. He looks over at me and sadly shakes his head. "Will no one rid me of this meddlesome priest?" he says to me. I know exactly what he's talking about. Henry II of England was becoming more and more disenchanted with Thomas a Becket, his Archbishop of Canterbury, and in a drunken rage, said those fateful words in the presence of several of his loyal barons. The barons took it as a royal order, though it most likely was not, and raced off to murder Becket.

Ford looks over at MacGruder, "If I had wanted Mr. Capra to step down as director of this picture, I would have said so to his face and we'd have hashed it out. This note of yours is cowardly and despicable, far worse than the Bette Davis release you sent out last week painting me as an arrogant condescending prick."

"Aw, come on, Glenn—"

"I should have fired you then but I'm making up for it now. Get out, Chick. I no longer need your services."

"Look, I—"

"Leave now, Chick, Don't make me call security."

MacGruder stands, then looks over at me, hatred seeping from every pore.

"Thanks, Bernardi. You've really done it, you and that bitch. I'm not going to forget this, no, sir, not for a second." With that, he balls up the letter and throws it on the floor, then turns and strides out of the room.

Ford picks up the letter, then turns to me.

"Tell Frank I had nothing to do with this. Or if you prefer I'll tell him myself though he might not believe me."

"No, I'll handle it," I tell him.

Ford may be legit or he just put on a bravura performance. I tend to think he knew nothing about this letter but I know he's worried that Capra doesn't trust him. If the denial comes from me, he might get the benefit of the doubt.

He and I chat for a few minutes. Since Chick MacGruder is no longer connected to the film, Ford hopes that I will step in on his behalf. I tell him I most certainly will. He says he is dining with Hope Lange, his lady friend, as soon as she is finished filming and invites me to join them. I beg off politely. My wife and daughter and I are going out for spaghetti dinner at the local pasta joint this evening, a Wednesday night tradition. Ford understands. Some other time.

I check my watch. It's not yet five-thirty. The company will be shooting for another hour. I decide to walk over to the sound stage where they are filming a scene with Bette Davis, Hope Lange and a dozen or so raggedy panhandlers. I hope I'm right about Ford. He seems genuine enough but he is an actor and all actors have something of the make-believe about them. If his firing of MacGruder was a performance, then I have been snookered, trusting soul that I am. I'll be interested to see what Capra thinks of the situation.

"I think he's fulla crap," Capra says irritably, "but it's remotely possible I'm wrong. Between the headaches and all the petty backbiting going around the set, I'm fed up, Joe. I can't think straight."

He's sitting in his director's chair and I'm sitting across from him. The crew is repositioning the lights for a two-shot of Bette and Hope and he's taking the time to drink a cup of coffee.

"You may be right, Frank, but let me worry about it. I've been at this for years. If Ford's responsible, I'll confirm it. If MacGruder did this on his own, I'll find that out as well, but leave it to me. You have enough to worry about."

He smiles and pats my knee.

"You're a good man to have around, Joe Bernardi," he says as he gets up from his chair. Bob Bronner has just signaled that they are ready to go. I also get up and after a wave to Bette, I head for the stage door. Enough is enough. I'm through for the day.

I'm walking out just as he's walking in and there is fire in Dexter's eyes.

"Just who I want to see," he says, grabbing my arm and pulling me outside to the studio street. He has a newspaper rolled up in his left hand.

"I sense a problem," I say.

"Yeah, you could say that, Joe. This time she's gone too far. Did you read Fidler this afternoon?"

Jimmie Fidler, the gossip columnist, is carried in the *Herald-Examiner* and while his claws aren't as sharp as Hedda's, they'll do. I confess I haven't had a chance to catch today's column.

"He's got three paragraphs on Bette and the picture, all very nice and complimentary. He also has an anecdote Bette recounted to me about Leslie Howard and her when they were filming 'Of Human Bondage', a story she'd never told before. Yet here it is in Fidler's column."

"Maybe Miss Davis gave it to him," I suggest.

Dexter shakes his head vehemently.

"She wouldn't do that to me," Dexter says. "No, this is the work of Heather Leeds. She must have rifled my briefcase, maybe even ran off a xerox copy."

"But why?"

"To collect more Brownie points. Puffing herself up is an obsession with that woman. Get in good with Fidler and someday it may pay off. Get rid of her, Joe. She's bad news. If you're not careful, the stink may rub off on you."

"Before we take this any further, I suggest we check with Miss Davis just to be sure she didn't personally pass this item on to Fidler."

"She didn't," Dexter growls.

"We'll ask her anyway," I say.

Thirty minutes later we're in Bette Davis's dressing room as she sits in her robe at her vanity scanning the newspaper item. One of the girls has removed her wig and is carefully combing out her hair. A wardrobe assistant is tending to her moth-eaten costume.

"Jimmie Fidler, that horrid little man. I haven't spoken to him in years. No, Dexter, I certainly did not give him this anecdote."

She hands the newspaper back to Dexter.

"I knew it. I'm telling you, Joe. This is Heather's work. Maybe she's trying to kill my deal with Vogue just because I won't put up with her crap."

"Now Dexter, calm down," Miss Davis says, "I must have dozens of stories just like that one and if I don't I'll make one up. Let me see, George Arliss is dead. He won't mind a little harmless fiction. Not in the least. You see, no harm done."

"It's more the principle of the thing, Miss Davis. I swear to God I'd like to kill the bitch."

"That, my young friend, sounds like a line of dialogue from one of my early B-movies with Bogie."

"Can I jump in here?" I say. "I'll call Fidler and find out where he got the item. Until then, Dex, keep your temper under control."

Grudgingly he agrees and the two of us leave Miss Davis in the hands of her attendants. I walk Dexter to his car and in the interim he has calmed himself. He'll wait to hear from me before he does anything stupid. I watch him drive out the gate and then I walk back to the production office. I check with the Paramount publicity office which supplies me with Fidler's phone number and when I dial it, a woman answers. Her name is LaVerne and she is Fidler's private secretary. She tells me Fidler left this morning on Sterling Hayden's yacht for a few days of deep sea fishing at Cabo San Lucas. He'll be returning in a week and until then he is unreachable. When I try to tell LaVerne that my need to speak to him is urgent, she just laughs. She says she fields dozens of calls a day and they're all urgent. With a pleasant 'Have a good day", she hangs up on me.

Since Heather is not within sight in the production office and there's no note from her on the message board, I get her home phone number from Mitzi and dial it. After ten rings, no answer. I try again in case I misdialed. Same result. I replace the receiver. I'm beginning not to care where she is. Maybe she's on a yacht headed for a fishing trip at Cabo. I wouldn't put it past her. I decide to go home.

It's past six thirty when I pull into the driveway and when I walk through the back door into the kitchen, Yvette dashes toward me and leaps into my arms.

"You're late, Uncle Joe. The spaghetti will be all gone," she says breathlessly.

"Not a chance, sweetheart, I promise. Here, let me look at you,"

I put her down and she pirouettes for me. She's sporting a red corduroy dress with a white lace collar and Mary Jane shoes on her feet. To top if off, her hair has been styled in an updo, just the way Jill used to wear it.

"I love your hair," I say.

"Just like Mommy's " she says. "Aunt Bunny fixed it for me."

"A labor of love," Bunny says from the doorway to the dining room. "I hope you're hungry because we are starved."

"Can I change?" I ask.

"No," they say in unison.

"Okay, okay," I say, "but I have one phone call I have to make. Three minutes, no longer. Promise."

"Three minutes," Bunny says with an edge like a Gillette blue blade, "and then I rip the phone from the wall."

"Absolutely," I say reaching in my pocket for Heather's home phone number and dialing it. After two rings a man answers.

"Buddy?" I say.

"No, Seth."

"The writing partner," I say.

"That's right. Who are you?" I tell him. "The flak," he says.

"I prefer professional motion picture publicist but let's not quibble over labels. I'm looking for Heather."

"Not here."

"Any idea where I can find her?"

"Not a clue."

"Can you put Buddy on the phone?"

"Not at the moment. We've been working here all afternoon but made the mistake of ordering in some rotten Mexican food. He's in the john fighting Mother Nature and I'm on my way home."

Bunny is looking at her watch and tapping her foot. Not a good sign.

"Then can I leave a message?"

"You can leave it," Seth says, "I'm not sure she'll get it."

"Tomorrow morning. The production office. Nine o'clock sharp. If she's a minute late, I'll allow Mr. Capra to fire her. Got it?"

"Got it."

"Good," I say, just as Bunny is reaching for the wall unit.

CHAPTER SEVEN

I don't know what possessed me to go to Lila's office but I did.

When I awakened at seven-fifteen this morning, I was all set for a leisurely breakfast before I bearded my ambitious underling at the studio. But I had a card and a key and something drove me to make a detour before driving to the Paramount lot. The card carried the address of Lila James and Associates. The key, which Lila had given me, would open the office door. Dex had said something that was eating at me, that maybe Heather had xeroxed his article and if she had, maybe the copy was in her company office where it would be safe from discovery. A long shot? Sure, but worth the effort which was minimal.

Lila's digs are definitely low-rent. The office building on Western Avenue near Beverly looks to pre-date Hoover's Great Depression and even a quick glance tells me that maintenance is not high on management's list of priorities. Brick and mortar, two stories high, it is located next to a furniture store which is 'Going Out Of Business' and apparently has been doing so for decades. The foyer is dimly lit and smells musty. The directory next to the out-of-order elevator lists six tenants; Lila, two lawyers, a CPA, a travel agency and something called the Bookbinders Association of America. Twelve offices are apparently empty.

I climb the stairs to Suite 202 which, from the hallway, appears to be slightly larger than a broom closet. Lila's name is neatly printed on a plaque on the door. I take out the key and am about to insert it in the lock when I turn the handle. Oddly It gives. Immediately I sense something's wrong. Gently I push the door open.

The suite consists of one room and it is dim and unlit. The window at the far end of the room looks out upon a brick wall which belongs to the furniture store. In the gloom I spot a couple of desks, a settee and coffee table, some filing cabinets, a table upon which sits a xerox machine, a fax machine and a hot plate and coffee pot as well as a pile of papers and magazines. I flip the switch by the door. Overhead fluorescents sputter and flicker and then light up the room. Illuminated, the office looks even worse. The walls are dingy and the cheap motel artwork doesn't help. To my left are two closed doors which I check out. One opens into a closet, the other into a tiny bathroom.

I walk over to the xerox machine and when I do, I spot a wadded up sheet of paper in the waste basket. I pluck it out and un-wad it. One look and I know this is going to be my lucky day. It is off-center and half-printed but when I see Bette Davis' name scattered throughout the copy, I have no doubt as to what this is, how it got here and who is responsible. I smooth it and fold it and slip it into my jacket pocket. Unbelievably only five minutes have elapsed and my work here is done. I turn to go back to the door when I see it. On the floor, beside the far desk, a woman's shoed foot is barely visible. I freeze for a moment, then cautiously walk to the back of the room.

Stuffed into the corner behind the desk is the lifeless body of Heather Leeds, her half-open purse lying by her side. Her eyes are staring toward the ceiling and her expensive white cashmere sweater is awash in blood having dried from a crimson red to a dirty brown. What was it I had just thought to myself? The wrong place at the wrong time. I suddenly feel like some kind of Jonah. I resist the urge to check her body temperature. This is a crime scene and I don't belong here. Nonetheless her features are so pale I am certain she has been lying here like this for hours.

I glance at the typewriter sitting atop her desk. A sheet of paper has been inserted in the platen and something has been typed on it. As a precaution I jam my hands in my pockets, then lean closer to read what had been written.

Dear Lila:

I hate to bother you while you are laid up in the hospital but I have to share my fears with someone and I honesty feel you are the only one I can turn to. I believe I am in real danger. It's not only the looks I've been getting but the way he talks about me behind my back. I don't even feel secure within the confines of the studio. I know if I try to drag the police into this it might cost you this job and that's the last thing I want.

And there it ends. A cry for help. A woman in fear of her life but from whom? She never got a chance to say. I feel a chill and start to back away from this grotesque scene. I keep backing until I'm near the door and then I stop, thinking about the crumpled xerox copy in my pocket. Taking it for Dexter's sake is one thing. Removing it from a crime scene is quite another. I slip the paper from my jacket and use my handkerchief to wipe it down, then wad it up again and drop it into the wastebasket. I realize it may tend to involve Dexter in what happened here but hiding evidence in a murder investigation is not in my genes. Besides I don't believe for a moment that Dexter could have anything to do with Heather's death.

I exit the office and look around for signs of life. Sounds of typing come from the office across the way. I check my watch. Seven-fifty-five. The Bookbinders Association of America likes to get an early jump on the day. I turn the handle and walk in. A dowdy grey-haired lady in a frumpy dress is typing away but looks up at me, startled and then wary.

"What do you want?" she manages to get out.

"I'm sorry to barge in like this," I say. "but I need to use your phone."

She shakes her head unconvincingly.

"No, I'm sorry but—"

"It's an emergency, ma'am. There's a dead body in the office across the hall."

Her eyes widen and she rolls her chair back several feet from the desk, pointing to the phone as she does.

I thank her and dial Aaron Kleinschmidt's home number. At this hour he may not have left for his office in the Homicide Division at the Police Administration Building.

"Yeah, who's this?" he says when he picks up the phone. Aaron is divorced and with no wife around to monitor his manners, he displays a few rough edges,

"Your favorite Hollywood feather merchant," I say.

"Jesus, Joe. Do you know what time it is? What can be so damned important at this hour of the morning."

"The usual," I say.

A long pause,

"No," he says.

"Yes," I reply.

Aaron and I have been good friends for years ever since 1947 when he tried to frame me for murder. In those days he played ball with a crooked police chief but he finally got fed up and decided to play it straight. Since then he and I have been involved in a few cases in which I had the bad fortune to stumble across corpses. The last time it happened, he warned me if there was a recurrence he was going to take me off his Christmas list.

"Joe, I warned you—"

"I know, Aaron, but this one's not my fault," I say.

"They never are. Okay, Jonah, fill me in."

I do so as the Bookbinder's secretary continues to roll further and further away from me, listening in disbelief and horror as I describe the scene in Suite 202.

When I finally hang up, the secretary, whose name is Gladys, reluctantly permits me to sit in her office while I wait for Aaron and his army of technicians to arrive.

"Poor dear Lila, I felt so bad when I heard about her accident on the staircase. A lovely woman. I sent flowers. That is, WE did. The Bookbinders, I mean."

"Very thoughtful," I say.

"As for the other one—" She sniffs and harrumphs and then continues, "I suppose one shouldn't speak ill of the dead but she had no use for anyone. Coming and going, I would try to greet her with a cheery hello, but not a peep, not even a glance. Not a word, except for the day before yesterday, of course, when you could hear her screaming up and down the hallway, she and that man and, my word, the mouth on that woman, the language she used."

"What man are you talking about, Gladys?"

"Why, the man with the beard, of course. An older gentleman, very nicely dressed, very distinguished."

An image of Travis Wright pops into my mind.

"And what were they yelling about?"

"Everything. Marriage, divorce, money. Everything. It was awful. They'd still be at it if it wasn't for Mr. Beck. He's a lawyer down the hall. Elderly but a big man. Very imposing. He told them to quiet down or he would call the police. Miss Leeds went straight into her office and locked the door and the bearded man hurried to the staircase and left."

"Gladys, could you be a little more specific about what was

said?" I ask.

"Dear me, no," she replies."I was trying to shut them out. I finally went into Mr. Fasselbender's private office and shut the door. He wasn't there, of course."

"Of course."

Interesting. A man who may or may not have been an ex-husband and who threatened to kill her knew exactly where Heather's office was.

Just then I hear them coming and I step out into the hall. Aaron has three men in civilian clothes with him as well as a uniformed officer. I point to the open doorway of 202. He gives me a look and then he and the guys in civvies walk in carrying their equipment. I start to follow. Aaron holds up the palm of his hand and throws me a glare that would panic Vlad the Impaler. I stop in my tracks.

For a few minutes I pace up and down the hallway and then Aaron emerges.

"Okay. Slowly and concisely, what were you doing here?"

Slowly and concisely I tell him everything.

"Did you touch anything?"

"Doorknobs."

"That's it?"

"That's it," I say.

"The unfinished letter in the typewriter, what's that all about?" Aaron asks.

"The lady was working with me at Paramount on a movie being directed by Frank Capra. After only a week she had alienated just about everyone within spitting distance. If it had been up to me I would have fired her on Day One but it wasn't within my power to do that."

"So you have no idea who the 'he' might be in the letter?"

"Could be a dozen guys," I shrug.

"Or none of them," Aaron says. "I'm fascinated by the image

I have of her sitting at the typewriter, stopped in mid-stroke by what? A knife to the chest? And yet there's no blood on the typewriter and none on the letter. Odd."

I smile. Aaron's nobody's fool and never has been.

"I'll need you at the Hollywood Division for a formal statement," he says. "Let's say two o'clock. One of their detectives, probably Brubaker, will be taking the lead. I'll be on hand In case he tries to arrest you on sight."

"Thanks," I say.

"What are friends for?" he smiles. "You can go now."

"Go? Does that mean I have to leave the building?"

"Joe, I don't care where you go," he says. "Just go." And with that he ducks back into Suite 202.

Able to take a hint, I turn to leave just as a heavy-set man with white flowing locks and thick rimless glasses is coming down the hallway carrying an attaché case. He stops at the open door to 202, peers in, cranes his neck at the activity for several seconds, then looks at me and without comment, continues on his way. I watch as he stops in front of Suite 204, takes out a key and enters. I amble over to the door and check his plaque. It reads: Zachary Beck, Attorney at Law. I knock on the door. No answer. I knock again. Still no answer. Hesitantly I open the door and peer in.

"Mr. Beck?" I say.

I hear running water which suddenly stops and at that moment, Zachary Beck emerges from the bathroom, wringing his hands to dry them off. He looks at me annoyed.

"Damned building. They're supposed to supply towels to the tenants. Guess I'm lucky I've still got a half a roll of toilet paper left by the crapper." He squints through thick glasses. "Do I know you?"

"No, sir," I say.

"Are you the one who croaked the babe next door? If so you've come to the right place. Homicide is my specialty. Pull up a seat."

He walks over to his desk and plops down in his chair.

"I'm not a client, Mr. Beck," I say.

"Not yet," he replies. "You will be. Wrong time, wrong place. It happens all the time to really fine people. Nothing to worry about. What'd you say your name was?"

"I didn't but it's Bernardi and I'd like to talk to you—"

"Of course you would and any consultation is free, no obligation, and don't look so jittery. There isn't a case that can't be beat if you go about it the right way."

I lean forward, hands spread on his desk and stare him down in a loud voice.

"Mr. Beck, I did not kill anybody and I don't need a lawyer," I say as emphatically as I can.

He looks up at me with a puzzled expression.

"Then why the hell are you standing there wasting my time?" he asks.

"I came to ask you about that raucous shouting match that took place in the hallway a couple or days ago. Maybe you remember it."

"Hell, son, I could hardly forget it. I was just getting ready to take a nap on the sofa when they started going at it."

"Can you remember anything that was said between them?"

"Well, of course, I can. I'm a licensed attorney. It's required of my profession to listen, to pay attention, to assess and analyze."

"And might you share with me what you felt you overheard during that confrontation?"

He squints up at me.

"You a cop, son?"

I laugh.

"Didn't you just observe me outside the open doorway to the murder scene? Tell me, counselor, what would I be doing here if I weren't a cop?" I haven't lied. Not exactly.

He hesitates, then nods.

"Well, it wasn't pretty, I can tell you that. I didn't get it all, not word for word, but it was pretty obvious what happened. These two birds had been married for several years. I'd say he had her by a good twenty years, maybe more. He was some kind of investment maven who got caught with his hand in the molasses jar. He got sent off to prison and she disappeared, apparently taking with her a large chunk of hubby's money which he had salted away unbeknownst to the Internal Revenue Service. He's screaming I want it, she says she doesn't have it. He calls her a thief. She calls him a name I won't repeat. Also it seems she got married again without benefit of divorce. He keeps saying he wants his money, she keeps saying she doesn't know what he's talking about though I'm sure she does. This is a great situation for a divorce lawyer which I happen to be, it's my specialty, but the more I listen the more I realize I want no part of either of them which is when I go out in the corridor and threaten them with the cops."

"Fascinating," I say. "You've been a big help, Mr. Beck."

"Anything to help," he says with a smile. "By the way, Officer Bernardi, are you married?"

"Happily so," I reply.

His face falls a little but nonetheless he takes a card from a holder on his desk and hands it to me.

"Well, take my card anyway," he says. "You never know."

With a smile and one more thank you, I leave lawyer Beck and go in search of Aaron. He's in 202 talking to one of the techs. He looks up and sees me. I beckon him to the doorway. He walks toward me, scowling.

"I thought I told you to go," he grunts.

"I'm going," I say, "but before you leave, spend a few minutes with Gladys across the way and Zachary Beck in the office next door. It'll be worth your while."

I smile and walk down the hallway toward the stairs wiser by far than I was when I walked into this building earlier this morning. I knew I recognized Travis Wright but I didn't connect the name and the face, a face that was front page news for weeks on end in both San Diego newspapers, the Union and the Evening Tribune. Travis Wright, self-describing himself as an investment manager, fleeced millions from the pockets of San Diego's elite using that tried and true chestnut, the Ponzi scheme. Created by Charles Ponzi, investors are guaranteed high returns on their money which in reality do not exist. Initial investors are paid handsomely using money invested by a second generation of suckers. The second tier gets paid by the ever expanding third tier who are breaking down doors to get in on this foolproof get-rich-quick proposition. And it works. It is brilliant in its simplicity. It cannot fail, provided that the perpetrator of this fraud knows when to get out and book passage on a slow boat to China. The trouble is, these guys never do and Travis Wright is just another example of greed run amok. Now he is out of prison and has been looking to lay his hands on some assets which his wife Heather apparently promised to protect for him. Given the situation I would guess that here is a fellow who is going to attract close scrutiny from the boys of the LAPD and in the process, pay less scrutiny to my friend Dexter Craven.

CHAPTER EIGHT

I head back to Paramount as speedily as possible. Mindful of my two o'clock appointment at the Hollywood Division, I need to chat with Dexter beforehand. Not that I think Dexter is involved, I don't, but the police may not share my confidence in the innocence of my normally easy-going friend. Overburdened by too many cases and with too little time, some officers of the law allow themselves to be seduced by what they see as an obvious solution. Worse, once a target has been applied to one's back, it's almost possible to be rid of it. I should know. It's happened to me a couple of times.

He's not in the production office. I check the call sheet and he's not with Bette Davis. Benny, the gate guard, says he hasn't seen him all day. I call the security office and Al Rhinehalter gives me Dexter's home phone. I dial it and after four rings, a woman answers.

"Cissy?" I ask.

"This is Cissy," she says.

"It's Joe Bernardi."

"Oh, migosh, Dexter said he'd run into you, Joe. It is ever so nice to hear your voice. How are you?"

"Fine."

"And married," she says with a smile in her voice.

"Absolutely. And very happily I might add."

"I always liked Bunny," she says. "I am so happy for the both of you, I really am. We must get to together, the four of us."

"Yes, we must, Cissy, and sooner rather than later. Meantime I need to speak to Dexter."

She hesitates for just a moment. Not long, just enough for a little 'ping' to go off in my head.

"I believe he's at the studio, Joe," she says.

"No, he hasn't showed all day. When was the last time you saw him,. Cissy?"

More silence.

"Is there something wrong, Joe?"

"Why would you ask me that, Cissy?"

"I'm not sure. Something in your voice."

"You didn't answer my question."

"What's wrong? Tell me."

"Is he there, Cissy? He has to talk to me. Now."

"He's not here, Joe. The truth is, I haven't seen him since last night."

"What happened?"

"I'd been expecting him for dinner. He came home around nine, stinking drunk in a foul mood. Not like him at all. I asked him where he'd been, what he'd been up to. He wouldn't answer me. He just kept muttering "that bitch this" and "that bitch that" and finally I had enough and I went into the bedroom and locked the door. He started pounding on the door. I told him to sleep it off. Finally he got tired of it and the house became quiet. I'd never seen him like this, Joe. To tell you the truth I was afraid. A long time passed and everything was silent and I figured he had passed out on the sofa but I wasn't about to open the door and look. Eventually I climbed into bed and fell asleep."

"And the next morning?"

"He was gone. I have no idea when he left, He might have caught some sleep on the sofa but I couldn't swear to it."

"And you haven't heard from him?"

"No."

"And you say he's never done this before?"

"Never. Normally he's a happy drunk. Not like that."

"Okay, Cissy." I say finally. "If he calls you tell him to phone me at Paramount right away."

"What's wrong, Joe? What's going on?"

"I can't tell you, Cissy."

"He's in trouble, isn't he? Bad trouble."

"Not yet," I say, "but make sure he calls me."

With that I hang up. I don't want any more questions I can't answer. I check my watch. It's still early, not even ten o'clock. Unless some reporter gets lucky and stumbles onto the story, news of Heather's death won't reach the public for several hours. As a courtesy I owe a couple of phone calls.

I get Glenda Mae on the phone and ask her to trot over the *L.A. Times* morgue and ask my biggest fan, the adorable but matronly Priscilla Watkins, to dig up everything she can on Travis Wright and the San Diego embezzlement scandal. 1957 or 1958, Priscilla will know. In my bottom right hand drawer Glenda Mae will find a glossy photo of Howard Keel autographed "To Priscilla". I have been saving it for a special occasion. This is it. Priscilla collects Hollywood glossies the way a hound dog collects ticks. This will make her day.

I ask her to switch me over to Bertha. It's bad enough that I have to tell my forebearing partner I am embroiled in yet another homicide not of my doing, I have to apprise her of Dexter's possible involvement. As I suspected, this does not sit well. She knows Dexter, albeit casually, and likes him. She, too, is positive he knows nothing about Heather's death and I have her tacit approval to poke around to help prove it. She also volunteers her participation if needed. Another reason why I love the old gal.

I almost ask Glenda Me to connect me to the hospital but then reconsider. Lila's entitled to a face to face to get this news no matter how she might have felt about Heather personally. I head out, leaving behind the usual instruction: If Dexter calls, get a number.

When I arrive at Lila's room I discover she has company. Peter Falk is standing by her bed and the two of them are sharing a laugh. Lila brightens when she sees me.

"Joe! Good morning," she says.

Peter also tosses me a smile.

"How're ya doin', Joe?" he asks.

"Just fine," I lie, unwilling to destroy the festive atmosphere.

"Peter brought me a lovely box of chocolates," she says.

"Here, have a piece," Peter says scooping up a two-pound box of Whitman's from the bedside table and thrusting it under my nose. I notice that there are five empty wrappers.

I wink at Lila.

"What happened to your diet?" I ask.

"Oh, Lila, didn't do this, Joe," Peter says. "I bought this box half off at Rexall's and I've been making sure the candy is still fresh. I don't want anybody getting sick on my account. Here, try this one. I think it's a chocolate covered cherry."

"No, thanks, I'm fine."

"I'll just check it out," Peter says, popping it in his mouth. "Mmmm. Cherry. I was right."

I consult my watch. The time is ten to eleven.

"Look, Pete, I hate to interrupt your breakfast but don't you have an eleven thirty call at the studio?"

"Yeah. Eleven thirty. So what?" He glances at his wrist watch. "Oh, boy, " he says in a panic, "I'm in trouble now. See you guys later." He hurries toward the door, then comes back and gently replaces the candy on the bedside table, then hurries from the room.

"One of a kind," Lila says with a smile.

"Without a doubt," I say.

"Well, it was very sweet of you to drop by, Joe, but you have enough on your plate without checking on me. I'm fine. I really am," she says.

"Lila, this isn't exactly a social call. Tell me everything you know about Heather."

"Oh, my God," she says in dismay, "what has she done now?"

"She's dead, Lila. Murdered."

Lila gasps, shaking her head, her eyes widening in disbelief.

"No," she manages to say quietly.

"I'm sorry. Apparently it happened some time last night at your office."

"How—?"

"She was stabbed to death."

Lila turns her head away, anguished.

"Oh, God, the poor kid. Do they know who did it?"

"No, but superficial evidence seems to point to Dexter Craven."

She looks at me sharply.

"Dexter? Ridiculous."

"I know," I say.

"Dexter's a churchmouse," she says.

"That's why I need to know everything you can possibly tell me about Heather. She must have submitted some kind of resume."

"Sure, but It was mostly lies, Joe. I hired her without checking. Big mistake. When I started having little problems, I pulled out the resume and started making phone calls. She'd put down Jules Stein as a reference but when I checked with MCA they had no record of her employment. Maybe he was a personal reference though I doubt it. I was set to fire her then and there when she walked in with a signed contract to publicize a low budget biker movie they were shooting out in the Mojave. It wasn't much but it was going to keep the lights on for a while. I put her resume back in the drawer. Guess maybe I shouldn't have."

"How about her husband? What do you know about him?"

"He's a screenwriter, I believe. Very successful, too. He's had major deals at several studios over the past four years."

"He and his partner," I say.

"She didn't mention a partner. She said Buddy had a Tony Curtis project with Columbia, something for Audrey Hepburn with Ross Hunter at Universal and I think she mentioned a European co-production with Sean Connery to be shot in Austria. I think the money dried up on that last one."

"And the other two?"

She shrugs.

"Went into turnaround, I guess. I'm pretty sure they didn't get made."

"And he did all of this while writing several dozen television scripts?"

"Television? Oh, no, she said Buddy wouldn't be the least bit interested in television."

Some people lie because they are delusional. Heather Leeds was not one of those people. Her lies were cold and calculating and well thought out. At its heart I believe her life had been a never ending self-serving charade.

"Then you didn't double-check with Northwestern," I say.

"No, why should I have? She made no mention of Northwestern on her resume. In fact, she made it a point to tell me that she hadn't gone to college."

That brings me up short, I would have expected this female Walter Mitty to have cited Vassar or Columbia or maybe even Harvard. But to deny going to a prestigious midwestern university from which she apparently graduated, that was out of character and I wonder why.

We chat for a few more minutes but it's clear that Lila knew nothing about Heather that Heather hadn't invented. Besides she's obviously getting tired so I say goodbye and promise to stop by tomorrow.

It's shortly past noon when I get back to the production office. That makes it two o'clock in the Midwest and I place a call to the Registrar's office at Northwestern. I pass myself off as a prospective employer attempting to verify Heather Leeds degree and a few minutes later I learn that she did indeed matriculate at the School of Communications but she didn't graduate. She dropped out early in her junior year. Odd, I think. Claire Philby wants to honor her as Alumna of the Year;, an honor most third year dropouts wouldn't exactly be eligible for. I ask about the exact date when Heather left the school. I'm told a partial refund of her tuition was returned to her on October 23, 1955. Okay, so Heather was not exactly who she said she was, but what about the woman claiming to be Claire Philby? Remembering what Buddy Lovejoy had said, I ask to be connected to the office of the Dean of the School of Communications. A woman answers the phone.

"Mrs. Philby?" I say.

"Oh, no," she says. "This is Myra Brown. I'm afraid Mrs. Philby is no longer with us. I mean, that is to say, are you a friend?"

"Not really," I say.

"I regret to tell you that Mrs. Philby passed away four months ago."

Another shocker.

"I didn't know," I say. "So sorry."

"Would you like me to connect you to the Dean?"

"Not necessary," I say. "Were you a close friend of Mrs. Philby, Mrs. Brown?"

"That's Miss. and we were colleagues for many years."

"In the School of Communications?"

"Yes."

"And do you remember a student named Heather Leeds? She left the University abruptly about six years ago."

There is a long silence on Miss Brown's end of the line.

"To whom am I speaking?" she asks, suddenly wary.

"My name is Joseph Bernardi. I'm calling from Los Angeles and our firm is considering Miss Leeds for employment."

"I see." Again there is a long silence. "I'm afraid I have nothing to say regarding Miss Leeds," she says coldly.

Interesting. I merely asked if she remembers Heather. A simple yes or no would have sufficed. But apparently she does remember Heather and not fondly and moreover she wants me to know it.

"I sense there was some sort of problem," I say, playing straight man.

"You would have to ask someone else about that," Miss Brown replies stiffly.

"Would that involve some sort of legal problem?" I ask.

"I'm sorry, Mr. Bernardi. I'm very busy and I really can't help you."

And with that, she hangs up.

I stare at the phone for several minutes. Who was this college dropout with a singular talent for alienating everyone she came in contact with and perhaps more important, who is this imposter who has followed her here from Evanston, supposedly to bestow an award which I now seriously doubt even exists.

A light goes on in my head. A very dim one to be sure but a light nonetheless. I reach into my jacket pocket and retrieve the phone slip upon which the ersatz Claire Philby wrote her local contact number. I dial it.

"Cromwell Arms Hotel," comes a man's voice.

"Claire Philby, please."

"I'm sorry, sir, but Mrs. Philby checked out early this morning."

Not good news.

"Do you have any idea where she went?" I ask.

"Our courtesy car drove her to the airport. I assume she flew back to Chicago."

"Of course," I say. "Oh darn, I seem to have lost her home address. Can you give that to me?"

"I'm sorry, sir," the voice says, "but we do not give out that information. Thank you for calling the Cromwell Arms."

And he disconnects with an audible click.

I put my head in my hands. I feel one of Frank Capra's headaches coming on.

CHAPTER NINE

I arrive at the Hollywood Division, fashionably early by four minutes. Aaron makes up for it by being ten minutes late. He shows up with a colleague in tow who I learn is Detective Sergeant Willis Brubaker and when I am introduced, I know him immediately. He's tall, slim, athletic and wears his blonde hair in a military style buzz cut. Ten years ago he was a standout wide receiver for the UCLA Bruins and in the intervening time, I doubt that Willie B. has put on one pound that isn't muscle. He greets me with a warm and disarming smile and a firm handshake and when we enter the squad room, the three of us huddle around Brubaker's desk which is in a partitioned section in the back of the room.

"The lieutenant tells me that on more than one occasion you have been helpful to the police in putting away some very bad people," Brubaker says.

"The lieutenant exaggerates," I say, feigning modesty. I smile at Aaron. He smiles back.

"Nonetheless, we in the department are grateful for your cooperation, Mr. Bernardi, which is why I am going to bend way over to give you a fair shake in this investigation."

The smile is still there but the words are a clear warning. Whatever Aaron might have said to this guy is going to get me so far and no further.

"Let's start with an easy question," he says. "Where were you last evening between, say eleven p.m and one in the morning?"

"Is that the time of death?" I ask.

Brubaker waggles a finger at me, again smiling.

"Uh,uh,uh," he says. "I ask the questions, Mr. Bernardi."

"Then I'm a suspect," I say, careful to phrase it as a statement.

"In my book, every taxpayer in Los Angeles is a suspect until I say they are not," Brubaker says. "Last night?"

"Home in bed with my wife."

"Bed with wife," he mumbles as he makes a notation on a yellow pad in front of him.

"This one's a little tougher," Brubaker says, "What were you doing at that office at eight o'clock this morning?"

I glance over at Aaron who is quietly watching and listening and it's then I figure out what he's doing here. This is not his investigation and he's not going to interfere but he's going to act as my advocate in case I need one. So far he doesn't think I need him. That's my best guess. Or maybe he just likes to watch me squirm.

"I was looking for something," I respond.

"And what would that have been?"

"Some paperwork in conjunction with my duties as a publicity spokesman for a motion picture."

Brubaker smiles some more.

"Mr. Bernardi, that is perhaps the neatest non-answer I have ever heard. Bravo. I understand that you also write fiction."

"On occasion."

"Tell me about Dexter Craven."

"What about him?"

"Did he kill Miss Leeds?"

"Of course not."

"You seem pretty certain of that."

"I know the man."

"Then you two are close."

"Close enough."

"In that case, maybe you know where he is."

"No, I don't."

Brubaker leans back in his chair lacing his hands behind his neck and staring at me thoughtfully.

"By ten o'clock this morning I had two of my men at Paramount Studios this morning, asking questions about Miss Leeds. Mr. Craven's name came up often."

"Among many others, I'm sure."

"Granted, but Craven was the only one who had threatened to kill her in front of witnesses."

"Who told you that?"

"A hairdresser and a wardrobe lady and then after some gentle coaxing, Bette Davis as well. Oh, and all three said you were in the room and also must have heard it unless, of course. you have a severe hearing problem in which case I would suggest you get to an otologist as soon as possible."

"It wasn't a threat. Not exactly," I say.

Brubaker leans forward and now the smile is gone.

"No? Then exactly what was it, Mr. Bernardi? Your friend Mr. Craven was certain that the victim had stolen material from an article he was writing about Miss Davis. He was furious with the victim for undermining his work and this encounter wasn't the first time he'd gone after her in public. Earlier they'd gotten into an ugly shouting match on the set."

"In a work environment, tempers flare—"

"What were your fingerprints doing on that discarded xerox copy wadded up in the wastebasket in the victim's office?"

It hits me like a blow to the solar plexus. i start to stammer but I can't get the words out. The truth is, I have no words to get out. I look over at Aaron for help.

"Whatever the hell it is, Joe, just tell him," Aaron says.

So I do. About finding the door unlocked, then finding the xerox and putting it in my pocket to take back to the studio and confront Heather Leeds, maybe even get her fired, then finding her body and realizing that I can't remove evidence from a crime scene so I do a half-assed job of obliterating my prints and putting the xerox back where I found it and then going across the hall to call Aaron.

Brubaker listens attentively.

"Okay," he says, "for the moment, I'll buy that. But I ask you again, where can I find Dexter Craven? Even if you don't know for sure, what's your best guess?"

I tell him I haven't got one. I also tell him there are plenty of people who had little or no use for Heather. I start to tell him about Travis Wright when he puts up his hand to silence me.

"We know all about the so-called ex-husband," he says "I've read the police report about that altercation at the Howard Johnsons. We're waiting to pick him up when he returns to his hotel. We've also taken a statement from a press agent named MacGruder who has motive but also has an alibi for the time of death. And we've also questioned the studio's security chief."

"Rhinehalter? What for?"

"Five days ago Leeds filed a complaint of sexual harrassment against him, a charge he's violently denied, but it's not the first time he's had a run-in with women at the studio. My guy heard that management has him on a short leash and we're digging a little deeper. So you see, Mr. Bernardi, despite what you may think, I am an equal opportunity bulldog."

"Then there's someone else you really ought to know about, Sergeant, a woman from out of town—"

Just then Brubaker's phone rings. He puts up a hand to silence me as he answers it. His expression turns to a scowl as he grunts a couple of times and then says, "I'm on my way." He hangs up and rises from his chair.

"Sorry, gentlemen, this will have to keep. Another case. We've spotted the perp near an abandoned storefront on Century Boulevard." He hesitates and looks down at me. "Oh, and Mr. Bernardi, that letter in the typewriter which you scanned, that is a deep dark secret which you and I and the rest of the LAPD will withhold from the press and everybody else. Do we understand one another?"

"We do," I say.

"I thought we would."

With that he hurries from the squad room. I look over at Aaron with a frustrated look. He smiles at me.

"Don't worry, Joe, I think you're safe from arrest for at least one more day."

"Great. Look, Aaron, there's this woman—"

"Don't tell me, Joe. I warned you. This is not my case. I only get to butt in if I think Brubaker's fucking up and so far he's right on top of things."

"But—"

"No buts, amigo. Whatever you think you have, take it up with Willie B. and not me. Now come on, let's get out of here."

We head for the parking lot. Once again I try in vain to get Aaron to listen.

"Joe, I know you're worried about your friend but trust me he's not going to be railroaded. If he's not involved he'll be cleared. I know Brubaker. He's tough but he's open minded."

"Okay, I'll take your word for it, at least for the moment."

"Good. Now go home, have a beer and relax. Leave this mess to us."

"I'll think about it," I say.

As Aaron drives away in his unmarked Dodge Charger, I slip behind the wheel of my Bentley. Maybe he's right. I've been wound up like a cheap watch since early this morning. Maybe I need to step back and take a deep breath. Yes, a good idea. I'm going to head for home and sack out on the chaise lounge just as soon as I can locate a phone booth and check with the office for messages.

"Mr. Craven called in about twenty minutes ago," Glenda Mae tells me. "He sounded scared to death."

So much for the chaise lounge.

"Did he leave a number?" She gives it to me. "Okay," I say. "You haven't heard from me and you don't know where I am."

"Haven't a clue," she says.

"Good girl. I'll touch base with you later."

I hang up and dial the number she gave me. The voice that answers tells me I have reached the House of Windsor Hotel. I am pretty sure this is old, dingy and rents rooms by the hour. Years of experience have taught me that the fancier the name, the bigger the cockroaches.

"One-oh-two," I say.

"You a cop?" he asks.

"No, but it can be arranged."

"Hang on."

A moment later Dexter comes on the line.

"Dex?"

"Joe, thank God. Oh, Jesus, this is awful."

"This hotel, Dex, where is it?"

"I'm not sure. Near the airport. Maybe Inglewood. Joe, I didn't do it, swear to God."

"Do what, Dex?"

"Haven't you been listening to the radio? Leeds is dead. Somebody killed her."

"Take it easy and sit tight. I'm on my way."

I hang up and grab the phone book. I find the hotel listed in the yellow pages. Two minutes later I'm in my car and headed for Inglewood.

As I weave my way through the afternoon traffic that generally clogs Western Avenue at this time of day, I tune my radio to an all-news station. Dex was right. The newshounds are all over this story. They haven't got it right but they're close enough. Attractive Hollywood publicist slain in her swank office in a high-powered industry office building. Police discount robbery as a motive. A search is underway for a possible suspect. His name is being withheld. A guy from the mail room at 20th remembers her and has nice things to say about her. Obviously he didn't know her well or his brain has turned to mush. It goes on like that with a gory description of the murder scene, all in the name of the public's right to know. When I've had enough I switch to a local disc jockey who is spinning Roy Orbison's 'Only the Lonely'. Now that's more like it.

The guy at the desk at the House of Windsor is what I expected. Short and dumpy, balding, hooded suspicious eyes and a shirt that hasn't seen a washing machine in weeks.

"One-oh-two," I say to him.

"The guy owes me twelve bucks for a late checkout."

"Chalk it up to one of life's teachable moments. Which way?"

"You a cop?"

"We've had this conversation."

"Oh, you're that guy."

"That's me," I say.

He points.

"Top of the stairs."

I toss him a mirthless smile and hurry up the staircase to the second floor landing. To my right I spot Room 102. I rap on the door.

"Dex?"

A moment later the door opens a crack and Dexter peers out from the darkened room. When he sees me he opens the door wide to let me in, then quickly closes it and throws the deadbolt. It's obvious he's terrified and when he turns to face me, I can see in the dim light from the window exactly why. One of his eyes has been blackened and he has a nasty cuts on his forehead and cheek.

"What happened to you?" I ask, flipping on the lights.

He recoils, shading his eyes.

"Long story," he says.

"Tell me."

"I didn't kill her, Joe, I swear to God."

"I know that. What happened?"

He sits down on the disheveled bed, hands folded abjectly between his legs. He stares at the floor.

"I got drunk," he says.

"I know," I say. He gives me a look. "I talked to Cissy."

"Oh, God," he mutters.

"So?" I say, waiting patiently.

He sighs.

"I was so damned furious with Heather I stopped off at a bar before going home. You know, I never do that, and I had a few drinks. Well, maybe more than a few and when I got home, Cissy was mad. Very mad."

"I know."

"And she started yelling about how that woman was ruining my life and I started yelling back, which I never do, saying I can take care of myself and suddenly she's in the bedroom and locking the door and I'm banging on the door and so I'm thinking, well, the hell with you, lady, which I never would have thought if I'd been sober. I love her, Joe. Love her very much."

"I know that, Dex."

"Anyway I leave the house to go find a bar to have a drink. Well, maybe more than one. So I find this bar and when they close I go find another one because I'm not going home. That's what I was thinking. Teach Cissy a lesson. If I wanted to have a few drinks and stay out all night, that was my business, you understand?"

"I understand, Dex."

"I even call home to tell her I'm staying out all night and where I am and what I'm doing is none of her business. But she's dead asleep and doesn't answer the phone so I hang up. Next thing I know I'm buying drinks for this very nice lady, or at least, that's what I thought, and then when I said I didn't want to go home she said she knew a hotel nearby where I could get a room for the night so I said sure because I was out on my feet. You know, I never do things like this, Joe, swear to God."

"I know."

"Anyway we get to the hotel and I pay for the room and we go upstairs, me and this lady, and we go in the room—" He looks around. "THIS room, Joe."

"Right."

"But when I walk in there's this guy in here and I don't know who the hell he is and when I ask him he hits me and when I hit the floor he picks me up and hits me again and then he starts going through my pockets and he takes my wallet and my keys and my watch and my wedding ring and that's all I remember until I woke up. That was like one o'clock. Maybe later. I hurt all over and when I see my face it all starts to come back to me and all I want to do is get out of here. So I go downstairs and I'm starting to walk out when the guy at the desk says I owe him money for a late checkout. I say he's crazy and try to go but he grabs my arm real hard and I think I'm in for another fight and that's when I hear the guy's radio, about Heather being killed. Now the guy's threatening to call the police and I realize I want no part of that so I tell him I'm going upstairs and call my wife to come and get me and she'll pay whatever I owe. And that's when I called your office."

He looks up at me like a three-year old seeking absolution for stealing a chocolate chip from the cookie jar.

"I believe you, Dex, and aside from getting crocked and then letting yourself get rolled by a couple of pros, you haven't done anything wrong. But you're going to have to talk to the police."

He shakes his head.

"I think I need a lawyer," he says.

"If it turns out you do, I can get you a good one but I can promise you, the minute you say lawyer to a cop, he puts you in his crosshairs and that's somewhere you don't want to be."

"Okay," he says. "Whatever you say."

At that moment there is a loud knock on the door. Dex looks up at me fearfully.

"Open the door, Mr. Bernardi," comes the voice from the corridor. I don't need to see his badge to know who it is. I walk over to the door and open it. Sgt. Willis Brubaker eyes me with disgust and pushes past me into the room. Two uniformed cops linger in the doorway. Brubaker stares down at Dexter.

"Dexter Craven?" he asks.

Dexter nods.

Brubaker turns to me.

"You should have called me, Mr. Bernardi," he says. "A big mistake. A very big mistake."

CHAPTER TEN

The good news is, I don't get arrested. Neither does Dexter. We face a lot of tough questions, but we are spared the hot lights, the rubber hoses and the water treatment. Brubaker doesn't like our answers but he has no choice. After two hours he lets us go because he has nothing to hold us on. Well, almost nothing.

As he escorts us to the squad room door leading to the stairs to the lower level and as Dexter goes on ahead, he pulls me aside and speaks quietly in my ear.

"I could slap you with obstruction of justice and see you put away for ninety days, maybe longer. As a courtesy to Lieutenant Kleinschmidt I'm not going to do that but I suggest you keep your nose out of this investigation, Mr. Bernardi, or next time you'll be staring at the walls in county jail."

"I hear you."

"Good," he says. "Then you must have paid a visit to that otologist I suggested. Good night, Mr. Bernardi, don't let me see you again."

I can feel him staring at me as I descend into the lobby below.

"What was that all about?" Dexter asks.

"Nothing important," I say. "Come on, I'll drive you home."

I'm doing this because Dexter has no idea where his car is. It's nowhere near the House of Windsor and he can't remember the name of the last bar he was in. It's likely that the B-Girl and her buddy found the car and drove it away in which case they will most likely have ditched it and the cops will eventually find it. In the meantime, I play chauffeur. Several times I check my rear view mirror but if Brubaker is continuing to follow me I see no sign of it.

Dexter lives in a modest but neat three bedroom house in Encino in the Valley. I visited several times years ago and I recognize it right away. It's past seven o'clock, dark, and the lights in the living room are shining brightly. Dexter is nervously staring at the front window.

"Come in with me," he says.

"I can't, Dex—"

"Please. You don't have to stay long. It'll make it easier. Besides Cissy would love to see you again."

I hesitate.

"Sure, why not?" I say as I start to get out of the car.

Dexter needn't have worried. When Cissy opens the front door, she takes one look and rushes into Dex's arms. holding him close. He starts muttering apologies, she keeps saying it's all right and I feel as useful as a Frigidaire in an igloo. But as I start to walk away she grabs my jacket.

"Joe Bernardi, don't you run away before you even say hello," she chides me in that precious Savannah accent of hers.

"Just leaving you two lovebirds to your own devices," I say.

"I will hear of no such thing," she says. "You come in here right now and let me look at you." All the while she's tugging at my sleeve. I don't have much choice.

Once inside I pose for inspection and apparently pass. She takes me in her arms and squeezes me tight.

"Thank you," she says quietly in my ear. And then louder, "Now what can I get you to drink?"

"Really, Cissy, I can't stay."

"We have Coors," she says brightly.

"I should get home—"

"One cold beer and I do insist," she says. "Dex, darling. will you get Joe a beer from the refrigerator?"

"Sure," he says.

When he's out of earshot, her expression darkens. Cissy is one hundred percent Southern belle but like most young ladies of the south, there's considerable steel beneath the crinoline.

"I must know what happened, Joe," she says.

"It's a long story."

"Then it will have to keep until tomorrow. I will call you at the studio."

"I'm sure Dex will tell you—"

"Dexter will tell me what he thinks I want to hear. Please."

The look in her eyes is anxious. I nod.

"I'll call you in the morning. We'll have lunch,"

"Fine," she says, then switches gears as Dex enters carrying my beer. "Dex, you will never guess. Dear Bette Davis phoned a couple of hours ago, desperate to know what is going on. She is so worried about you."

"That was kind of her," he says, handing me the bottle of beer and retaining one for himself. "I'll thank her tomorrow."

We spend the next fifteen minutes talking about nothing consequential. Despite Cissy's obligatory hospitality I know I'm in the way and I try to down my beer in record speed. I finally make it to the door, hugs and handshakes all around, and I get myself out of there.

By the time I arrive home Yvette's already in bed and my pork chops are being kept warm in the oven. Bunny gives me a big hug and a bigger kiss and then sits me down at the kitchen table so I can impart a blow-by-blow account of today's events. With no way to wriggle out, I eat and talk and swill Nehi, not even a Coors to comfort me. Her eyes narrow in displeasure when I start talking about my misadventures with the police but brighten when I relate the warning delivered to me by Sergeant Brubaker.

"There, you see, Joe," she says. "That sergeant has it right. The woman's death is none of your concern. I hope you're going to listen to him and stay out of it."

Absolutely, I tell her, and I mean it. But I have this niggling feeling that, like it or not, I may be in this thing up to my ears.

When I arrive at the studio early the next morning, I find myself in for another surprise. Benny, the gate guard, puts up his hand to stop me and tells me I'm wanted in the security office. When I ask what it's about, he shrugs. No idea, he says. He's lying.

When I walk in a guy in a grey flannel suit is standing by one of the filing cabinets thumbing through the contents. A uniformed security officer is at Rhinehalter's desk carefully going through the contents of a file folder. I see no sign of Al Rhinehalter.

The guy in grey flannel turns to me.

"Can I help you?" he asks.

"Benny on the gate told me I was needed."

"Name?"

"Joe Bernardi."

A flicker of recognition crosses his face and he stops what he's doing and approaches me.

"Sit down," he says pointing to a chair near the desk. He does not offer his hand. "Johnson," he says sharply in the uniform's direction, head nodding him out of his chair. Johnson goes off and grey flannel sits down across from me.

"Noel Peabody, head of studio operations," he tells me.

"Nice to meet you," I say. "Where's Al Rhinehalter?"

"Terminated. Last Wednesday at five p.m. The studio conveys its condolences on the death of your associate."

"Why?"

He looks puzzled.

"Why what?"

"Why was Rhinehalter terminated?"

"Charges had been lodged against him. Following an incident on Wednesday afternoon, we felt we could no longer retain Mr. Rhinehalter in his present position."

"What sort of incident?"

"I don't really see where this is any of your business, Mr. Bernardi,"

"What sort of incident?" I ask again. This prissy little weasel is getting on my nerves.

"A shouting match near the commissary. He accused Miss Leeds of lying about him. His choice of words was unsavory, not the sort of thing we expect of a Paramount employee."

"She'd accused him of sexual harassment."

"Yes."

"Without proof."

"Where there's smoke there's fire."

"You deprive a man of his livelihood and blame it on smoke?"

"I don't believe Paramount has to answer to you for the implementation of its policies."

"The charge against Rhinehalter was totally bogus."

"And you know this how, Mr Bernardi?"

"Because I knew Heather Leeds. Keep a sharp lookout, Mr. Peabody," I say as I get to my feet.

"For what?"

"For a lawyer and a million dollar lawsuit for wrongful termination."

And with that I turn on my heel and get the hell out of there. I'm sick. Even in death Heather Leeds is still ruining people's lives.

As soon as I walk into the production office I find a message from Frank Capra. He needs to see me right away. I stop long enough to grab a container of coffee and start to walk over to the sound stage. Several people on the way give me funny looks, some smiling, some concerned, some flashing me a thumbs up. Peter Falk comes dashing up the street in his well-worn brown overcoat and beat-up fedora heading for makeup but he stops long enough to tell me not to worry and that he's with me all the way. Anything I need, just ask. I have no idea what he's talking about but before I can get him to explain, he's racing away, his new "old coat" flapping behind him.

Capra is sitting alone on his folding chair studying his script. The crew is laying dolly track for the next setup and the Best Boy is working the lights with DP Bronner. He looks up as I approach and gestures to the chair next to him.

"Are you okay?" he asks.

"Sure. Why not?" I reply.

"We were told you'd been arrested," Capra says.

"No, Dexter Craven and I were questioned, that's all."

"Craven. He's the one doing the story on Bette."

"That's right."

"Ever since the cops swarmed all over the lot yesterday, a lot of crazy stories have been floating around."

"I'm sure," I say.

"Look, Joe, I heard from UA this morning. They're not happy. Squabbling on the set is one thing, a murder is something else and this kind of publicity could really tar the picture. God forbid it turns out she was killed by someone attached to the company."

"I don't think that's the case."

"Good. Give me an abusive husband or an irate boyfriend any time."

"Probably not that either."

"Too bad. Well, whatever it is, Joe, we have to minimize this story."

"That'll be hard, Frank. You know how America loves their gory murders."

"I always thought they loved Longfellow Deeds and Jefferson Smith," he snorts. "I guess times change."

"That they do."

"Well, do what you can," he says. He looks past me. "Excuse me, our star has just arrived and we must talk." I look. Glenn Ford has just walked onto the sound stage. Capra stands and looks down at me. "The guy ties a knot in my gut every time he bounces into a scene like a musical comedy funny man." With that he walks off to make nice with his leading man.

I grab this opportunity to duck out and go in search of Bette Davis. I don't have to look any further than her dressing room. I knock and she bids me enter and when I do, I am stunned. She is sitting at her vanity in a silk evening dress and when she turns to face me, she is a vision. I know the script. I know she is transformed from a hag into a Park Avenue socialite but this is Capra at his best. This radiant lady is once again the glamourous star of the 30's and 40's.

She smiles knowingly.

"Not bad for an old bag of 53, eh, Joe?"

"You defy time and gravity, Miss Davis. I am overwhelmed but not surprised."

"Well, get over it, Joe, and for God's sake stop calling me Miss Davis. Those I like and respect call me Bette and you've made the list."

"Honored."

"Now where's our pal? We have an article to finish and don't tell me he's in the pokey."

"He'll be here by noon," I say, "and the pokey is not in his future."

"Good. I have no idea what happened to that woman or why but I am damned sure Dexter had nothing to do with it."

"His wife told him about your call. He's very grateful."

"What? Grateful that I don't think he's a cold blooded killer? I'll support him with more than words if it comes to that. Now, Joe, I have a problem which you must deal with. Louella wants me to lunch with her."

"Excellent," I say.

"Excellent? Me sit down with that fat old walrus with claws on her flippers? I can see that you don't know me very well. I'm a lousy interview, Joe, because I say what I mean and mean what I say and Louella is the best, the very best,at what she does and her bullshit detector is operational at all times. Now even though I was far from first choice for this role, I can probably pick my words carefully enough while discussing Mr.Capra and the film but If queried about Mr. Ford, I will do this venture no good. No good at all."

"Perhaps if you were to—"

"Perhaps if I were to NOTHING!" she says angrily and launches into a tirade about Ford that includes such terms as son of a bitch and shitheel.

"Yes, I see where you're coming from," I say. "Suppose we do this. We have lunch at Scandia's, the three of us, and I set a few ground rules. Like, for instance, you express an admiration for Mr. Capra and for the original film and delight at the chance to pay an homage to a woman who was once a dear friend, May Robson."

She stares at me for several moments.

"You sure know how to sling it, don't you Joe?"

"When I have to. We'll make this lunch all about your grand and glorious career."

"But no talk of comeback," she says firmly.

"Absolutely not."

"I've been choosy, not rejected."

"Of course."

"Ten years ago I should have won my third Oscar for 'All About Eve' and I would have, too, if it hadn't been for Judy Holliday, if she hadn't been so damned good and so damned funny. Poor kid." She moves from wisecrack to genuine sympathy in a mini-second. Several months ago Holliday had been in Philadelphia trying out a Broadway-bound play about actress Laurette

Taylor. She fell ill and the production was cancelled. A month later Holliday underwent throat surgery.

I check my watch. I have a full plate this morning if I'm going to get to my lunch with Cissy Craven. Again I promise Bette I'll handle the Louella Parsons situation and head for the production office.

I leave word with Louella's secretary and then spend thirty minutes trying to quell the fears of the money guys at UA. We had an almost identical situation two years ago while filming 'Some Like It Hot" and the notoriety didn't hurt the box office one bit. When I finally get to hang up, I think I have them half-convinced. Next I call Phineas and several other influential columnists and ask them to ignore or at least soft pedal Heather Leeds connection to our film. They tentatively agree barring any egregious developments. Finally I call Cissy and ask her to meet me at Biff's All-American Diner which is in the Valley and close to her home. She asks if I can swing by and pick her up. Her car-less husband had to borrow her Volkswagen to get to the studio and she has no wheels. I tell her I'll be by at twelve-thirty.

When I arrive, Cissy has a surprise for me. She leads me to the rear patio where she has set up lunch on an umbrella table. Chicken salad sandwiches, hardboiled eggs and a seven layer chocolate cake. And oh, yes, an ice bucket holding three long neck Coors bottles.

I've taken one bite of my sandwich when Cissy gets right to the point.

"They're watching him, Joe."

"Who?"

"The police. There was a car parked out front this morning. When Dex pulled out of the driveway and started for the studio, the car followed him."

"Maybe it's just procedure. They may be keeping a tail on some others as well," I suggest.

"It's not procedure, Joe. Some sergeant called early this morning and wants Dexter to come in for a lie detector test."

That brings me up short. When a cop suggests lie detector, he's got you squarely in his sights.

"What did Dex say?"

"He said he'd have to check with his lawyer which is a big joke because we don't have a lawyer."

You will have as soon as I call my friend, Ray Giordano, I think to myself. In the past ten years Ray has risen to the top of the heap when it comes to criminal law. If I ask him, he'll take on Dexter and it now appears that Dex is going to need him.

"So what happened yesterday, Joe. You said it was a long story."

I pop the cap on a Coors and take a deep swallow.

"I won't sugarcoat it for you, Cissy."

"I beg you not to."

And so I tell her. All of it. The gal in the bar, the sleazy motel, the beating at the hands of the woman's boyfriend. Her expression, stoic, never changes and when I'm finished she lights up a cigarette and blows a cloud of smoke into the air.

"Dex didn't kill that woman, Joe, of that I am sure but I am very glad someone did. If that sounds heartless, so be it but she was trying to destroy my husband and by extension, me. For that there is no sympathy and no forgiveness."

The steel beneath the crinoline.

I look at her closely and I realize that there is nothing she won't do for Dex, that his foolishness came out of frustration and too much liquor, and that she will fight for him no matter what it takes. And that's when it occurs to me, how to put Cissy to good use.

"How's the Sennett book coming along?" I ask.

"Exceptionally well, at least my end is," she replies.

"Does that mean you could put it aside for a day or two?"

"I suppose. Why?"

I tell her about my visit from a woman claiming to be Claire Philby but isn't because Claire Philby is dead. I tell her about the so-called Alumna Award she was planning to present to Heather Leeds which makes no sense because Heather dropped out of Northwestern at the beginning of her senior year. I cite the phony Philby's obsession with meeting with Heather personally. I recount Myra Brown's reluctance to say anything bad about Heather and saying it in such away that she made sure I knew here was something bad to learn. And finally I reveal that the faux Mrs. Philby checked out of her hotel room on the morning after Heather was killed and made a beeline for her home in Chicago, odd behavior since she had yet to meet with the woman she had flown all these many miles to meet, odder still because the press had not yet aired the story of Heather's death. And oh, yes, Heather had denied going to college, why I don't know. I say she is hiding something and ask Cissy what she thinks. She, too, thinks that Heather Leeds' past needs to be investigated and the identity of the phony Claire Philby revealed.

"All I really have is the date Heather officially dropped out of school. October 23, 1955. It isn't much."

"More than enough," Cissy says.

"I want to pay your airfare to Evanston," I say.

"No," Cissy replies.

"I insist," I tell her.

"I don't need any airfare, Joe. I'll do it all from here and if I'm lucky I should have everything you need within 24 hours."

"You're sure?"

"Positive."

"Well, whatever you need, just ask."

"Only one thing. A description of this woman who was passing herself off as Claire Philby."

I give it to her as best I can and then just as I'm ready to leave the phone rings. Cissy picks up and listens and then quickly signals me not to leave.

"Yes, I see," she says. "Is it drivable?... When can I pick it up?... Who would I have to call about that?... Yes, I understand. Thank you for calling." She hangs up and faces me.

"They found Dex's car. It's being held at an impound lot on Santa Monica Boulevard. The gentleman says I can't claim it until the police have a chance to go over it."

"Damage?"

"He says not much. They found it abandoned at the top of Lookout Mountain Avenue. A lot of food wrappers and empty beer cans in the back seat. He thinks some kids stole it off the street and took it joyriding."

I nod.

"I'll see what I can find out."

As I head out the door, Cissy is already on the phone with AT&T information, trying to get the number for the Evanston newspaper.

Finding the car is a good first step in establishing a rock solid alibi for Dex. The muggers had the car keys. They might have been the joyriders. If the police can find identifiable prints, they might be able to pick them up and just maybe get them to admit rolling Dex and leaving him in that hotel room. In fact Brubaker may already be on top of it.

When I arrive back at the production office, the first thing I do is call the police.

"What the hell are you calling me for?" Aaron growls on the other end of the line.

"Because Brubaker won't talk to me. In fact he warned me to stay away from the case under penalty of jail time."

"Man's smarter than I thought he was," Aaron says.

"Aaron. the guy is trying to railroad my friend and he's not going to get away with it." I tell him about Brubaker's demand for a lie detector test. Silence on the other end.

"I didn't know about that," Aaron says quietly.

"As soon as I hang up, I'm going to phone Ray Giordano and ask him to represent Dexter," I say.

"I think that's a good idea," Aaron says.

"Meantime, as a friend, Aaron, don't shut me out. Off the record, what have they found out about the car?"

"You're not to go off playing detective," Aaron says sternly.

"Of course not. I just want to be able to tell Dex and Cissy what's going on."

"Okay," Aaron says, "off the record, they've pulled some prints out of the car but so far no match."

"And what about the hotel desk clerk? What's he saying?"

"Nothing. Guy's name is Herman Sherman. Brubaker sweated him for over an hour and came up empty. He thinks the guy was scared out of his jock but he wouldn't budge."

"Okay," I say. "Tomorrow or the next day, I may have something new for you."

"Not me, Joe. Brubaker."

"You, Aaron. Brubaker wants me for Sunday lunch and not as a guest. Anything I get, you get next, like it or not."

And I hang up.

I sit quietly at my desk, drumming my fingers in frustration. There are things the police can do and some they won't do and more and more I'm beginning to realize it's up to me to fill in the blanks. The phony Claire Philby is one of them. Herman Sherman is another.

CHAPTER ELEVEN

It's quarter to three on a Friday afternoon and my chances of finding Ray Giordano at his office range from highly unlikely to 'Who are you kidding?' Over the past ten years his practice has expanded in tandem with his waist line and he now has a dozen or more subordinates toiling beneath him, billing an outrageous number of hours at equally outrageous rates. Only in the legal profession does a day consist of more than 24 hours and Raymond Giordano and Associates has the receipts to prove it.

I get lucky. I find him in and he comes on the phone immediately. I describe Dexter's plight in colorful terms and when I am finished, Ray reluctantly agrees to represent him even though he is up to his size 19 collar defending a sleazy slumlord from a wrongful death suit involving an 83 year old grandmother who fell to her death because of a faulty bannister on a rickety staircase. Two things sway him. First I am probably his best friend. Secondly, and more to the point, I suggest how good he's going to feel representing someone who is actually innocent. We agree to meet at my house tomorrow afternoon, even though it's a Saturday, and I will have Dexter and Cissy in tow.

I hang up. Next stop, the House of Windsor Hotel.

I hope I get lucky again and I do. Behind the cluttered reception desk is the same short and dumpy bald guy I had dealt with earlier. The guy must love his work. He seems to be here every hour or every day.

"Good afternoon, Herman," I say as I approach his desk, taking an educated guess.

He looks up from his comic book with hooded eyes and obvious disgust.

"You," he says.

"Me," I say.

"How come you know my name?"

"I know many things," I say ominously, stealing a line which I am pretty sure comes from the old 'Shadow' radio program.

"Well, know 'em someplace else, buddy. I'm busy."

I reach in my wallet and take out a crisp new fifty dollar bill and lay it on the counter. Herman's eyes flick from the latest adventure of the Green Arrow and Speedy to the green on his desk.

"One thing I don't know is the names of the two people who brought my friend here the other night."

"I already told the cops, the guy checked in by himself. There wasn't nobody with him."

"What time was this?"

"Late. I don't remember exactly. What time would you like it to be?"

"Eleven o'clock?"

"Sure. Why not?"

"After two?"

"That, too. Whatever makes you happy."

He reaches for the bill. I slam my fist down on the back of his hand and he screams in pain.

"How about if you stop bullshitting me and tell me what I want to know."

I pick up the fifty and stick it in my shirt pocket.

"How about if you go fuck yourself," Herman Sherman says.

"That really the way you want it?"

"Get lost."

He turns his attention back to the Green Arrow.

"Okay, Herman, your option, Starting tomorrow night I am going to have a very capable photographer stationed somewhere close by and he is going to be photographing every person who enters this hotel which I presume will be almost exclusively hookers and their johns."

He looks at me angrily.

"I know my rights," he says. "You can't do that!"

"Wrong. The police can't do it. I can. And when I get the pictures, I'm going to examine them very closely. Some I am going to mail to the wives of the johns with the compliments of the House of Windsor, but most I will pass along to the vice squad. In short I am going to make your life a living hell and if I'm lucky, put you out of business."

"This photographer of yours—" Herman starts to say.

"This photographer of mine is always armed with a .45 automatic and when on the job, is accompanied by an associate who carries a sawed off shotgun nestled in a leather sling underneath his raincoat. Any other questions?"

Herman shakes his head in defeat.

"Okay, okay. Gimmee the fifty," he says.

"Names, Herman."

He hesitates, then says, "The chick is named Cora. I think the guy's name is Wendell but I'm not sure." He puts out his hand.

"For fifty bucks I need more than that."

"I'm pretty sure they're college kids. I overheard 'em talking one night when they didn't know I could hear 'em. Maybe UCLA. I think they're livin' together in Westwood. The girl's okay. Gotta rack on her that won't quit but kinda squirrely. The guy, he thinks he's a hard case. Carries a knife with a foot-long blade. He made a point of showing it to me one night, like keep your mouth about me and Cora or else. So what I'm telling you here, you didn't get it from me, you understand?"

Yeah. I understand. Just a couple of clean-cut students working their way through college.

"And the time, Herman?"

"Maybe a little before midnight. I ain't exactly sure."

"When the cops come back asking, make real sure."

I take the fifty from my pocket and lay it back on the counter, then hurry to the front entrance to get away from the stink of the place.

It's quarter to five when I get back to the office. I half expect Glenda Mae to be gone for the weekend but no, she's still here and there is a thin manila envelope on my desk.

"Priscilla was delighted with the photo of Howard Keel," Glenda Mae says. "He's one of her absolute favorites ever since 'Show Boat'. She says she's sorry she hasn't got more on Travis Wright but it's really a San Diego story. She suggested I drive down and check out the morgue at the Evening Tribune."

"We'll see," I say.

"Uh, Boss—"

Uh, boss, can only mean one thing. Glenda Mae needs an itsy-bitsy, teeny-weeny meaningless little favor from me or at least that's the way it seems to her.

"Okay, Gorgeous, let's have it," I say.

"Well, you know Sunday is me and Beau's anniversary—"

I did but I'd forgotten it. Thank God she reminded me.

"— and Beau made reservations at this nice place on Catalina for Saturday and Sunday and so uh,—"

"And so you'll be coming in late on Monday if you come in at all, is that about it?"

"Well, yes, but I can stay late the rest of the week—"

I smile at her.

"Go. Have a good time. Come back when you want."

"Are you sure you don't mind?"

I take her in my arms and give her a huge hug.

"Happy anniversary, Glenda Mae. Tell Beau for me he's one lucky son of a bitch."

"He knows it. I keep reminding him."

"Good. Now before you disappear from my life completely, get me Aaron on the phone and then scram."

She reaches up and gives me a sisterly kiss on the cheek and then wiggles from the room. And how I love to watch that woman wiggle.

"If this is more good news, I can hardly wait," Aaron says as he comes on the line.

"I only hope you appreciate everything I am doing for you in your investigation."

"Dammit, Joe, I keep telling you, it's not my case."

"Well, it ought to be. I keep coming up with great stuff but if I should mention it to your boy Brubaker, I risk incarceration."

"And what great stuff have you go for me now, Joe?"

I tell him all about my tete-a-tete with Herman Sherman and there is a substantial pause on Aaron's end of the line.

"No bullshit?"

"No bullshit, Aaron."

"Okay, I'll pass it along without mentioning where I got it. Between the prints in the car and the first names, Brubaker ought to be able to find these two birds."

"Thanks. Now what have you got for me?"

"What are you talking about?"

"The police report. You've seen it, Aaron, don't tell me you haven't."

"I may have."

"She was moved. She didn't die in that office."

"You think not."

"The post-mortem lividity didn't fit. You could tell just by looking at her. Not only that, the letter's a fake."

"Letter? What letter?" Aaron asks.

"Get off it, Aaron. I was there, remember? I read the damned thing. Heather covered with blood and her letter and her typewriter are without a splatter, not so much as a drop of blood even though she was supposedly killed in the middle of typing. To which I say, bullshit."

"You'll be pleased to know that Brubaker agrees with you," Aaron says.

"Does he? Good. Then he also has to realize that this clumsy attempt to point a finger at Dexter now does the opposite. Being false, that letter points away from him."

"Maybe yes, maybe no," Aaron says. "But in any case you"ve been warned to keep your nose out of this."

"And I will as soon as Willie B. starts focusing on someone besides Dexter. And by the way, Ray's taking his case."

"Good," Aaron says. "so unless your buddy is a stone cold killer, he's going to be just fine."

When we finally hang up, I empty the contents of the manila envelope from Priscilla, my reliable babe at the newspaper morgue, onto my desk. There are a dozen or so xerox copies of news articles about Travis Wright, his arrest, his trial and his subsequent conviction. I pore through them. For several years he had been a high flying financial advisor, rubbing elbows with the elite of the San Diego power structure. When his world came crashing down on him the record showed that he had defrauded his clientele of close to twenty seven million dollars. About eighteen million was retrieved from safe deposit boxes, foreign banks and other entities. Nine million could not be accounted for. In the initial stages of the prosecution his attractive young wife, Heather Leeds Wright, was named as a co-defendant but charges against her were dropped when she agreed to testify for the state. It is an axiom of law that a wife cannot be compelled to testify against her husband but in this case, Heather was all too glad to pin the tail on her husband in a place where it would really hurt. Weeping on the stand she said she wanted only to do what was right for the people of San Diego. It took the jury only eighty-seven minutes to find Travis Wright guilty on all counts and he was sentenced to six years at the state prison in Tehachapi. In the aftermath of the trial Heather Leeds Wright disappeared from the public eye. Authorities continue to search for the missing nine million dollars but to date, none has been recovered. The final item notes Travis Wright's release from prison on parole. It is dated February 17, 1961. One week ago.

I lean back in my chair. Granted, Travis Wright has every reason to despise his ex-wife but other than that I'm having trouble plugging him into a murder scenario. Assuming Heather has the nine million or knows where it is and how to get it, it makes no sense for Wright to kill her. Secondly the note in the typewriter alluded to danger from someone connected with the film. If the note is a red herring designed to throw the police off, Wright couldn't be expected to know about her troubles at the studio. Do I think the note is a phony? I do but I'm pretty sure Travis Wright had nothing to do with it.

Nine million dollars. A huge sum of money. Not something you would bury in the backyard or stuff in your mattress. If she has it, and that's still a very big if, she's either banked it or invested it and certainly not under her real name. Which brings me to her husband, Buddy Lovejoy. How much does he know about Heather's past and does he know anything at all about Travis Wright? And if he does, then what does he know or not know about the money?

Enough is enough. I'm getting a headache. I slip the news copies back into the envelope and shove it into the bottom drawer of my desk. I'll get at this again later. Meantime I have an overwhelming urge to go home and see my family.

CHAPTER TWELVE

On the sixth and seventh days, Hollywood rests. The unions insist. On location away from the studio, the rules are different. Saturday shoots are obligatory. The costs involved in feeding and housing a veritable army of artists and technicians is far too high to let a perfectly good day go to waste. Time was, years ago when I was an ambitious dynamo trying to make a name for myself that I would use Saturday to whip up a lot of self-serving projects, research current industry activities, butter up my sources and stay in touch with influential columnists in every part of the country. Not so these days. Now I spend a few hours on the chaise dozing or reading or, better yet, allow myself to be hustled into a picnic or a day at the beach with my two best girls.

Today is different. Today is the day we try to get Sergeant Willie B. off of Dexter Craven's back. Ray Giordano and I are sitting on my back patio working on a pitcher of lemonade and swapping war stories about the good old days when Saturday morning meant basketball at a downtown sports center. The game broke up several years ago for a variety of reasons. Two actors left town, one for Minnesota and the other for Florida. Our six foot two CPA got caught misreading some tax figures and was chased out of the business by the IRS. Last I heard he was painting houses for a living in Eugene, Oregon. Ray caught the case of the decade when he successfully got an acquittal for a crooked city councilman accused of bribery despite the fact that everyone in Hollywood with the exception of Lassie knew he was guilty. After that Ray had to beat off sleazy would-be clients with a stick. Still, some slipped through and now he is the go-to-guy for well-off movers and shakers with a defective moral compass. Me, I just got very, very busy. I also got a busted knee which cut my court speed down from lumbering to barely moving.

At precisely 2:28 Bridget escorts our visitors to the patio. Dexter looks better than he did but not great. Cissy is on his arm, holding tight, showing solidarity with her man. I make the introductions and when Dex asks about Bunny, I tell him she has taken Yvette to the local park to feed the ducks. I offer something beside the lemonade and get no takers. We are here to do business and so we get to it.

Ray instructs Dexter in no uncertain terms to refuse to take the polygraph test. Dexter's attitude toward the police should be respectful and courteous but answer no questions. If they start throwing their weight around Dexter is to clam up and call Ray immediately. Dex signals that he understands.

I've already told Ray about my contact with Herman Sherman and my subsequent chat with Aaron Kleinschmidt. Now I fill in both Dex and Cissy. When I finish, Ray says, "I believe there's a very good chance Brubaker will find these two. I think we can assume they are college students, we have first names, and since they live in Westwood we're probably looking at UCLA. If their prints match the ones taken from your abandoned car, Mr. Craven, game over."

"You make it sound simple, Mr. Giordano," Dex says.

"Not really. Finding them will be time consuming grunt work and getting them to confess before they hook up with some buck an hour shyster won't be easy. I should know, a lot of those creeps are acquaintances. But those kids'll crack. if not for the police, then for me. It's what I do."

At this moment Cissy tentatively raises her hand.

"Joe, would this be a good time to discuss Claire Philby?"

"Why, Cissy? Do you have something?"

"I have everything," she says proudly.

Ray looks at her curiously, then at me.

"Who the hell is Claire Philby?" he asks.

I tell him and when I finish I look over at Cissy.

"Tell Ray what you've got."

"For one thing, a juicy scandal. For seven months prior to dropping out of school Heather Leeds was having a secret affair with one of her professors. She was twenty-two. He was forty-seven. His name was Axel Burley and he taught English Literature. When the affair became public knowledge, the University terminated him, citing a morals clause in his employment contract. Even so he would show up on campus trying to continue his relationship with Heather, several times in crowded places in front of students and faculty members. This, despite the fact that he was a married man. Rebuffed, he put a pistol to his head and pulled the trigger."

This is ugly, very ugly, and I can tell by the expression on his face that Ray concurs.

"Shortly thereafter," Cissy continues, "the professor's wife Diana suffered a nervous breakdown and was committed to a mental institution where she remained for the next six years. Then, due to overcrowding, she was released from the state facility over the objections of her doctors. The date of her release was January 4. Seven weeks ago."

I nod.

"And may I assume the woman who passed herself off as Claire Philby was actually Diana Burley?"

"Based on your description, Joe, I'm sure of it," Cissy says, "but to be certain, a very accommodating young lady at the newspaper is sending me a morgue photo for confirmation."

"You are sure of your facts, Mrs. Craven?" Ray asks.

"I have three different sources, Mr. Giordano. Yes, I am quite satisfied."

Ray looks over at me.

"What do the police know about this woman, Joe?"

"Nothing. I tried to tell Brubaker but he cut me off. Wouldn't listen."

"And Aaron?"

"The same. Not his case. Tell Brubaker, he said."

"And now she's out of our reach," Ray says.

"That's it?"

"That's it, Joe, The police have no power to force her back here and unless we go to trial, neither do I. And even then I might not be able to do it."

A pall of uncertainty hangs over the rest of our meeting although Ray continues to be optimistic. If the police can find those two muggers, Dexter will be alibied and no longer a suspect. He's probably right but I'm a chronic worrier. Suppose those two suddenly drop out of school and move to Florida for the warm weather. Suppose Herman Sherman knows them a lot better than he claims and warns them the cops may come looking for them. The last thing we need is Dexter on trial, not just because he's innocent as well as my friend, but also because every news story will somehow find a way to mention 'A Pocketful of Miracles'. Whoever said there is no such thing as bad publicity didn't know what he was talking about. Films are fantasy, murder is grim. and Kipling had it right, the twain should never meet.

Our little gathering breaks up around three-thirty and the first thing I do is phone Aaron. He is not happy to hear from me.

Aaron is an aide to the Commander of the Homicide Division working out of the Police Administration Building. He works with and oversees the homicide detectives from the city's many local divisions but except in extraordinary situations, he doesn't interfere with the lead detectives on a case, even if they seem to be making a mess of things. Already annoyed with me, in a minute or two he is going to be apoplectic.

"What now?" he growls.

"More help from a concerned civilian."

"Oh, God," Aaron groans. "I talked to Brubaker this morning and gave him what you'd passed on to me about the two muggers."

"I'm sure he wasn't happy about it, " I say.

"Wrong, Joe, he's a good cop first and last and he was grateful for the information but he is frustrated by you. He's never had a civilian mucking around in one of his cases before and it makes him very uneasy. I told him he'd get used to it. I don't think he believed me."

"Well, I have another suspect for him to worry about. What do you suggest I do?"

I hear him sigh.

"Okay, lets hear it."

I spend the next five minutes telling him all about the loony widow passing herself off as a dead woman trying to get face-to-face with the murder victim and then her sudden and unexpected departure from Los Angeles, long before Heather's demise was reported on the news.

There's a long silence and then Aaron says, "Tell him."

"Actually, Aaron, I thought maybe you—"

"No, sir, I've done my good deed for the week. Suck it up, Joe. You're the one who wants to play Dick Tracy."

"But—"

"No buts, Joe. This is something Brubaker needs to know about but I'm through playing go-between."

Now it's my turn to sigh.

"Okay, if you think so, I'll touch base with him Monday morning but if I end up in the pokey, I expect you to bail me out." Silence. "Aaron?" More silence. "Aaron?" He's hung up on me.

I don't have time to get annoyed because at this exact moment, Yvette comes bounding in the front door, bubbling over with a story about a mama duck and some baby ducks while a frazzled Bunny follows her in and plops down in an easy chair, out of gas. I vow then and there to forget about Heather and Dexter and all of the rest of it until Monday and devote myself to my girls. The vow lasts for all of two and a half hours.

I'm sprawled on the sofa watching the final minutes of the Laker game. They have just relocated here in Los Angles from Minneapolis and I am impressed. With players like Jerry West and Elgin Baylor, they have a good chance to win the championship. I can hear Bunny in the kitchen wrestling with dinner and I'm about to get up off the couch to turn off the television when the local news pops onto the screen. A guy with a microphone is standing in front of a suburban one story home. Off to the side I see an LAPD squad car with it's rooftop light array blinking and a dozen or so people milling about. At his side is Buddy Lovejoy, Heather's husband. What now, I ask myself.

"Behind me is the West Hollywood home of slain movie publicist Heather Leeds whose murder this past Wednesday is the subject of a city wide investigation. In a strange twist in an already bizarre case, Miss Leeds' husband returned home a short time ago to find a burglar ransacking the residence. Standing here with me is Miss Leeds' husband Mr. Buddy Lovejoy and Mr. Lovejoy, can you tell our viewers what happened here?"

"Yes, it was about an hour ago. I was returning home after an all day session with my writing partner. It was just getting dark when I pulled into the driveway and I noticed some lights on inside the house which they shouldn't have been. I hurried to the front door, walked in, called out and then heard a noise in the back bedroom. I grabbed a poker from the fireplace and hurried back there, ready for anything. The lights were on and I could see right away that the room had been thoroughly trashed. The back door leading to the patio was wide open and when I stepped outside I barely got a glimpse of a man running across the lawn and into the backyard of my neighbor. That's when I went back inside and called the police."

"Did you recognize the man who did this?"

"No, it was too dark. The police have asked me for a description but I never saw his face. He was a burglar, that's all. These things happen here in West Hollywood."

"Can you tell us what, if anything, was stolen?"

"No, not yet, but it can't be much. Heather and I didn't really own anything worth stealing outside of her jewelry and there wasn't much of that."

"Do you think there is any connection between this break-in and your wife's unfortunate death earlier this week?"

Buddy shakes his head.

"I would have no way of knowing anything like that," he says.

It goes on like that for another minute and then Bunny yells "Dinner!" and I walk over to the TV set and turn it off. Running through my head is Zachary Beck's recounting of the argument between Heather and Travis Wright in the office corridor. "Where is it?— "I want it. It's mine!"—"What have you done with it?"— "You're a damned thief! You won't get away with this."

Before I was curious. Now I am obsessed. I am reasonably sure that whatever "it" is is probably worth in the neighborhood of nine million dollars.

CHAPTER THIRTEEN

I have a busy day ahead of me at the studio. Three press releases are in the works. One touts Peter Falk's nomination for Best Supporting Oscar for 'Murder, Inc.' while liberally quoting his enthusiasm for his current film. A second involves Glenn Ford and real life gal pal Hope Lange and how delighted they are to be working together professionally on Frank Capra's latest film. The third is a puff piece basically extolling Capra's delight in having Bette Davis as his star reprising the role originated by Mae Robson in 'Lady for a Day'. Not a word of acrimony. No hint of discord. The atmosphere on the set is warm and fuzzy, take my word for it. Ninety percent will accept my releases at face value. Ten percent will dig a little deeper. Those are the ones I worry about.

But before I can deal with the picture I have to come to some sort of detente with Brubaker which is why I find myself sitting on a bench across from the information desk at the Hollywood Division station house awaiting the sergeant's arrival. It is five past eight. He may not show for an hour or two but he is not going to slip by me and he is not going to duck my phone calls. I'm pretty sure he won't slap the cuffs on me but I'm prepared for anything.

He wanders in at eight twenty-five and the first thing he sees is me. He stops short, eyes me uncertainly and then with a nod of his head, invites me to follow him as he heads for the staircase. I do so and soon we are seated at his desk, staring at one another.

"You want coffee?" he asks, pouring himself a mugful.

I tell him I don't. There's a long pause.

"That was a good tip on the mugging at the hotel," he says.

"Thanks."

"We think we know who those two birds are and where to find them. As soon as they show we'll grab them."

"Good."

"Anything else?"

"Yes, something you need to know about but first I'd like to confirm a few things," I say. "Time of death. Still pegged between eleven and one?"

"I've already told you, Mr. Bernardi, we don't need any additional detectives on this case."

"And I believe I told you, Sergeant, that until my friend Dexter Craven is in the clear, I am going to be asking a lot of questions of a lot of people about a lot of people whether you like it or not and if you want to toss me in a cell, now's your chance."

Again, Brubaker stares at me.

"Between eleven and one. A single thrust with a knife to the heart and that's official," he says.

"And she was not killed in the office, her body was moved from somewhere else."

"Who told you that?" Brubaker asks.

"Sergeant, I was there. I discovered the body, I know something about lividity and I am not blind."

"Okay, she was moved," Brubaker says.

"And the note in the typewriter. She didn't write it."

Brubaker frowns.

"Where are you getting all this?"

"Observation. No blood spatters on either the typewriter or the note and besides that, I will bet there were no fingerprints on the paper, not even the victims, which is a good trick if we're supposed to believe that she inserted the paper into the typewriter herself. Tell me I'm wrong."

"I can't."

"And since the misleading note is a plant designed to erroneously implicate a man with a studio connection, then it stands to reason that Dexter Craven is not involved."

"It would seem that way unless your friend is a lot smarter than we give him credit for. Now, you said you had something important for me."

"First, tell me about Travis Wright," I say.

"What about him?"

"You tell me."

"He was in his hotel room sleeping at the time his ex-wife was killed and before you ask, he was playing chess with the guy across the hall at the hotel at the time the Lovejoy house in West Hollywood was being ransacked. Yeah, we know about the missing nine million. Wright couldn't have made it more public if he'd put an ad in the yellow pages. Again, I ask you, Mr. Bernardi, what is it you think I ought to know about?"

I tell him all about the widow Burley who came to L.A. posing as a dead woman named Claire Philby. At first he is patronizing, then curious and then finally involved.

"So this award was a phony?" Brubaker asks.

"I assume so. Everything about the woman was false but her insistence on getting face to face with Heather was all too real."

"You think she came here to L.A. to kill Leeds?"

"I couldn't say for sure but Heather had destroyed her husband and her marriage and Diana Burley was only a few weeks removed from being locked up in a sanitarium."

"You're sure of your facts?"

"Positive."

Brubaker leans back in his chair. His expression is grim and I can see a hundred different thoughts going through his mind.

"No way I can bring her back here, not without a warrant, and no judge is going to issue a warrant based on what you told me."

I nod.

"That's what Ray said."

"Who's Ray?"

"Ray Giordano."

"What's he got to do with this?"

"He's representing Dexter Craven."

Brubaker looks at me in disbelief.

"Ray Giordano is representing your buddy? What the hell is he afraid of?"

"You," I say.

Brubaker glares at me for a moment and then he shakes his head.

"Look, Bernardi, you've got this crazy idea I'm trying to railroad your friend. Believe me, I'm not. Craven is one of a dozen suspects I'm looking at, some you know about, a few you don't. I may not have a bedside manner but I'm thorough and I'm tough to bullshit. I would love nothing better than to strike Mr. Craven from my list. Just one less suspect to deal with but he's not there, not yet, and until he is, I'm keeping my eye on him."

I nod.

"Okay, I'll take your word for that," I say. "What are you going to do about Diana Burley?"

"I don't know," Brubaker says.

I get to my feet.

"Well, she's your problem now, Sergeant. I gave you everything I have. Thanks for talking to me."

I start to go. Brubaker's voice stops me.

"Bernardi."

I turn back toward him.

"I underestimated you. My mistake. You've been a big help."

"Thanks."

"I presume you're going to keep poking around."

"You presume correctly."

"And if you learn anything, I presume you'll share it with me."

"Absolutely," I say.

He nods thoughtfully.

"If there's anything you need, call me."

"I'll do that," I say.

"Okay, now get out of here," he growls.

I give him a smile and a little salute and head for the staircase. Just as Brubaker admitted that he misjudged me, I'm beginning to think I've had the wrong take on him. Time will tell.

When I get back to the studio Mitzi hands me a pink telephone slip with Louella Parsons' number of it. The lady and I are deep into a game of telephone tag which might continue for weeks. I sigh and with little hope of getting through, I dial her number. I'm astounded when the lady herself picks up. She is gracious and complimentary and her conversation is peppered with a lot of "darlings" and "dears" and what she has in mind is a very flattering column about Bette and she wants this interview today and how about Chasen's because she knows Bette has a very late call to the set and besides she's already made the reservations. In the face of all this I tell her that Bette and I would be delighted to lunch with her. When she makes noises like I will be unnecessary, I explain that if I'm not there, Bette won't be either. In that case she will be delighted to see us both at twelve noon.

Over the next hour I check a couple of things with both Frank Capra and Glenn Ford in order to gird myself for lunch. Bette's right about one thing, Louella's a first rate reporter and knows how to dig but she also likes to dig for scandal even when there is none. She and Hedda and Fidler are not the make-or-break powerhouses they once were but even a featherweight can throw a hard punch every once in a while. It's my job to make sure it doesn't happen. I'm so into this lunch and my actual career that I've forgotten Dexter's problems with the law. When I do remember them I feel confident that Brubaker is going to find and deal with the two college kids and get Dex off the hook.

Lunch starts out harmoniously. Louella has already arrived and Dave Chasen, the owner, leads us to her table which is prominent in the main dining room. Dave loves it when celebrities spruce up his establishment, they are good for business, and Louella and Bette Davis are a coup. Louella is working on her first old-fashioned. Others will follow. Compliments fly back and forth like a shuttlecock in a badminton game and it isn't until Louella's second old-fashioned and appetizers that the bonhomie starts to tatter.

"I do hope everything is going well for you on the set, Bette," Louella says sweetly spearing an escargot.

"Couldn't be more pleasant," Bette says lighting up a Camel.

"One hears such awful rumors," she continues. "Discord, petty jealousies, I just hope it isn't hurting the work."

I jump in.

"Yes, we've heard the same scurrilous rumors, Louella, and we've pretty much traced them to a publicity agent that Glenn was forced to fire. I asked Glenn if he was planning to sue for slander and he told me he will be meeting with his lawyer this evening to discuss that very subject. I doubt much will come of it, though. No reputable journalist is going to pay any attention to the man's unfounded allegations, it's much too risky not only for the sake of one's reputation but the money involved in possible litigation."

Louella smiles. She knows a threat when she hears it. She signals our waiter for another old-fashioned.

"And you, dear Bette, you must love the challenge of portraying

Apple Annie but does it bother you at all that you were the sixth choice for the part?"

"Actually, third, Louella. Dear Shirley Booth was scared to death of the part and my dear friend Helen Hayes was forced to drop out when the shooting schedule was changed. As for me I had made it plain for the past several years that I was through with Hollywood so I am not surprised in the least that dear Frank Capra didn't consider me immediately. But of course when he did I accepted with alacrity. Apple Annie is one of the great female characters of the film world. I am flattered that I was considered."

Behind the thoughtful and interested look on my face, I am silently laughing my ass off. Bette Davis can sling it with the best of them. I am in total admiration. But at that moment my eyes flick past Louella to the bar where I see a bearded man staring at me and my unvoiced laugh disappears. As soon as our eyes lock he turns away but he's not quick enough. What the hell is Travis Wright doing here? Following me? And if so, why?"

"Shirley Jones."

I realize Louella is talking to me.

"What about her?" I ask.

"Is it true that Shirley was already signed to play the part of Queenie when Glenn stepped in an demanded that the part be given to his girlfriend of the moment?"

"Really?" I say, feigning ignorance."I could be wrong but the way I heard it, Shirley had already been committed by her agent to do John Ford's 'Two Rode Together', something she didn't know about when she first talked to Frank about the part. But as I say, Louella, I would have to double check this. I wouldn't want to mislead you."

At that moment, Bette kicks me under the table and when I look at her she is blithely looking up at the ceiling, puffing on her cigarette, and, I think, trying to stifle a huge guffaw.

Just before our lunch arrives I leave the table on the pretext of using the facility but instead I place a phone call back to the production office. I tell Mitzi to get a hold of transportation and have a limousine waiting outside Chasen's no later than one-fifteen. When I return to the table, I find that Louella has tried to insert the tragic death of Heather Leeds into the conversation. I suggest that such an unpleasant subject has no place in a column about Bette Davis and her on-going contributions to the film industry. Louella says her interest was merely idle curiosity. I don't believe her for a moment but she backs off and doesn't mention the subject again. Good thing. I was prepared to bring up the 1924 murder of Thomas Ince, the director, aboard William Randolph Hearst's yacht, the Oneida. A dozen famous people were aboard at the time. Although the official version had Ince dying of a heart attack, off the record some of those aboard would later relate that Hearst, in a jealous rage, fired a pistol at Charlie Chaplin and hit Ince instead. In the aftermath dozens of conflicting stories arose but of one thing there is no debate. Louella, a local gossip columnist, was an eyewitness to what occurred but made no mention of it in her column. Within a matter of days Hearst decided to syndicate Louella's column to every Hearst newspaper in the country and thus, a legend was born.

Louella is on her fourth old-fashioned when I glance at my watch. It's twenty after one and I suggest to Bette that we get back to the studio. I lard more flattery on Louella and she responds accordingly. My sense is we'll get good press out of this luncheon without any mention of Heather's death because in the Hollywood of 1961 these gossip columnists need us as much as we need them. Access is all important and it works both ways.

We get up from the table and head for the main entrance by walking through the bar. I am trailing the ladies and as I pass by Travis Wright I put my hand on his shoulder and whisper in his ear.

"Save me a seat. I'll be back in a moment."

Outside, Louella's car and driver is waiting for her. We say our goodbyes and off she goes, I start to trundle Bette into the limo citing company business off the lot that demands my immediate attention. She reaches up and kisses my cheek and with a sly smile.

"Nice going, tough guy." she says. "You can work my corner any day of the week."

I watch as the limo disappears down the street and then head back inside to have a friendly chat with a big time thief and maybe even a big time killer.

Wright is digging into a wooden bowl of peanuts like he hasn't eaten in a week. I slip onto the stool next to him.

"I'll have a Coors on tap," I say to him. "You're buying."

"You're the guy with all the money," he says. "I'll have a double scotch neat, water back."

I signal the barkeep and place our order and then turn to him. "Why are you following me?" I ask.

"I'm not," he says. "I drove to the studio hoping to con my way onto the lot. Just then you and the old lady drove out so I did a U-ey and followed you here."

"That old lady was Bette Davis."

"No kidding. Never one of my favorites. Lana Turner, Rita Hayworth. More my speed."

"Okay, so you tailed me here to Chasen's. What for?"

"You might have something of mine."

"And what would that be?"

"Not sure."

"Might it be worth roughly nine million dollars?"

"It might."

"What makes you think I have it?"

"You were in her office and it wasn't in her home."

"Who told you that?"

"I'm psychic."

"What happens if the guy across the hall is asked by the police to actually play a game of chess?"

"He'll fake it. The cops aren't all that bright."

"Don't bet your life on it. What exactly is it that you think I have?"

"If I had to guess, I'd say a pouchful of high quality diamonds. It was the last thing Heather and I discussed before I was hauled off to the calaboose and she disappeared from the face of the earth."

"She may have changed her mind?"

"I doubt it. Diamonds require no paperwork and you can carry them in your purse."

"In either case, I don't have them," I say.

"Maybe yes, maybe no," Wright replies.

I slide off my stool and toss a Hamilton onto the bar.

"If I see you following me again, Mr. Wright, I'm going to be forced to call the cops."

"You won't see me," he says.

I head for the front door and step out into the afternoon sunlight. Wright follows me, close behind.

"I want my money, Bernardi. I'm going to get it. I promise you."

"News flash, pal. It's not your money. It belongs to those poor bastards you fleeced in San Diego."

"They were anything but poor and they didn't get that way playing by the rules."

"Nice try, Mr. Wright, but you're still a sleazy thief."

I'm at my car now and unlocking it as he presses close to me, his eyes revealing undiluted menace.

"If you have it, Bernardi, I'll get it from you and I won't be polite about it."

"The way you weren't polite to Heather?"

"I didn't kill her," he says.

"Maybe yes, maybe no," I say with a smile and open my car door. Wright backs away and as I pull away from the curb I can feel his eyes continue to follow me as I merge into the Beverly Boulevard traffic. I can't really see Wright killing Heather. It would be an act of lunacy if he hadn't yet procured the nine-million and if he had, he wouldn't be tailing me around L.A. or ransacking houses, he'd be on a veranda in Puerto Vallarta swilling double scotches neat, water back.

CHAPTER FOURTEEN

I check with Mitzi at the production office. There are no frantic messages, no urgent phone calls to be returned. no squabbles to be quashed so I head back to the office to catch up on a few things left undone when Lila had suddenly pressed me into service. Glenda Mae is delighted to see me, even though I have interrupted her reading which today is something called 'The Mistress of Mellyn'. I can tell from the lurid dust cover it won't be up for the Pulitzer any time soon.

She lays the book down.

"Hi, I'm Glenda Mae Brown.," she says. "I work here."

"Joe Bernardi. So do I."

"Coulda fooled me," she says.

It's a game we play when I spend an inordinate amount of time away from my desk. Poor girl, she gets lonesome when I'm not around. I try to humor her.

"You know a cop named Brubaker?" she asks.

"Unfortunately."

"I left his number on your desk. He said it was urgent."

"Of course he did."

I start into my office.

"Coffee?"

"You betcha."

The woman is a treasure. Brubaker, however, is not.

"Tell me again about the Philby woman," he says when he comes on the line.

"First of all her name isn't Philby, it's Diana Burley."

"Yeah, yeah. I got that. You said something about a photograph."

"Cissy Craven was supposed to get one from the local newspaper. She may already have received it. Why? What's going on?"

"It's possible the lady did not fly to Chicago and is still here in L.A."

Now there's a turn of events. Before I can register my astonishment Glenda Mae comes in with my coffee. I tell Brubaker to hold while I ask Glenda Mae to call Cissy and see if the photo has arrived.

"I'm working on the photo," I tell Brubaker. "So what the hell happened?"

"Like you said, the hotel courtesy car dropped her off at the airport but she didn't know that O'Hare had been socked in by a freak snow storm. No planes in or out. The flight finally took off at four o'clock but according to the passenger manifest she wasn't on the plane. You have any idea why she'd stick around?"

"None. Are you sure she's not in Chicago? Another flight? The train?"

"I have no idea," Brubaker says. "We leaned on the desk clerk at the hotel for the address she used when she checked in. No such street anywhere in the city and since she's only a few days away from six years in the looney bin, she's not in the phone book. If we had to scour Chicago for her, we wouldn't know where to begin but if she's still here in Los Angeles, we have a chance even if she's using a phony name. That's why I need the photo, to canvass the hotels. She's got to be staying somewhere."

"If Cissy Craven has received it, I'll get it to you."

He thanks me and hangs up and I stare at my coffee mug. It seems unlikely to me that Diana Burley killed Heather. For one thing she could never have moved her body into the office without help even if she knew where the office was, which I doubt. And then there's the phony letter, since she was not privy to any of that information. No, there's no logic to Diana Burley as a suspect. On the other hand there's also no logic to her remaining in Los Angles, especially if she had heard on the news that Heather was dead. But there's a reason. There has to be. I'm the one who saw the icy look in her eyes.

Glenda Mae buzzes me.

"Mrs. Craven just got the photo special delivery," she tells me.

"Good. Call Sergeant Brubaker and tell him I'm bringing it over."

"Will do. Meanwhile I have two gentlemen out here who would like a few minutes of your time."

"Names?"

"One of them gave me his card. Buddy Lovejoy," she says.

"Send 'em in."

For a guy who has been a widower for a little over three days, Buddy Lovejoy seems to be in pretty good spirits. He's wearing a sharkskin sports jacket and white flannel trousers with a golden bandana tied around his neck just above an open collared baby blue silk shirt. Color by Technicolor. His hair is still combed over and he smells of Aqua-Velva. The guy with him is big and broad shouldered, wearing blue jeans and a grey sweatshirt that look like they came from a yard sale. He sports traces of a five o'clock shadow and his unkempt dark brown hair refuses to lie down quietly. Buddy introduces him as Seth Donnelly, his writing partner, and I invite them both to sit down.

"First of all, let me express my sympathy on your loss," I say to Buddy.

He shakes his head.

"Oh, no, you have it wrong, Mr. Bernardi. The deal was signed the first thing this morning. The picture's a go." He stops, frowning. "Oh, you mean Heather. Yeah, thanks a lot. It's been rough."

"Very rough," Seth chimes in.

"Have you made any final plans? About interment, I mean."

"Oh, sure. The cops said I could pick up the body late today. Forest Lawn's handling the whole thing. Burial on Wednesday or Thursday. Seth and I will be there, maybe a preacher to say a few words. She didn't have any family, you know."

"No wake, then," I say.

"For who?" Buddy asks. "Listen, Mr. Bernardi, me and Seth aren't here to chat about Heather. We're hoping we could talk to you and your partner about career management, now that we've arrived."

Arrived? George Hamilton as a 21 year old spy in a film aimed at pubescents?

"We have another deal going," Seth says.

"Oh?"

Buddy jumps right in. "Our agent's in New York confabbing with Keith Michel. He's starring in 'Irma La Douce' on Broadway, you know." No, I didn't know. "We have a tentative go-ahead into story if we can attach a British star to the project. Okay, so Keith's Australian. What's the difference? He'd be perfect for 'Behind Nazi Lines'."

"Is that the name of it?"

"Catchy, huh?"

"A spy movie?"

"Of course. We envision a lot of action, special effects to heighten the suspense, a love affair with a continental type leading lady. We're thinking Gina Lollobrigida."

Twice I have looked over at Seth Donnelley to see if he had anything to say but no, he seems to be content to keep his mouth shut. Buddy is the spokesman for this duo.

"Speaking of Milt—" Buddy says. "Milt Schlepper, that's our agent. I know you've heard of him." I haven't. "He's supposed to call Seth some time after three." He looks over at his silent partner. "Maybe you'd better get home so we don't miss him."

Seth gets to his feet and reaches across the desk to shake my hand. "It's going to be a pleasure working with you, Mr. Bernardi," he says and then he's out the door.

"He's quite a guy," Buddy says. "I think I told you, we've known each other since grammar school in Philadelphia."

"You mentioned that."

"We have this kind of thing where sometimes we finish each other's sentences, that's how close we are. Of course, he's a little quiet but I make up for it."

"I've noticed."

"So what do you say, Joe? Are you interested? I mean, Seth and I are on the edge of a big breakthrough and you and Mrs. Bowles can help make it happen."

I am about to politely toss Mr. Buddy Lovejoy out of my office when a thought occurs to me and I hesitate in mid-toss. Instead I ask Buddy about his career and then his marriage to Heather which he is loath to talk about. He finally admits that he thinks Heather married him only because he was a very important television writer which is a bigger oxymoron than 'military intelligence'. I buzz Bertha and ask her to come in to my office for a meet-and-greet. She obliges and is all smiles and warmth while giving me furtive looks that say, who is this guy and why are you wasting my time?

Having buttered him up like a peach danish I am ready to apply the coup de grace. I tell him I have to run an errand but I'd be glad to drop him somewhere. Since Seth obviously took the car, he jumps at the invitation. He'd like me to drop him off at Seth's apartment. No problem, I say.

As soon as we're heading east on Santa Monica Boulevard I spring it on him.

"I know you're anxious to have the police capture Heather's killer," I say.

"Absolutely," he says.

"I think there's something you can do."

"What's that? Left at the next light."

"Schedule the burial for Thursday noon and place a notice in the local papers on Wednesday that there will be a two hour viewing in a chapel at Forest Lawn prior to the interment."

"And why would I want to do that?"

"Because there's a crazy lady running around who might, just might, be your wife's klller and I have a hunch she might show up for this wake if we give her the opportunity.

I tell him all about Diana Burley, her husband's suicide and her obsession with Heather. Buddy listens attentively.

"Yeah, I could do that if it would help," he says. "Right at the next corner."

"I think it's worth a try."

"Sure," Buddy says. "I'll take care of it. We're here. Pull over."

I do as I'm told and it's only then that I realize that I'm on La Cienega Boulevard, sitting in front of the same apartment house where only five days ago, I dropped off Heather Leeds to visit her lawyer.

"You two live quite a distance from one another. Isn't that a little inconvenient?" I ask casually.

"We're close, Joe, but we respect each other's privacy," Buddy says as he gets out of the car. "Besides the rent's pretty cheap here, not that that's a problem. Not any more."

He smiles and gives me a thumbs up and closes the door. I watch as he walks up the same path that Heather took the other day. Something tells me that if I suddenly needed a lawyer, I wouldn't be able to find one in this building.

I pull away from the curb and head for the Craven house in the Valley. Cissy meets me at the door with a manila envelope which had been sent special delivery from Evanston. I check the contents. The photo is six years old, taken at the height of the scandal and even though Diana Burley is six years younger it is an excellent likeness. I ask about Dex and she tells me that he's at the studio finishing up with Bette Davis for which she is very grateful. The sooner he ships the article off to Vogue, the sooner they'll get a check and the sooner he'll get back to work on the Mack Sennett book.

It's past three when I get to the Hollywood Division station house and Brubaker's not at his desk. A nearby cop thinks he may be across the street having a late lunch so I go looking for him. Alvin's Deli may not be haute cuisine but the sticker inside the door from the Board of Health says you probably won't die from the french fries. The place is pretty much deserted so I have no trouble spotting Brubaker sitting in a booth by the window. He looks up when I slide in across from him.

"Please. Have a seat," he says with a half smile on his face.

"Thanks. I will."

He takes a spoonful of what looks like cream of chicken soup but could just as easily be gruel. For a beverage he's drinking milk. Both signs of a man nurturing a stomach ulcer. He gestures toward the envelope.

"That it?'

I slide it toward him. He cleans off his hands before pulling out the photo. He nods approvingly.

"This'll do," he says. "Thanks."

"Happy to help," I say. "I've had a thought."

"Oooh, a thought," he says. "I can't wait."

A waitress comes by and I order coffee and a prune danish. As she walks away I tell Brubaker my idea for luring Diana Burley into the open by staging the wake at Forest Lawn. Right away I have his attention.

"What makes you think she'll show?" Brubaker asks.

"A hunch. One, she flew all the way from Chicago to confront Heather and two, she's crazy."

"That's thin."

"Thin but worth a try. If you're not interested, I can handle it on my own."

He laughs.

"She'd eyeball you in a second."

"I have friends."

"Nice to know," Brubaker says.

"Mick Clausen for one," I reply. Mick's a bailbondsman, married to my ex-wife and one of my closest friends.

"Mick's a good man but you won't need him. It's a longshot but I'll play along."

"Thanks."

"Don't mention it."

"Speaking of longshots, what's going on with Cora and Wendell?" I ask, referencing my two favorite muggers.

"I've got a couple of plainclothes sitting on their apartment in Westwood. When they show we'll grab them."

"Nice work. Thanks again." I hesitate for a second.

"Anything else?" Brubaker asks.

"Just out of curiosity what do you know about the husband?"

"Buddy Lovejoy? What about him?"

"I guess you checked him out."

He looks at me disbelieving.

"I realize murder is only a hobby with you, Mr. Bernardi, but even rookies at the academy know that when a wife dies, you look really hard at the husband and vice versa."

"So he's clean."

"Unless he hired somebody to do the deed, yes, he's clean even though he and the victim had a fight at their house earlier in the evening. A real screamer, he called it.

"What about?"

"He wouldn't say. Personal. None of my business."

"You let him get away with that?"

"I pressed him. He wouldn't budge. I backed off knowing I could come back at him any time I wanted. Anyway, he walked out and went to one of those artsy-fartsy movie theaters that start showing old artsy-fartsy movies at ten o'clock."

"Alone?"

"He hooked up with a couple of friends outside the theater just before ten. Afterwards the three of them went to some bar for an hour or so. I checked him upside down and inside out. He's clean."

"And forensics checked out the house for signs of a struggle. Or worse."

He nods.

"It's procedure."

Our waitress returns with my coffee and my prune danish along with a check for fifty five cents. I make her day by handing her buck and she walks off happy.

"Okay, Buddy walks out and heads for the theater leaving Heather at the house. Does she stay? Does she go out?"

"No idea."

"Does she make a phone call?"

"Phone company says no."

"I can tell you this, Sarge, the white sweater and blue skirt she was wearing when she was killed was the same outfit she'd been wearing all day."

"You sure about that?"

"Positive. So in or out, she doesn't change." I hesitate for a moment. "What do you know about his partner?"

"Donnelly? We checked him out. He was home asleep in bed."

"Any witnesses?"

"No. What are you getting at?"

"Maybe nothing."

"I don't like the sound of that maybe."

I know I may be clutching at straws and being unfair to the guy but reluctantly I tell him about the coincidence of her lawyer, if she actually has one, and her husband's writing partner living in the same apartment complex.

"Meaning what?" Brubaker asks.

"Come on, Sarge. I haven't met a cop yet who believed in coincidence."

Brubaker pushes the bowl away.

"What I wouldn't give for a bacon cheeseburger," he says. He takes another sip of milk and stares off into space. "A guy diddling his partner's wife, that's a real recipe for trouble."

"The thought occurred to me," I say.

"And a knife wound like that, there'd be a lot of blood, no matter where she was killed," he says.

"I expect so," I say.

"No way I could get a judge to issue a warrant to find out."

"Probably not."

"Doesn't mean I couldn't drop by unofficially for a chat with the guy," Brubaker says.

"Just to say hello," I say.

"That's right."

Brubaker takes a heathy swig of his milk and then shoves it over next to the bowl.

"The ulcers. How long have you had them?" I ask.

"Since I met you," he deadpans. and then he smiles. "They come with the job, Joe. I agonize over the ones that get away. Stupid, I know, but I can't help it."

"This one's not getting away, Sarge," I say.

"Not with you helping," he says.

The man is a master of the dead pan.

CHAPTER FIFTEEN

Sometimes Jack Paar is funny. Some nights he just whines about the state of his world. Tonight I'm not quite sure what he's doing. Bunny and I are laying in bed watching Paar fence with Charlie Weaver. I can't tell you if they are funny or not because my mind is light years away. It's at this moment that I realize Bunny is jamming her elbow into my ribs.

"Okay, what?" she asks.

"What what?"

"You've been staring at the TV for the past ten minutes with your eyes glazed over. What's going on? Trouble at the studio?"

"No more than usual. In fact things seem a little better."

"How's Lila?"

"Up and about on crutches. She says another few days and they'll let her go home."

"Even better, back to work," Bunny says. "It'll be nice to have your full attention again."

I make the mistake of not responding and feel the sharp point of her elbow back in my ribs.

"Okay, its not the picture. Then what?"

"I heard from Stu Rosenberg late this afternoon."

She looks at me, then gets out of bed and crosses to the TV, switching it off. She turns back to me.

"And?"

"We lost Rod Taylor."

Stu had been working for a couple of months with Universal who had shown some interest in our project and also in doing something with the Australian actor Rod Taylor who had just come off a breakthrough part in "The Time Machine". Rod had read the script and expressed interest in playing Walt, my protagonist.

"Shit," Bunny mutters in a most unladylike fashion. "What happened?"

"Twentieth offered him the lead in a TV series called 'Hong Kong'. Big bucks, steady work for at least a year and financial security if it turned into a hit. He told Stu he couldn't turn it down. Stu told him his future was in films, not television. It made no difference, Taylor had already committed."

"Oh, Joe, " Bunny says climbing back into bed.

I manage to force a smile.

"Onward and upward, Bunny. Stu's going back to Universal tomorrow to see if he can hold this together. He's had a nibble from George Peppard's people."

"Who?"

"He co-starred in Bob Mitchum's latest picture with good notices. Whether that'll be enough, who knows? I hear the guy's a pain in the ass to work with."

"Just what you need," Bunny says, snuggling up against me. We lay quietly like that for a while. Then she says, "You know, we've got enough money for a dozen lifetimes."

"I suppose so."

"If you chucked it all tomorrow it wouldn't really affect us."

"Probably not. But why would I do that?"

She looks up at me.

"Because you want to."

"You're so sure of that," I say.

"Positive,"

I look down at her and then lean in and kiss her tenderly.

"Don't change the subject," she chides me.

At the moment I am not interested in Stu or George Peppard or Lila James. Little Joe has sent me a message which I have no intention of ignoring. I kiss her again and start groping underneath her nightgown. She responds in kind and once again I am reminded of the reason I spent nearly ten years chasing this woman all over the country.

The next morning we're having breakfast on the rear patio. Bridget is getting Yvette ready for school and I have just heard from Lila. The doctors have cleared her to go back to work next Monday at which time I will be released from my act of charity. Bunny is now coming at me with guns blazing. Next Monday we will take off for a week's vacation, just the three of us, at some beachside bed and breakfast in northern California, maybe Mendocino or Fort Bragg. I remind her that I still owe Walt Woods three more weeks on his picture. Fine, she says with jaw set firmly, and marches over to the wall calendar and counts off the days, then circles March 24. She turns to me with a look that dares me to argue. Fine, I tell her, remembering last night. A week at a cozy little bed and breakfast with Bunny doesn't sound half bad.

I'm at the studio by ten o'clock and there's a spring in my step. Four more days and this mess of a picture is Lila's problem. Actually I'm being unfair. Things are quieting down and tensions are easing. Frank Jr. tells me his Dad is still having headaches but they are less severe. Glenn and Bette have forged an unspoken truce and filming is right on schedule. True to my word, I invite Bunny onto the lot for lunch and we spend twenty minutes chatting with Bette in her dressing room. I am no longer worried about Dex. As soon as they pick up those two college kids, he'll be off the hook. As for the rest of it, Heather's murder is Brubaker's problem, not mine.

Everything is wonderful right up to three minutes past three when I receive a phone call at my desk in the production office.

"We picked up those two kids at their apartment at eight o'clock this morning," Brubaker says.

"Great," I say.

"Not so great. We've been hammering away at them but they're denying everything."

"That's ridiculous. What about the fingerprints?"

"Oh, they match, all right. but they claim they found the car at curbside with the keys in it and took it for a joy ride. They know zilch about any late night bar or the House of Windsor hotel."

"Bullshit," I say. "How about if Dexter eyeballs them in a lineup?"

"I could do that but I already know how it'll play. Your friend will ID them and their lawyer will argue that Dexter was dead drunk at the time, mentally impaired, and couldn't identify Santa Claus in the Macy's Thanksgiving Day parade."

"They're got a lawyer?"

"Walked in twenty minutes ago. He's in with them now. I booked them on a charge of grand theft auto until we can get things straightened out but I have a feeling they'll be walking out of here by six on bail."

"Back where we started," I say.

"Not exactly," Brubaker says. "We think the bar where the woman supposedly picked up Craven is called Giovanni's."

"That's something," I say.

"My guys are leaning on the help. So far not much. I think they are more afraid of the owners then they are of the police."

"Oh, that kind of place," I say.

"Yeah. But just so you know, I pretty much believe your pal's not involved. Still I gotta go by the book so I can't tell you he's off the hook. Not yet."

143

"Well, thanks for that much," I tell him. "Any luck with Seth Donnelley."

"Not yet and I'm up to my ass with two other cases. I think I can get to him late tomorrow."

"How about if I take a swing at him this afternoon?" I ask.

"Dammit, Bernardi, we've been down this road," he barks.

"And we're going down it again," I say loudly. "Look, Sarge, this guy and his partner came to my office practically begging me to represent them. If I knock on his door he'll roll out the red carpet, believe me."

"And what do you do after you get in? Take pictures? Ask him where the bloodstain is?"

"We chat. I look around, admire the decor, pry a little about his relationship with Buddy because if we take these guys on as clients I don't want any surprises like a Martin and Lewis surprise, stuff like that, and if I see anything out of the ordinary, i'll let you know about it. Look, Sarge, if he's involved, he's going to be really careful about what he says and does in front of you but me, I'm just a Hollywood feather merchant. I'm no threat to anyone."

There is a long silence on the other end of the line.

"He's home now. Alone," Brubaker says.

"And you know that how?"

"I've got an unmarked across the street watching his building."

"I'm on my way," I say.

"Bernardi, don't do anything stupid."

"Not my style," I say.

"Lieutenant Kleinschmidt tells me you have a license to carry."

"I keep it in the glove box."

"Leave it there," Brubaker says.

"Will do," I reply and hang up.

The unmarked black Ford Fairlane parked across the street from the apartment house is about as subtle as the wart on the end of the Wicked Witch's nose. I suppress an urge to wave at the guy behind the wheel and head up the pathway to the main entrance. Inside the lobby I find a bank of mail boxes and the one for 2D is labeled "Donnelley". A moment later I'm knocking on his door. At first there's no response and I'm about to knock again when I hear stirring. The door opens a crack and a suspicious looking Seth Donnelley peers out. Something tells me he doesn't get much drop-in company. He smiles when he recognizes me.

"Mr. Bernardi."

"Hi, Seth. Mind if I come in?"

"No. Sure. I mean, yes, come on in."

He steps aside and I enter. I'm immediately struck by how small his apartment is. There's no foyer. I step directly into a cramped living room which is sparsely furnished with thrift shop specials. One sofa, one easy chair, a coffee table and a 21" floor model Admiral TV set. To the left is a kitchen area with a tiny round walnut table and two chairs. Obviously Seth doesn't do much entertaining. Off to the right is a short corridor that leads to a bathroom and what appears to be a single bedroom. I put the total square footage at three hundred but perhaps I exaggerate.

"Is there something wrong?" Seth asks, not a man to dilly-dally with small talk.

"No, why should there be?" I ask.

"I don't know. I just thought, I mean, that is, I don't usually get company and, well, this is a surprise."

I think for a moment that he is flustered. Maybe wary. But very quickly I decide that he is inarticulate, ill at ease with small talk even as he is probably very facile with the written word.

"I just came to chat, Seth, that is, if you have a few minutes."

"Oh, sure. Can I get you something to drink? I have tea."

"No, thanks." I say. "Nice little place you have here. Where do you do your writing?"

"The bedroom," he says, pointing.

I smile and walk to the open doorway and peer in uninvited.

An old-fashioned rolltop desk is set up in the corner holding a vintage Smith-Corona typewriter. To the left of it is a table upon which are piled newspapers, magazines, a dozen hardcover books and three times as many paperbacks. A double bed, neatly made, is shoved up against the wall and a foot or two away is a chest of drawers. I walk in my eyes casually scanning the floor which is polished hardwood without benefit of carpet or rugs. I see no signs of a stain or excessive scrubbing.

"Nice machine," I say to him admiring his typewriter. "I once had one just like it."

"Bought it when I went to college. Lotta scripts came out of that thing."

"I'm sure. You know, maybe I will have that tea."

"Not a problem."

"Mind if I use your facility?"

"Help yourself."

He heads off to the kitchen and I go into the bathroom, locking it behind me. The tub is white porcelain and it looks unblemished but nonetheless I run my finger along the inside of the drain looking for traces of blood. There are none. I look for stains on the floor tiles, particularly the grout. They're a little grimy but no blood residue. I turn my attention to the medicine chest. You can learn a lot from what you find there and I find something right away. An open bottle of Midol. I try to think of a reason a big strapping guy like Seth would have Midol in his medicine chest and only one comes to mind. The questions is, was her name Heather Leeds? I know one way to find out. I tear off about a dozen squares of toilet paper and carefully wrap them around the bottle, then slip it into my jacket pocket.

A few minutes later Seth and I are drinking mugs of Earl Grey at his kitchen table and I'm grilling him about his relationship with Buddy, and by extension, Heather.

"So you and Buddy starting writing together in junior high."

"Junior high, high school, Northwestern. We've been at it a long time."

"And Heather," I say. "She was there at the same time."

"Yeah."

"Buddy told me he actually never dated her back then. How about you, Seth?"

"Me?"

"Why not?"

He hesitates for just a moment.

"Yeah, well, once I took her to a party at the Sig Ep house."

"Once?"

He shrugs.

"She really wasn't tuned into undergrads."

"Yeah, I heard there was some trouble with one of the professors."

His eyes narrow.

"Who told you that?"

"Buddy, I think. Not sure. She dropped out when? Junior year?"

"I don't remember. Look, Mr. Bernardi, she's dead, okay? In my opinion she was a very troubled lady and I'm not going to say anything bad about her and frankly I don't think her past is any of your business."

"I understand, Seth, but she's dead and somebody's got to answer for that. Right now the police have their sights on a good friend of mine and he is innocent and if it's within my power I will not see him railroaded for a crime he did not commit."

He nods.

"I understand. It's just that I'm a little touchy when the conversation involves Heather."

"I understand she and Buddy had a big fight earlier in the evening the night she was killed."

"Buddy didn't kill her," Seth flares.

"I didn't say he did."

"He was at the movies with friends."

"Take it easy, Seth. I'm not accusing anyone. I'm just trying to sort out the truth. What was the fight about? Was he seeing someone on the side and she found out about it, something like that?"

Seth snorts derisively.

"Hell, no. Nothing like that. She knew we were about to sign the movie deal and she wanted in. Associate Producer, some title like that. To tell you the truth, Mr. Bernardi, I think that's the only thing she ever cared about. I think she hooked up with Buddy because she thought he was going to make it big and take her along for the ride. Did she love him? I don't think so. She was a sexual animal, no question about that, but that's all she had to give. The rest was take, take, take. I said to her one day, Heather, that overweaning ambition of yours will be the death of you yet. I wonder now if that isn't what happened."

"How?"

"Got no idea but that's what drove her, that and nothing else. She had a knack for making enemies and maybe one of them just got tired of it."

"But not Buddy," I say.

"No, not Buddy," he says looking me in the eye. "Not Buddy and not me."

"Like I said, Seth, I'm not accusing anyone."

I finish my tea, thank Seth for his hospitality and get the hell out of there. At the first opportunity I call Brubaker.

"If anybody got killed in that apartment, I saw no sign of it," I tell Brubaker.

"You sure?"

"I was pretty thorough. On the other hand, I'm pretty sure something was going on between Donnelly and Heather. He didn't want to talk about her and got defensive when I pressed him about her."

"Doesn't mean much."

"I also liberated a bottle of Midol from his medicine chest. You might want to dust it for prints."

"Jesus H. Christ, Bernardi," he explodes. "Are you nuts? You can't tamper with evidence like that."

"Evidence of what? Is he an actual suspect? Until now I don't think he was. Besides, I'm not the police. I'm a friend who merely borrowed it without telling him. Do you want me to bring it over or not?"

I hear him sigh.

"Sure, why not? Too late now. I'm going home and reintroduce myself to my family so leave it with the sergeant at the front desk and try not to manhandle it."

He hangs up.

One of the things I like best about working with the poiice is the gratitude they show when you have helped them out. Now I hang up. If he can visit his family, I can visit mine. Besides tonight Bridget's cooking pot roast.

CHAPTER SIXTEEN

Regrettably, Tuesday passed without incident. Brubaker had the Midol bottle checked for fingerprints. They found two, both smudged and unidentifiable. Even so Brubaker's interest in Seth Donnelley has multiplied by a factor of ten but with three other live cases on-going and a morning wasted in court waiting to be called, which he wasn't, he hadn't had time to re-interview Donnelley. Meanwhile the temptress Cora and her bullyboy consort Wendell are free on bail on the auto theft beef and a lot of LAPD shoe leather has been wasted trying to get answers from a host of uncooperative lowlifes that make up the clientele of Giovanni's Bar and Grill. Travis Wright has completely fallen off the map proving that his threats are as empty as his pockets. And finally Louella's column in the Herald Examiner was a love letter to Bette, predicting she will be in the thick of things when Oscar nominations are announced for next year. Late in the afternoon Louella called me, hoped I was satisfied and quoted me her price for her sugar-laced column. If and when the police make an arrest in the Heather Leeds murder case, she wants to know about it first. Why is it all these gossip columnists want to be another Jimmy Breslin? Isn't one more than enough?

It's now Wednesday morning. The clock reads 6:55 and I'm brewing a pot of coffee, waiting to hear the clunk as the morning

L.A. Times hits the front door. Wally Pepper, our paperboy, has an arm the Rams would kill for. Despite the twenty-three yards between the street and the front stoop, Wally never misses. Clunk. There it is. I light the flame under the coffeepot and hurry to the front door. The paper is just where it's supposed to be and I scoop it up. I start to go back inside when I notice an old beat up white Plymouth Fury about halfway up the block, parked at the curb, facing this house. This is odd because I've seen this car before but not in this neighborhood. On the street when I'd left Seth Donnelly's apartment? Or earlier, near the police station? I can't remember or maybe it's just my imagination. I squint to see if there's someone sitting behind the wheel but the rising sun is glaring off the windshield and I really can't see inside the car.

I go back into the house, carrying the newspaper into the kitchen. While the coffee perks, I turn to the obituaries and there it is. Buddy has outdone himself. He's sprung for a black framed two column notice that includes a photo of Heather. Everything is there. The where, the time, the place, directions, a "Public Welcome" invitation. All we need is an appearance tomorrow morning at Forest Lawn by Diana Burley and maybe another piece of the puzzle will fall into place.

But will it? The one thing that will really erase suspicion from Dexter is solid evidence to back his alibi. Frankly, I really don't care who killed Heather Leeds. I know that's a lousy thing to say but she was an evil manipulative woman who played a dangerous game, lost, and paid a terrible price. I won't shed crocodile tears over her and if it weren't for my friends Dexter and Cissy I would have walked away from this sordid business days ago. No, to my mind, Cora and Wendell and Herman Sherman are the keys that will absolve Dex and a thought has been germinating in my fevered brain ever since the hour just before dawn as I tossed and turned in half-sleep waiting for sunrise. It is harebrained, almost ludicrous and most certainly dangerous but I can't get it out of my head. It is not an idea I would share with Bunny and certainly not with Brubaker, now that we are on speaking terms. What I need is an impartial, supportive and thoughtful sounding board.

"Are you out of your friggin' mind?" Aaron Kleinschmidt screams at me, even as I am trying to get a spoonful of Grape-Nuts into my mouth.

I have ambushed him at his home before he was able to leave for work. Oblivious to my intentions he invited me to breakfast with him and his son Josh, a gangly six-four twenty one year old who plays power forward for a very talented UCLA basketball team. When he hears what I have in mind, Aaron turns livid. Josh just smiles.

"Sounds kinda neat to me," Josh says. "I think I saw something like it on Perry Mason a couple of weeks ago."

Aaron glares at his son.

"Don't you have class or something?" he growls.

"Eleven o'clock." Josh says downing a tumbler of orange juice in two swallows. He has no intention of leaving his seat at the kitchen table.

"It'll be perfectly safe," I say.

"The hell it will and since when did you suddenly become an actor?"

"Hey, if Troy Donahue can do it, so can I."

In the simplest terms I have explained my idea for smoking out Cora and Wendell. Tonight I will show up at Giovanni's around ten o'clock, bleary eyed and moving slowly. I will sit at the bar and order several drinks over a thirty minute period, first having lined my stomach with a quarter pound of butter to ensure sobriety. I will be wearing my fancy Rolek watch which I bought in Times Square for ten bucks as a joke. I will prominently display a wad of cash that would fund a decent sized pension plan and hope that my presence will attract the attention of Cora and Wendell, if they are already there, or a confederate who might call them with the news that a fish is sitting at the bar waiting to be hooked. If all goes well, I will get up from the bar and head for the rear exit where presumably I will go out into the alley behind the bar to barf my brains out. When the criminal lovebirds follow me out and make their move, the police will arrest them.

"And what police would that be?" Aaron asks sarcastically.

"I assumed you could talk to Brubaker and—"

"Well, you assumed wrong, my friend. The LAPD has better things to do than baby sit some screwball civilian's wet dream."

"Look, if you won't help, I can always get Mick Clausen and his guys—"

Mick is a bailbondsman married to my ex-wife and employs a lot of ex-military and retired cops.

"Mick's not going to condone this any more than I will and if he tries, I'll have him arrested," Aaron says.

"I'll help, Uncle Joe," Josh pipes up. "Me and some of the guys from the team—"

Aaron whirls on him.

"You! Out! Go to class!"

"It's too early—"

"And don't come back until your brain is in working order!"

Josh hesitates.

"Now!" Aaron says loudly.

Reluctantly, Josh gets up from the table and tosses down his napkin.

"Jeez, you'd think I was two years old," he mutters.

"Aha!" Aaron says triumphantly. "The light dawns!"

Father and son glare at each other momentarily and then Josh grabs the keys to his Harley and heads out the door.

Aaron shakes his head.

"He's a great kid but sometimes I wonder what he uses for brains—" and with a look at me "—like some other people I know."

"I know you're just looking out for me, Aaron, but I am going to do this."

"Why?" Aaron demands.

"For Dexter."

"And why else?" he insists.

"There is no why else," I protest.

"And why else!" he shouts at me.

"Because I'm bored!" I shout back.

For a moment we stare at each other in silence.

"I thought it was something like that," Aaron says. "You've been acting squirrely for months now, Joe, but getting yourself killed is not the ideal way to relieve your boredom."

I get up from the table.

"I'm going to do this, Aaron, and I am not going to get killed. Thanks for worrying about me and thanks for breakfast."

I head for the kitchen door that leads outside.

"Joe, if I thought it would do any good, I would broach this to Brubaker for you but I guarantee if I did, he'd have you locked up for obstructing an investigation."

"I know," I say, "but thanks anyway."

I start to walk out, then stop.

"Speaking of Brubaker," I say. "any chance that the Hollywood Division is using a six year old white Plymouth Fury for surveillance?"

"On who?"

"Me."

"I doubt it unless he persuaded some undercover to use his own vehicle. It's been known to happen."

"But not often," I say.

"Not often, " Aaron confirms. "This car, it's tailing you?"

"I'm pretty sure."

"Next time you see him, get the plate number for me."

"Thanks, Aaron."

"Do not approach the vehicle. Get the plate number."

"I hear you," I say.

"Yes, my nitwitted friend, but do you comprehend?"

He glares at me. I go out the door and leave him to his glaring.

Like Aaron, my buddy Mick is dubious about my plan but not as apoplectic in his opposition. My guess is, Mick's past sixty and creeping up on Social Security. I've never asked his age and he's never told me but he's a vital kind of guy and Lydia, his wife and my ex, adores him. Ex-Shore Patrol, I know he loves a little action now and then and I can tell from the look in his eyes, this caper sounds like fun.

"If I were to help you out on this, Joe, and I'm not saying I will, I don't think we should let the wives in on it."

"Agreed."

"They'd just get all weepy and crazy, why I do not know, but it's something neither of us needs."

"I'm with you, Mick."

"Besides me, you'd need one other guy. I'm thinking Lou Moscovitz. He's been sitting around for week and I've had nothing for him."

"I've met Lou. Good man," I say.

"If we were to do this thing, you'd have to slip Lou at least a C-Note. Two would be even better. Me, I would do it as a favor for a friend, that is, if we were to do this thing."

"Not a problem, Mick."

"Be nice if we had photos of those two birds," he says.

"I have a pretty good description from Dex but you're right, of course, it'd be easier if we had copies of their mug shots but I don't know how to get them without arousing Brubaker's suspicions."

"Hollywood Division has mug shots?"

"Yes, but—"

"No buts. Leave it to me, I can get copies, that is, if we decide to go ahead with this thing."

"Right," I say. "You on the front door, Lou watching the back and me at the bar pretending to be drunk."

"No, Joe, sitting at the bar apparently drunk and pretending to be sober."

"Gotcha," I say. For a few moments I remain silent. Then I say, "So what do you think?"

"About what?" Mick asks.

"The thing."

"What about it?"

"Are we going to do it?"

Mick looks at me in disbelief.

"Of course we're going to do it," he says, "What do you think we've been talking about?"

I tell Bunny that I've been asked by Mick to fill in as the fifth man on their bowling team since one of his key guys is home with the flu. I have forgotten the bullshit Mick and I had prearranged because Mick tells Lydia that Mick and I have been invited to a raucous going away party for an old Warner Bros. colleague of mine. We'll be fine as long as the girls don't compare notes.

We meet at eight o'clock and grab a bite to eat at a burger joint a few blocks from Mick's office. Bunny fretted a little when she saw I was wearing one of my expensive suits. Not exactly what you wear to go bowling, is it, Joe? she had asked me with a dollop of suspicion. I mumbled something incoherent and quickly ducked out the door. The suit was dumb of me but I wanted to reek of 'money' in that bar and I was sure blue jeans wouldn't cut it.

Mick shows me the police mug shots. Cora and Wendell look about the way I thought they would. Lou Moscovitz takes the pictures in his stubby fingers, a long look, and then he has their faces committed to memory. Lou's a stocky little bald guy, as tough as a bouncer in a biker bar. He, too, loves to mix it up, especially with guys who tower over him by six to eight inches. All in all I'm pretty much in safe hands. At nine-thirty Mick and I order a second cup of coffee while Lou drives over to Giovanni's to check the place out. We already have a good idea of the layout. If there are any surprises, he'll come back and fill us in. Otherwise he'll order a meatball sub and a pitcher of beer and post himself at a table by the kitchen. A short corridor next to the kitchen leads to the rest rooms and the back entrance to the bar. By ten of ten Lou hasn't returned and we assume he's in place.

I drive to Giovanni's which is maybe six minutes away. Mick will be a few minutes behind me. I park in the alley behind the bar and then walk around to the front entrance. I walk in gingerly, not staggering, a bit slowly and carefully, and take a seat at the far end of the bar where I have a good view of the entire place. I had ingested my stick of butter on the way over and with my stomach properly lined, I can drink real booze in decent quantities without getting pie-eyed. This, in case the barkeep is part of Cora and Wendell's entourage.

The clock over the bar reads 10:06. I spot Lou sitting at a table in the rear but there is no sign of Cora and Wendell. For a moment I feel a twinge of stupidity. This may turn out to be a really dumb idea. Okay, maybe so, but I just arrived. We'll give it a half hour, maybe a little longer, then I'll put on my dunce cap.

"What'll you have?"

The barkeep is tall and bald with a needle nose and very unfriendly eyes. I order a Jack Daniels neat, water back and he grunts at me. He's back in a minute with my drink.

"Buck and a quarter," he says.

"How about if I run a tab?" I say.

"Buck and a quarter," he says again, those unfriendly eyes boring in on me.

"Sure. No problem," I mutter and as I fumble to take my wad of bills out of my pocket. I remove the rubber band and place it carefully on the bar, smiling at the barkeep as I do. The outer bills are a couple of fifties and a batch of twenties. I dig into the interior and pull out a fin and lay it on the bar. Then, meticulously, I roll up the wad and replace the rubber band and fumble the wad back into my pocket. I smile again at the barkeep who scoops up the bill wordlessly and heads for the cash register. As he rings up my tab, he reaches for the phone nearby and dials a number. I pretend not to be looking but he says something into the phone and then hangs up. When he brings back my three-seventy-five in change. I leave it sitting there, a sign I'm here to do some serious drinking. By now Mick has entered the place and he is sitting down at the other end of the bar wearing a loose fitting USC sweatshirt and an Irish cap. I know that beneath the sweatshirt a snub-nosed .38 revolver is tucked in his belt. Mick raps noisily on the bar and calls out to the barkeep. For the foreseeable future, he will be noisy and disruptive. I will sit quietly staring into my drinks. looking as if I will fall off my barstool if anyone so much as blows a smoke ring in my direction.

I look into the large mirror behind the bar and take in the place. Giovanni's is what I expected, a real dive. Three certifiable barflys are sitting on stools either mute or mumbling to themselves. The main floor features a dozen or so tables and a tiny dance floor. Most of the tables are occupied and two scantily clad waitresses are flitting from table to table keeping everybody well lubricated. A Wurlitzer is jammed against the far wall and at the moment is spewing out Bobby Vee's 'Take Good Care of My Baby'. A sailor and a babe in low cut silk are half-dancing in the middle of the floor. He's had a few too many and she obviously works for the house. Not a good outlook for the sailor. Across the room two tables have been pushed together and four guys in Italian silk suits are laughing and scratching with four babes who probably keep the peroxide counter at the May Company solvent all by themselves.

And just then, they enter. I pretend not to notice but Cora and Wendell make a lovely couple and they look just like their mug shots. They hesitate at the entrance and make eye contact with the barkeep, then glance in my direction, all of which I catch out of the corner of my eye. They grab a corner booth and wait for a waitress to take their order. Instead the barkeep brings them a pitcher of beer and two mugs and the conversation concerning me continues as Cora keeps looking in my direction. None of this escapes Mick or Lou and we make silent brief eye contact. Now it'll be up to me.

"Buy a girl a drink?" I hear.

I look up and a green-eyed blonde has slipped onto the stool next to me. She's looking at me with a toothsome smile and completely fouling up our well laid plan.

"Some other time," I manage with a trace of a slur.

"You look lonely," she says, putting her hand on the inside of my thigh and moving it northward.

"Sorry, sweetheart, but I don't care much for blondes."

Her smile never fades.

"I'm not a blonde, honey, and if you give me half a chance, I can prove it."

At this point, the barkeep returns and glares at her.

"Beat it," he says to her.

"C'mon, Manny—"

"I said blow!"

She gives him a fuck-you look and wanders off. The barkeep turns to me, forcing a smile.

"Sorry about that, sir. We try to keep girls like her out of here, ya understand."

"No problem," I say.

Manny smiles at me.

"Refill, sir?"

"Damned right," I mutter, tossing down the dregs of my first drink and slapping the glass onto the bar.

Out of the corner of my eye I see Cora get up from the booth and head in my direction. I lean forward and sag a bit more over the bar. I'm sure I'm a pathetic looking sight. She reaches the bar just as Manny arrives with my drink.

"Manny, got a pack of Pall Malls back there? I'm fresh out," she says.

"I'll take a look, Miss Crandall," Manny says walking off.

Cora takes the last remaining cigarette from her pack and sticks it in her mouth, crumpling the empty pack and tossing it on the bar. She turns to me.

"Got a light?"

I smile and look around in my pockets, finally producing a 24 karat gold lighter with my initials on it, a present from Jack Warner one Christmas many years ago when I'd temporarily taken up smoking. I had dug it out of my dresser drawer just for this occasion. Unsteadily I try to make it work. She puts her hands around mine helpfully and lights up.

"I really ought to give these things up," she says.

"Worst they can do is kill you," I mumble. I take a big swig of my drink and chase it with water.

"Yeah, that's funny," she says. "I'm Cora, by the way."

I nod my head.

"Nice to meet you, Cora. Jake Bloom."

"Jake," she says.

"Sometimes my wife mispronounces it 'Jerk'."

"Shame on her."

"Shame,shame,shame," I say.

Manny comes back with the cigarettes.

"Thirty five cents, Miss Crandall," he says.

"On me," I say, playing the big spender. I put two fingers on the two remaining quarters on the bar and push them in Manny's direction. "Keep the change, my good man," I say.

Manny smiles and picks up the coins.

"Anything to drink, Miss Crandall?"

"Sure," I butt in. "Anything she wants. On me."

I reach in my pocket for the wad which shows a fifty on top.

"No need, sir," Manny says. "We'll run a tab."

How quickly things have changed in this woebegone place. Cora orders a manhattan and we start to chat. Or rather, Cora begins to pump me and I tell her all about my lousy marriage and my two kids who hate me, the broken water heater and my never ending battle with crabgrass. I think things are going well but one manhattan, one Jack Daniels and two cigarettes later, I think I overplay my hand.

"Not going home tonight. No, sir. Won't do it," I say. "Gonna stay at a hotel. You know any good hotels around here, Cora?"

For the briefest of instants, her eyes narrow and her mouth tightens imperceptibly. Then she shakes her head.

"Can't help you," she says.

"Sleep, that's what I need. Just a little sleep. Are you sure you don't know any hotels, Cora?"

She smiles at me, shaking her head.,

"You know, Jake, you never did tell me what you did for a living."

"Didn't I?"

"Are you a cop, Jake?" she asks.

Smart girl, this Cora Crandall. If a cop is working undercover and is asked directly if he is a police officer, he is required to answer truthfully. It's the law. Unluckily for her, I'm just a snake oil salesman.

"A what? A cop?"

"A cop," she says firmly.

"Are you kidding me? A cop. Jesus. A cop. No, I'm not a cop, I sell insurance. Lots and lots of insurance to people who don't want it and don't need it but I sell it to 'em anyway."

She stares at me hard and I can see the wheels turning. She's just had a brush with the police and she may be gunshy. She may even be afraid of a set-up. Like I said, smart girl this Cora Crandall and I sense I'm about to lose her. I slip off the stool dizzily and reel a little.

"Damn, I feel lousy," I say. "Need some fresh air."

I lurch a little and then head toward the back of the room, toward the corridor by the kitchen that leads to the rest rooms, a pay phone and the rear door. I stumble near Lou's table and use it to keep from falling.

"Going outside, alley," I whisper unobserved and then continue on my way. I don't look back. If she's coming, she's coming. I can only hope.

I burst through the door out into the alley and I am struck by icy air. I am also confused because it seems exceptionally dark out here, not the way it was when I drove up a half hour or so ago, I look up over the doorway and the light has gone out. No, I'm wrong. It hasn't just gone out, the bulb has been smashed. Now who would do a thing like that?

"Put your hands where I can see them and don't move," comes a voice from the shadows where the garbage is disposed of. The voice sounds familiar but I can't place it. I start to turn.

"Don't turn around. I have a gun," the man says.

I freeze in place.

"The car straight ahead, parked beneath the light pole. Walk toward it."

I look toward it, squinting and I recognize immediately, a beat up old white Plymouth Fury.

"Move, Mr. Bernardi," the voice says insistently and then I recognize it.

Travis Wright.

CHAPTER SEVENTEEN

"Get away from me," I say without turning.
"I told you to walk to that car. Now move," Wright says.
"I'm trying to find out who killed your wife," I say. "You're ruining everything."
"I don't care who killed her. Move. I mean it."
I hesitate, then take a couple of steps in the direction of his car.
"People know I'm here." I say.
"Good for them. You won't be here long."
I feel the blunt muzzle of a pistol being jammed into my back and I realize I'm in big trouble. If Cora and or Wendell don't follow me out into the alley, then Mick and Lou are going to stay put. So far no sign of anyone.
"You sure must like prison to take a chance like this," I say.
"I'm not going back to prison," he says.
"What are you going to do, kill me?"
"If I have to," he says.
It's the way he said it, like a man at the end of his patience with nothing left to lose. This could get real ugly real fast.
We're halfway to the car now and I know if I get in it, I'm a dead man.
"It doesn't have to be like this, Bernardi," Wright says. "Just give me the diamonds."

"So now it's definitely diamonds."

"I talked to my man in Amsterdam. He sold them to her four and a half years ago, right after I entered prison. But then you already know that, don't you?"

"How many times do I have to tell you, I don't know what you're talking about."

"You have them, Bernardi. I tossed her house inside out. Nothing. But you were in her office. You discovered the body but why were you there at that hour of the morning? Looking for something? No, it has to be you. It can't be anyone else."

"You're wrong."

"We'll see."

We're at the car door now. I sense him close behind me, maybe no more than a foot away.

"Open the car door," he says.

I'm out of options. The man is delusional, no question, and I sense his nerves are totally frayed. I can turn on him and try for the gun but most likely he'll get a shot off. I can get in the car and hope for an opening later but if I do, I'm totally on my own and what he wants I can't give him.

"I won't tell you again," Wright says, jamming the pistol into the small of my back. If ever I was to have a chance this is it. I tense my body, ready to spin around.

"Freeze, asshole!"

A familiar voice close by cuts through the chill night air like a straight razor.

"Drop the weapon or I'll blow your fucking head off."

"Joe!" comes a shouted voice from afar.

I look to my right. Mick and Lou are emerging from the rear door of the bar.

"Stay where you are!" I shout. "Aaron's got this guy handled."

They stop in their tracks.

"Up to you," I say to Wright. "You can die right here with a bullet in your head or you can live to see another birthday."

A moment later I feel the gun being removed from my back.

"Drop the gun on the ground and back away," I hear Aaron say.

Slowly I turn as the pistol clatters to the pavement. Wright has moved away from me, hands raised, as Mick and Lou run up to us. Aaron has his revolver pointed at Wright's midsection.

"Mick, pat him down, just in case," Aaron says.

As Mick starts to search Wright for a second gun, I look over at Aaron.

"What are you doing here?"

"Did you really think I was going to let you three bumblers do this on your own?"

I share a look with Mick. He doesn't appreciate being called a bumbler.

"No need to thank me right away," Aaron says with a smile as he reaches for his handcuffs.

Forty minutes later Aaron has Wright at the Police Administration Building, booked on a range of charges including assault with a deadly weapon and attempted murder. I've tagged along to sign the complaint. Mick and Lou are headed for warm beds and warmer wives. Mick told me that less than a minute after I went out the back door, Cora and Wendell left by the front entrance. Maybe my performance was unconvincing though I doubt it. More likely they smelled a trap. Either way we are no closer to locking in Dexter's alibi.

It's past eleven-thirty when Aaron dumps Wright into an interrogation room and lets me into an adjoining room with a one-way window so I can watch the proceedings.

"Aren't you going to call Brubaker?" I ask.

"What for?" Aaron replies.

"It's his case."

"Not this one. My collar, my case, "Aaron says. "Don't bitch. This lets me slide into the Leeds case by the back door without promulgating disharmony."

I stare at Aaron in disbelief. He has just used two words I didn't know he knew. Maybe he does a lot of crossword puzzles.

"Pull up a chair," he says to me "then observe and learn."

He leaves me and I watch as he enters the interrogation room. Travis Wright is handcuffed to a u-bolt embedded in the table. Aaron sits down opposite him. Even before Aaron can ask him question one, Wright is demanding to see a lawyer. Fifty-one months in the slammer have educated him in the ways of the system and he knows his rights. Aaron tries to finesse him into cooperating. Wright wants no part of it. Lawyer, lawyer, he whines. After thirty minutes Aaron gives up and tells him he can have his one phone call. Wright says he doesn't want a phone call, he wants a free Public Defender. He has no money for a lawyer. A uniformed officer takes Wright back to a cell where he will be held until his arraignment tomorrow morning. Aaron joins me in the observation room.

"Tough cookie," he says.

"Just your typical jailhouse lawyer," I say, "but I don't think he killed Heather Leeds."

"And you know this how?" Aaron asks.

"That missing nine million was converted into diamonds and unless the guy is a world class actor, which I doubt, he hasn't found them. He never would have killed Heather without getting the diamonds first."

"And where are these diamonds?"

"I have no idea," I say. "Maybe in a safe deposit box somewhere under a false name but that would require a false set of papers. He ransacked her house and found nothing but something tells me the diamonds are close at hand."

I check my watch. It's quarter past midnight and I need to get to sleep. Forest Lawn is on the morning agenda and I need some sleep. Aaron wishes me luck and I head for home.

Thursday is a perfect day for a funeral. Rain clouds hang over Glendale like a grey shroud. The wind is blowing from west to east in fits and starts and anyone with half a brain has left his house with an umbrella in hand. My half a brain is inoperative. I'm wearing a black suit and a black tie, confident that the storm clouds will pass by without incident. I arrive at Forest Lawn at nine-thirty, drive up to the massive gate where I am stopped by a man in black. He's dressed like an undertaker but my gut tells me he works for Brubaker. My suspicions are confirmed when he recognizes me.

"Top of the hill, Mr. Bernardi," he says. "The sergeant's waiting for you."

I thank him and climb the winding driveway to the small chapel located next to Inspiration Slope, one of the cemetery's many fastidiously kept sections.

A dozen cars are parked in the lot and I spot Brubaker by the front door, apparently on the lookout for me because as soon as I park he makes straight for me. Uncharacteristically he is wearing a very un-coplike suede sport jacket and grey slacks. He sports a black mourning band on his sleeve.

"What's with all the cars?" I ask him.

"Off duty cops and their families. I decided to do this thing right. If she shows and the place is deserted, she might be scared off."

"Good thinking," I say.

"Thanks," Brubaker replies with a sardonic smile. "So, Lieutenant Kleinschmidt says the ex-husband surfaced last night."

"Matter of fact he did," I say as we head to the chapel entrance.

"While you and Mick Clausen were playing junior detectives at Giovanni's." He gives me a hard look.

"You've got a lot on your plate, Sarge. We were just trying to help out."

"Nice mess you made of it and by the way, your drunk act? I was told you can catch better performances in a Bugs Bunny cartoon."

"You weren't there."

"One of my undercovers. He was getting somewhere with one of the B-Girls when everything turned sour. Thanks for your help. Now the bad guys are on red alert."

"I meant well," I say.

"I believe that phrase is etched on Custer's headstone."

We go inside. Organ music is being quietly piped into the small chapel. There are a dozen pews and about a dozen assorted "mourners", most of them packing. Buddy and Seth are sitting together in the front row, somberly dressed. I make eye contact with Buddy before he looks away. Facing the pew is an open casket that sits on a flower festooned bier. On either side are several stand up floral arrangements. I walk over to the casket and stare down at Heather Leeds' lifeless face. The mortician has done a good job of reconstructing her physical beauty but somehow I am half afraid those eyes are going to suddenly open and she is going to snarl up at me like a rabid vixen.

I hear the crackle of a radio and Brubaker reaches inside his jacket and extracts a walkie-talkie.

"Go," he says.

"Subject coming up the driveway in a Valley Cab," the voice replies.

"Roger that," Brubaker says and then slips the unit back inside his jacket. He turns to the others. "The lady's on her way. You know what to do." He turns to me. "You, back of the room in the shadows. We don't want her spotting you."

I nod and hurry to the rear of the chapel, standing beside and slightly behind a life-sized statue of St. Anthony, a bluebird perched on his shoulder. Brubaker takes up a position a few feet from the casket, pretending to read the condolence cards that accompanied the floral arrangements. For several moments all movement is frozen. There is no sound save for the mournful organ. And then she enters.

She's wearing a light colored raincoat and rain hat and her eyes are obscured by dark glasses. A large purse is slung over her shoulder. She hesitates in the doorway and takes a slow look around. I press back into the shadows. If she has seen me she gives no sign of it. But she has seen Buddy Lovejoy and she stares in his direction for what seems an eternity.

Finally she walks slowly over to the casket and looks down at Heather. At least thirty seconds pass and then she opens her purse and extracts a small unmarked bottle containing some sort of liquid. Furtively, she starts to unscrew the cap. Brubaker is watching her and suddenly he leaps toward her grabbing her wrist just as the cap comes free. Diana Burley screams as the bottle slips from her grasp and falls to the carpet. Instantly a huge cloud of hissing vapor arises from the spot that has been soaked. Acid, no question about it, and it was intended for Heather Leeds.

I start forward but I'm not needed. Even as Brubaker is wrestling her to the ground, kicking and screaming, two cops jump in to help him subdue her. A moment later she has curled herself into a fetal position and is weeping inconsolably. A female officer joins them and kneels down and starts to talk to her quietly. After a minute or so her tears stop and she is helped to her feet, her visage now stoic. She is led outside to a waiting squad car even as I stare down at the hole which has been burned into the carpet. I shake my head. Even in death, Diana was determined that Heather would pay the price of disfigurement for her betrayal.

By three o'clock Diana has been taken to the psych ward at County General Hospital. At first she had been brought back to

Brubaker's office at the Hollywood Division but she refused to speak. Not a word, not a syllable of explanation or remorse. She sat for an hour staring transfixed at a wall. Finally Brubaker had no choice and the medics were brought in.

Now Brubaker and I are sitting in the hospital cafeteria drinking coffee and the sergeant is wolfing down a cheese danish. He shakes his head.

"I've seen hate before," he says, "but nothing like that."

"She snapped a long time ago, Sarge. The doctors thought she was ready to go back into the world and they were wrong."

"I don't suppose we'll ever know what's going on in her head."

"No, but I'd like to."

"She's not our killer," Brubaker says, "any more than Travis Wright is. A woman her age, alone in the city, too many things don't fit. Moving the body. How could she have handled that? That alone rules her out."

"But she knows something," I say.

"Such as?"

"I don't know but the way she was staring at Buddy Lovejoy when she first walked in, she knows something we don't and I want to know what it is."

"Not much chance of that. My guess is she's headed back to treatment. Maybe here. Maybe in Illinois."

"I'd still like to speak with her."

"Weren't you watching, Bernardi? She's mute."

"I'd still like to try. Five years ago Heather Leeds touched her life and very possibly touched Buddy Lovejoy's life as well. There's a connection. I know there is."

"And how do you expect her to open up to you?"

"I had a long talk with her at the studio. She seemed rational. We talked pleasantly. I tried to help her. Maybe she'll remember me. It can't hurt."

Brubaker hesitates, then nods.

"Give it a rest for today. Then if you can get by her doctors, it's okay with me. But if you get something useful, you share. Despite what you may think, you're not a cop."

"I hear you," I say.

"We'll see," he says as he shoves the check across the table in my direction. Sixty-five cents not including tip. Stuck again.

CHAPTER EIGHTEEN

I've had it.

Nearly four o'clock and I am done for the day. I call Mitzi at the production office to see if anything urgent has popped up. It hasn't. Lila called to say hi and tell me rehab was progressing well. She'll check back with me in the morning but barring any new calamity, tomorrow is my last day on this picture and Lila will be back, albeit on crutches, Monday morning. It can't come any too soon. Compared to "Pocketful of Miracles", a few weeks on the snowy streets of New York hustling for "The Hustler" will seem like a vacation. One more call before I head home. I catch Bunny at her desk and check her schedule. When she says she won't be home before seven o'clock I volunteer to bring in Chinese. This always makes me a popular guy, especially with Yvette who adores mushu pork, most of which she manages to get into her mouth. the rest ending up on the oversize bib we provide her on these occasions.

It's six-thirty when I approach the house. A strange car is parked at the curb with a man behind the wheel, his back to me. I pull into the driveway and stop, reach over and take my .25 Beretta from the glove box. I slip the little pistol into my jacket pocket and get out of the car. Then and only then do I see Al Rhinehalter, the recently fired head of security at Paramount, walking up the driveway toward me.

"Got a minute?" he asks. "I need a friend."

"Don't we all?" I reply.

He looks like hell. His eyes are sunken as if he hasn't gotten much sleep. His denim shirt sports deeply embedded coffee stains. His shoes could use a shine. His hair could use a comb.

"Look, Mr. Bernardi, I know I'm imposing. I need a couple of minutes. If you haven't got them, I'll leave. I don't want to cause you any trouble but I need to talk to someone and nobody else will listen."

I take my two sacks of Chinese from the back seat and head for the kitchen door.

"Come on in," I say.

I sit him down at the kitchen table and offer him something to drink. He shakes his head. Yvette comes bounding into the room. I pick her up and give her a huge hug and a kiss and tell her about dinner. She squeals with delight. I ask her to give me a few minutes alone with my guest and she nods and runs from the room. I look over at Rhinehalter who has witnessed this and I'm not sure if his face is reflecting sadness or envy. Maybe a little of both.

"Nice little girl you've got there," he says.

"Eight going on eighteen," I say. "As I recall you have a couple of girls."

"They're with their mother."

I don't like the way he said this and sure enough, he explains.

"She left for Seattle two days ago to be with her folks. Took the girls with her. Don't know when she's coming back."

The way he says it, it's not a visit. I can't think of anything appropriate to say so I keep my mouth shut.

"The cops are all over me," he says. "They've had me in twice for questioning, they're talking to the neighbors and I'm pretty sure I'm being followed."

"I know the feeling," I say.

"When Rose—that's my wife—found out I'd been fired because of the harassment charge, she just picked up and left. Years back I used to cat around a little but never since the kids were born. Made no difference. I swore to her it wasn't true. She didn't want to hear it." He hesitates. "I've got a pretty good idea who killed Miss Leeds, Mr. Bernardi. Maybe you could pass what I know along to that sergeant."

"Who are we talking about, Al?"

"Chick MacGruder, the press agent who used to work for Glenn Ford."

"You have proof?"

"Proof? No, " Rhinehalter says, "but I know things the cops should be told about. Like for starters, why the bitch pinned the sexual harassment charge on me."

"Tell me."

"She resented Ford having his own press person and she was determined to get rid of him so she came to me with the same bullshit sexual harassment claim she later used on me. I checked it out, talked to MacGruder, cross-checked some dates she'd thrown at me and realized she was lying. I told her so and warned her not to pull that crap on me again. That's when she tells her phony story about me to my boss, Mr. Peabody."

"I've met him. A mountain of marshmallow."

"You bet. He suspended me immediately without even hearing my side of it and then when she turned up dead, he terminated me."

"A man who never let due process get in the way of justice. Your wife finds out and skedaddles for Seattle."

"Right. But now I know somebody who had real good reason for killing her—"

"MacGruder."

He nods.

"So I started asking around and the word was out I was curious about MacGruder so that same day I get a call from a buddy of mine who works security at MGM and he tells me that he knows all about MacGruder who three years ago worked in the studio press office. Something of a ladies man or at least he thought he was and he had a thing for one of the secretaries there—Alicia Hernandez her name was—who strung him along for a few free meals and then dumped him. Only he wouldn't stay dumped and one evening when she was working late alone, he grabbed her and dragged her into one of the offices and tried to stick it to her. She fought like a tigress and Jack, that's my buddy Jack, heard her screams and broke it up. The next day they fired MacGruder but Jack told me he thought MacGruder would have killed her if he hadn't been there."

"And how come the police don't know about this?" I ask.

"Because they let him go quietly, no arrest, no fanfare and no bad publicity. Do I have to tell you how the studios play the game?"

He doesn't. Studios hate the kind of notoriety that belies the fairyland image of Hollywood. In its more sordid moments the movers and shakers have covered up abortions, bigamy, beatings, drug addiction, homosexuality and occasionally murder. Not that any of this involved me but some in my profession have not been so fussy about what they were called upon to do. Chick MacGruder is one of those people who facilitate the dark side of the silver screen and in doing so, apparently has developed a dark side of his own.

"I know that sergeant is trying to pin this on Mr. Craven but I don't see it, not him, not for a second, and I thought maybe you could get through to Brubaker because I sure can't."

"I'll talk to him," I say. "This is something he needs to know about. About MacGruder, do you know where I can find him?"

"Sure. Everybody who works at the studio has to be registered. He's living at the Concord Inn on Santa Monica. Pretty sleazy kind of a place. The cops call it 'Hooker Heaven'."

"Seems appropriate," I say.

Just then the door opens and Bunny comes in. She seems startled to find me with company. Al gets to his feet, a little flustered.

"Well, hello," Bunny smiles. "Am I interrupting?"

"No, ma'am," Al replies. "I was just leaving."

I introduce Al and Bunny being Bunny invites him to dinner. Al demurs.

"Kind of you, ma'am, but I have to be going. My wife will be looking for me." He turns to me. "You'll look into that matter?"

"Count on it," I tell him.

Al leaves and Bunny gives me a hug and a peck. She looks up at me, curious.

"Do I need to know?" she asks.

"Not really," I say.

"Then lets eat."

The next morning I'm up by eight and on the phone to the Hollywood Division. An underling tells me that Brubaker will be in court most of the day. Is there a message? I say no and hang up. This guy spends so much time in court he could give Perry Mason a run for his money. I had hoped to steer him toward Chick MacGruder but it seems that isn't going to happen. I also know that Brubaker doesn't work weekends. I can see my morning is now going to be spent at the Concord Inn.

The prevailing wisdom seems accurate. The Concord Inn is a dump, a third-rate motel with Hiltonian delusions. Nestled about twenty yards off of Santa Monica Boulevard between an Army-Navy store and a boarded up travel agency, it stands two stories high and is in bad need of a paint job. All twenty four rooms face the street, twelve at street level and twelve more on a balcony reachable by a single staircase next to the office. A half dozen cars, none newer than six or seven years, litter the parking lot. Enticing signs such as "Free TV" and "Half-Day Rates" are featured prominently in order to entice the weary traveler or, more likely, a bleached blonde hooker and her newest john.

I park my newly washed Bentley on the street and feed the meter a few nickels. I realize that the motel parking lot is free but it might also be contagious. I play it safe.

The babe at the registration desk is a heavy set redhead wearing a plus-plus size dress with a scoop neckline that leaves nothing to the imagination. Her makeup has been slathered on and an array of silvery bracelets hang from both her flabby wrists. She looks up from the morning paper with a smile when I enter but her expression quickly turns to one of caution. I am wearing a suit and tie and the message center in her brain is probably screaming, 'Cop! Cop!'

"Can I help you?" she says warily.

I sense this is one tough cookie and so I decide to play it hard-nosed.

"Chick MacGruder. What room?" I say curtly.

"You a cop?"

"No."

"Then I'm sorry. I'm not authorized to reveal that information."

I press my belly against the counter and lean forward, giving her an icy look.

"Does the name Mickey Cohen mean anything to you?" I ask.

She hesitates.

"You're not Mickey Cohen," she says.

I lean closer, grabbing her hand and pressing it to the countertop.

"I'm his nephew," I say very quietly. "Chick MacGruder. What room?"

"Two-oh-nine," she replies, just as quietly.

"Thank you," I say as I head for the door. I turn back. "And if you touch that phone, you'll be eating out of a straw for at least a month."

Outside I jog up the staircase and quickly locate number 209. I knock. No response. I knock again. Then the door opens a crack and MacGruder peers out. He's just woken up. His face is stubbled, his hair is askew and he smells like yesterday's tuna salad sandwich.

"What do you want?" he growls.

"Information," I say.

"Try the Brittanica," he replies attempting to slam the door in my face. I wedge in my foot and shove. The door flies open and MacGruder stumbles backwards into the room. I can get away with this because he's a little guy who'd make a toothpick look obese.

"Hey!" he yells, apparently outraged.

I close the door behind me and turn to him.

"How do you want to handle this? The easy way or the hard way?" I'm beginning to sound like Lee Marvin in "Bad Day at Black Rock".

He glares at me.

"Okay, tough guy," he says, "I'll give you five minutes. After that I call the cops."

I point to his bedside phone.

"Call 'em now," I say. "All I'm trying to do is save your ass from a murder conviction."

"I'll bet," he says with a sneer. "Thanks, sport, but no thanks."

"Here's a riddle for you, Chick," I say, "What's the difference between Heather Leeds and Alicia Hernandez?"

The color starts to drain from his face, the sneer disappearing from his lips as he sits heavily on the bed.

"What do you want to know?" MacGruder asks.

"Everything," I say. "The phony charges of sexual assault leveled at you, anything she might have said to you beginning with day one, anything you can tell me about her and her dealings with not only you but other people."

And so he tells me and basically his story parallels Al Rhinelander's. A woman striving to get ahead, able to switch from come hither to back stabbing in the blink of an eyelash, the epitome of a self-serving narcissist. She seemed to have had run-ins with everyone, commissary busboys and secretaries, script supervisors and teamsters but never with anyone who could further her career.

"I'll tell you who you should be looking at," MacGruder says to me. "The boyfriend, that's who."

"Boyfriend? What boyfriend?"

"The guy. The guy she was hanging around with for the last couple of months."

"Not her husband."

"Of course not her husband. Lovejoy, he's a little twerp. I mean the big guy. Over six feet. Built like a football player."

A picture of Seth Donnelley jumps to mind.

"Name?"

"Are you kidding? If there's a name on that register downstairs, chances are it's John Smith."

"And they came here a lot?"

"Four or five times that I know of. The last time was the day she died. I remember because of the fight."

"What fight?"

"It was about eleven in the morning. I'd had a tough night. Drank a lot. What the hell. No job, no money, all thanks to her. I got up and looked out the window. They were in the parking lot, yelling at each other. Couldn't really hear what they were saying and then he starts off and she grabs him and he shoves her and she falls down and he doesn't even bother helping her up. He screams at her,'Stay away from me or I swear to God, I'll kill you'. Then he just drives off and she's screaming after him and then she gets in her car and just sits there for a couple of minutes and then eventually she drives away."

"Do you know Seth Donnelley?" I ask.

"Who?"

"Lovejoy's writing partner."

"Is that who that guy was? Jesus."

"Maybe yes, maybe no. Sergeant Brubaker might want you to make an identification."

"That'd be good," MacGruder says. "If I help him, maybe he'll get off my back."

"You never know," I say.

I leave his room and go back down to the office where the mistress of the establishment is now checking out the funny papers. She looks up at me with contempt.

"Mickey Cohen doesn't have a nephew. I checked," she says.

"Good for you. For the last few weeks or so a woman named Leeds has been coming here now and then with her boyfriend."

"Get lost."

"Maybe you saw her picture in the paper. She was murdered last week."

That stops her but only for a second.

"Sorry, I forgot to send flowers," she says.

"I need to know what you can tell me about the man with her."

"Hit the road, Jack, or I call the cops."

I reach in my pocket, open my billfold and take out Brubaker's card. I lay it on the counter.

"Here's the number. Give him your address. Tell him Joe will be waiting for him in the office and bring the paddywagon. He'll need it to round up the hookers and the johns."

Her eyes turn into icy slits as she pushes the card back at me.

"I never met the guy," she says. "She did the registering. Mary Maloney from Beverly Hills. Paid cash."

"Big surprise. And the guy? You must have seen him at least once."

"No."

Once again I lean across the counter with my hard look.

"At least once," I say insistently.

She hesitates.

"Yeah. Once. A big man, over six feet. Not much of a dresser. Blue jeans, a sweat shirt with a big purple NW on it—"

"You sure about that?"

"Would I make that up?"

I nod and tell her the same thing I told MacGruder. Expect a police lineup identification. She says to me, only when pigs fly. I decide not to press my luck so I get out of there.

When I get back to my car, I see that I have a nickel's worth of parking still remaining so I sit behind the wheel, trying to make sense of what I know or, more precisely, what I think I know. Something tells me I am within a cat's whisker of sorting this thing out. Something also tells me I need to have another chat with Diana Burley.

CHAPTER NINETEEN

It's late afternoon and Brubaker is probably still in court. Even if he's not, I don't need him and I don't want him. What I have in mind is going to require a little delicacy. To Sergeant Willie Brubaker a little delicacy is a tiny hot dog wrapped in bacon. I actually like the guy but like a lot of cops, he galumphs through his duty days in size twelve brogues catching who he can and regretting the ones that got away. Subtlety is not part of his M.O. and when it comes to Diana Burley she needs to be handled gently and with understanding.

The guy sitting opposite me is, unfortunately, understanding very little. His name is Robert Reikes, M.D. and he is Chief of Psychiatry at County GeneralHospital. He has a round face and wears round rimless glasses, a sort of taller version of Peter Lorre as Mr. Moto. Because he is a doctor, he knows all the answers and conversation has been difficult.

"I couldn't possibly let you interrogate Mrs. Burley," he says to me, blowing smoke at me in more ways than one. He's puffing on a Viceroy using one of those long FDR cigarette holders. "Her condition is much too fragile."

"I'm looking for a chat, Doctor, not a grilling."

"You're not the police, Mr. Bernardi," he says.

"I have Sergeant Brubaker's permission to see her."

"But you do not have mine."

"I promise it will be low key. Put a nurse in the room with me if you like."

"How many times must I repeat myself, sir?" Reikes says.

"I would rather this situation not turn ugly, Doctor." I tell him.

"Damn it, sir. Are you deaf or just stupid? Please leave my office now."

"Is that your final word?"

"It is."

"Then may I use your phone to call the hospital administrator?"

"He has no authority over my department, Mr. Bernardi. It won't change things."

"Oh, I know that, Doctor," I say quickly, "but as a courtesy I want to warn him."

"Warn him of what?"

"That when I leave this office I am going to put in a call to Lou Cioffi, the crime editor at the *Los Angeles Times* with a major story for tomorrow's edition. It concerns the key witness in a murder investigation who is being shielded from interrogation by Robert Reikes, the chief of Psychiatry at County General Hospital whose psych ward has three times in the past five months released patients into the general population, ostensibly cured, who immediately went about repeating the heinous crimes for which they had been originally committed."

Reikes sputters and nearly chokes on his cigarette.

"Now wait a minute," he says.

"I'm pretty sure Lou will call for a thorough investigation of hospital practices in this area which include overcrowding, insufficient nurses and orderlies, and a criminal lack of medical judgement by a substandard psychiatric staff."

"I'll sue," Reikes blusters.

"Excellent," I exclaim. "Nothing Lou likes better than a knock down, drag out court case that keeps his name in front of the public. He dreams of winning a Pulitzer, you know. Maybe you're it. And by the way, Doctor, just how do you think the Administrator is going to feel about the hospital's good name being dragged through an ugly trial that will only serve to remind Los Angeles about Everett Jankowski, the child rapist who you personally released from this facility three and a half months ago only to see him molest two eleven year old girls in the basement of St. Timothy's Church?"

Fifteen minutes later I emerge from the elevator and start down the corridor toward Diana Burley's room, a registered nurse at my side. Crooked in my arm is a vase filled with a dozen tea roses and a half dozen carnations. I'm feeling pretty proud of myself. Anticipating a bureaucratic stone wall I had spent an hour researching Robert Reikes M.D. who turned out to be the self-important pedant that I anticipated he would be. I love pompous egotists like Reikes. At the first sign their spotless public image might be sullied, they collapse like a punctured hot air balloon.

At the door to her room, I identify myself to the cop on duty. He nods. I'm expected. I ask if she's awake. He says she was the last time he looked. The nurse, who was merely an escort, has warned me that Diana was sedated about two hours ago and even if she's awake, she may be incoherent. The nurse then takes her leave and I step into Diana Burley's room.

The room is small, utilitarian and dimly lit. Diana is propped up in her narrow bed, eyes wide open, staring at the opposite wall. Her wrists are tethered to the bed frame. If she's aware of me, she gives no sign. I walk over to the bed and stare down at her.

"Mrs. Burley?"

Only then does she look up at me and I think I see a flicker of recognition. Her eyes fall on the vase and she smiles.

"Flowers. How nice."

"A little something to brighten up the room," I say, placing the vase on her nightstand. I grab a nearby chair, pull it to her bedside and sit down.

"Do you remember me, Mrs. Burley?" I ask.

"I think so," she says. "Were you a friend of my husband's?"

"No. My name is Joe Bernardi. We met at Paramount Studios. You came looking for Heather Leeds."

"Oh, yes," she says after a long pause. "How are you?"

"Never mind me," I say. "How are you?"

"Tired."

"Do you remember coming to the cemetery?"

"Yes. It was stupid. I couldn't help myself. I didn't want her dead. I wanted her to know what she had done to me. I wanted her to pay."

"By throwing acid in her face?"

"Yes."

"You hated her very much,"

"Yes."

"Tell me about your marriage."

"Axel loved me deeply. I loved him. She destroyed all that. She took him away from me and then discarded him. Why did she do that? She didn't want him. She didn't need him the way I did. She already had her man, a young man, much younger than Axel. She threw him away, too."

I tense up. I realize I'm close. When she entered the chapel she had hesitated and stared across the room at Buddy Lovejoy. Now I'm sure it wasn't Buddy she had recognized, it was Seth Donnelley.

"This man of Heather's, this young man, do you know who he was?"

"I didn't know his name," she says.

"Did you see him again at the chapel?"

"Yes."

"A tall man, athletic looking?"

"That's right."

"And he and Heather Leeds had been lovers years ago at Northwestern?"

"I assume so."

"And she dumped him for your husband?"

"Axel was in a position to further her academic career. That young man wasn't. You must understand, Mr. Bernardi," she says, "Axel was a gentle man, soft spoken, unworldly. He never had a chance."

I nod and then reach over and grasp her hand.

"I'm sorry, Mrs. Burley. Truly I am," I say.

She just nods, lost again in her own thoughts as she resumes staring at the wall.

It takes me twenty-five minutes to drive to the Hollywood Division. I mount the stairs looking for Brubaker. He's not there. I'm told he's still in court. I pull up a chair next to his desk and say I'll wait. For the next fifty minutes I get a lot of curious looks but I don't move, not even to pee. Having gotten this far, I don't intend to let the momentum slip away. I am positive that Seth Donnelley killed Heather Leeds. I know when and how. I don't know where and why but I intend to find out.

Brubaker shows up at ten after five and to suggest that he is glad to see me is also to suggest that a vegetarian rabbi loves pork chops. He slips out of his suit jacket and hangs it on the back of his chair, grabs a sheet of paper and slips it into his typewriter.

"I have to file this report," he says without looking up. "Goodbye."

"I need to be wired," I say.

He looks over at me.

"What?"

"Wired. I know who killed Heather Leeds. I also think I can get him to admit it."

"Bernardi, you live in a fairyland. Who is this doofus who is going to suddenly confess a homicide to you?"

"Seth Donnelley," I say.

I let him have all of it starting with the relationship eight years ago at Northwestern right up to the recent affair, despite the fact that she was married to Donnelley's childhood buddy and current writing partner. At first he half-listened. By the time I was finished he was staring at me with arms folded across his chest, absorbed in every word.

"Great theory," Brubaker says. "It might even be accurate. Where's your proof?"

"Where's my wire?"

"Even if he's guilty, the guy isn't going to confess to you. not after all the trouble he went to to deflect suspicion. Maybe in some nickel and dime B movie but not in real life. Besides which he could be dangerous."

"You'd be nearby."

"I'll mention the fact in your eulogy."

"Do you want to close this case or don't you?"

"The guy will keep until Monday. I'll pick him up and apply some pressure."

"Is that before or after he screams for his lawyer?" I ask.

We go around like this for a few more minutes until Brubaker finally explodes.

"Listen to me, Bernardi, and listen closely. I do not work at this job seven days a week. I do not work on Saturday and I do not work on Sunday. This weekend I am taking my family to Disneyland. If I do not take my kids to Disneyland tomorrow they will hate me for the rest of my life and my wife will divorce me. Do I make myself clear?"

"This evening is fine with me, Sarge," I say calmly.

His eyes turn into beady little slits and for a moment I think he is going to get up from his chair and throw a set of cuffs on me. And then he sighs and shakes his head in defeat.

"I'm going to do this, Bernardi, if for no other reason than to shut you up. But if this doesn't work, if it goes south for any reason whatsoever, I want you gone. Disappeared. Out of my face forever. Do you understand?"

"Got it," I say.

We set H-Hour for nine o'clock. It'll take that long to get set up. An unmarked with a couple of undercovers has driven to the apartment house to make sure Donnelley is home alone. If he's not we abort. The only chance this has of succeeding is to get him talking one on one. I'll drive up just before nine, already wired by a technician. I've done this before. I know the drill. A surveillance van decked out as a water company emergency vehicle will be a minute or two behind me. Brubaker and the technician will be in the back operating the radio and recording equipment. An armed uniform will be behind the wheel. As we go through our preparations, Brubaker becomes less contentious. Maybe he senses this might work although I know he is having reservations about having to work with a dim-witted civilian.

At ten to nine I park at the curb in front of the apartment house. I've already phoned and told him I'm coming. I want to talk to him about representation by Bowles & Bernardi and for the moment I want this chat to be between the two of us and not Buddy. There had been a long silence before he said to me that he and Buddy were a team, always had been and always would be. When I told him I knew that and that I had no intention of breaking them up, he relaxed and invited me over.

I exit my car and walk up the path to the front entrance. The van has just pulled up behind my car. I hesitate before stepping inside.

"Going inside. Flash if you can hear me," I say.

The van blinks its high beams twice. Satisfied I step into the building. This is going to be a one-way transmission. For Brubaker to talk to me I would need a plug in my ear, a sure giveaway that something was amiss. I'll just have to trust that they get it all and nothing goes wrong.

I knock on the door and it opens immediately. Seth smiles and invites me in. He's wearing sweat pants and sweat shirt, his face is damp and his hair still needs combing. On the living room floor is an exercise mat and a pair of dumbbells.

"I've been working out," he says. "Need to stay in shape."

"Absolutely" I say, me who hasn't worked out since Eisenhower was President.

"Can I get you something?" he asks. "I still have that tea. Also put in some carrot juice."

"Maybe a glass of water," I say.

"Okay."

I follow him into the kitchen and sit down at the little table with two chairs. Seth brings me my water and sits opposite me.

"I want to tell you how nice it is, I mean, how proud I am that a great company like yours wants to represent us, Mr. Bernardi. I can't thank you enough."

"And if things work out, that's exactly what we're going to do, Seth."

Seth furrows his brow.

"What do you mean, if things work out?"

I put on my most concerned face.

"You have a right to know. It's one of the reasons I'm here this evening. The police are looking at your partner for the murder of his wife."

He shakes his head.

"That's crazy."

"I'm afraid not. They have evidence that she was running around behind his back for at least two or three months. They think he found out and killed her. That's what the big fight was about the night she was killed."

"No, that's all wrong. Buddy wouldn't do anything like that. Besides he just didn't care. He told me he was fed up with her, that he hadn't slept with her for over a year. If she'd wanted to leave, he'd have held the door open for her."

"Sorry, Seth, but the cops don't see it that way. Right now they're trying to track down the boyfriend, The sergeant says they have a lead, a matchbook from a place called the Concord Inn which they'd found in her purse. Just the kind of place you'd go if you didn't want to be seen."

"They have it all wrong."

I shrug.

"Maybe so. Tell me about her."

"Me?"

"You knew her back at Northwestern. You said you dated her once. I've been told you knew her a lot better than that."

"Who told you that?" he says testily. He's beginning not to like this conversation.

"Diana Burley. You saw her yesterday at the chapel. She tried to throw acid in Heather's face."

"A crazy woman."

"Six years ago you and Heather were close. Then she dumped you to go after Diana Burley's husband."

"Okay, so I knew her. And yeah, we were very close. But that was a long time ago and she didn't dump me. I walked away from a lousy situation."

"Last week at the Concord Inn was not a long time ago, Seth."

That brings him up short.

"What are you doing here, Mr. Bernardi?"

"Trying to get to the truth about Heather Leeds death," I say.

Our eyes lock. The hospitality that he had shown me when I first walked in the door is gone. I see only hardness and I am beginning to feel a little uneasy.

"Buddy didn't kill her," he says.

"Perhaps not," I say. "But someone did. Until proved otherwise he's at the top of the list."

I don't look away. Neither does Seth and then he gets up from the table and crosses over to the kitchen counter. He hesitates, staring down at it and then he opens a drawer and takes something out and when he turns to look at me, he is holding a very sharp, very ugly kitchen knife with an eight inch blade.

"Buddy didn't kill her, Mr. Bernardi." Seth says. "I'm responsible and this is the knife that killed her."

CHAPTER TWENTY

This is an unexpected and unsettling development. I find myself thinking fast.

"Why are you threatening me with that ugly looking kitchen knife?" I ask loudly so that even Brubaker can't miss it.

Seth steps toward me. I try to squiggle back in my chair but I'm already up against the wall. And then I discover my fears are for naught. He lays the knife down on the table and resumes his seat. I stare at the knife, then at him.

"There's no blood," Seth says. "I scrubbed it clean."

"You want to tell me about it?" I ask, still edgy.

"Sure," he says.

He picks up a pack of Chesterfields from the table and taps one out, then lights it with a kitchen match.

"We started seeing each other about eight weeks ago. Her idea, not mine."

"But you went along with it."

"Sure. Why not? She was a fantastic piece of ass and she started coming on to me like I was fucking Errol Flynn. Besides, Buddy didn't have any problem with it."

"Buddy knew?"

"Sure he knew. Didn't I just tell you he was fed up with her?

Maybe he figured I'd take her off his hands."

"But after six years, after your aborted relationship at the university and the breakup—"

"Northwestern was still an open chapter in my life, Mr. Bernardi. Look, I was a shy nineteen year old freshman with all the experience of a choir boy, she was a twenty-two year old junior who'd been around the block a few times. It was exhilarating, at least for the first few weeks but then she started getting demanding. Be here, do that, don't do that. She'd make a date and then not show up. She was unpredictable. Euphoric highs, miserable lows. I thought if I did whatever she wanted we'd get along. Like I said, choirboy. Not smart enough to recognize manic depression when I saw it. And then one night she went too far. We went to that party at the Sig Ep house and she started playing up to this senior on the varsity basketball team and finally I just walked out and went back to the dorm. Enough was enough. The next day she was all peaches and cream and wanted to make up but by that time, I was onto her. I told her to go find another plaything. We had a screaming argument. She even threatened to kill me. That's when she took up with that Englsh professor."

"And all this time you and Buddy were working together, writing as a team—"

"Oh sure, and we were roommates. He kinda liked Heather. He told me I was crazy for breaking up with her but he didn't know her like I did. I really think he was about to make a move on her but then, like I said, she was seeing the professor and everybody knew it so he just backed off. A couple of months later the affair spilled out into the open. The professor got canned and Heather dropped out of school. I really thought that was the last I'd ever see of her."

"And then a year ago——" I let it hang.

"Yeah. A year ago we ran into her at a press party. She was working for Columbia and me and Buddy were doing Zorro. Next thing I knew Buddy was taking her out and getting all serious and I warned him. I said, she's not for you, Bud, but he wouldn't listen and one weekend they sneaked off to Vegas and came back Mr. and Mrs. And then it started."

"What started?"

"The looks, the remarks, the phone calls for Buddy when she knew he wasn't there but I was. Subtle at first, then not so subtle, like she never met a man like me and she spoiled everything back at school and if she had to do over—that kind of crap. Coming on to me, even though she's now married to my best friend. Yeah, it took me a while but I finally figured what she was up to. She wanted to break us up."

"You're sure about that?"

"Oh, yeah, like I was so talented and why was I letting a second rate hack drag me down and I'm never going to make it big with Buddy hanging onto my coattails."

I shake my head,

"But why would she do it?"

Seth almost laughs.

"Why do dogs chase cars? Because they can."

"But you and Buddy were on the verge of making it big, Seth. This is a community property state. If Buddy got rich so did she."

" I don't think she cared. It was an obsession. Call it jealousy, revenge, wounded pride. She wouldn't let it go. That's what the big fight was about in the parking lot. I told her I never wanted to see her again."

"And yet?" I say.

"Yeah. And yet," Seth says bitterly. "It was the night she died. She and Buddy had had a fight. Mean, nasty. The kind you can never forget about or take back. She'd told Buddy I'd been bad mouthing him behind his back, that I wanted out of the partnership, that I'd found somebody else to work with who was a lot better writer. All of it lies and Buddy didn't believe any of it. Not for a second. Buddy told her he was going out for a few hours. When he returned he wanted to find her gone. Her possessions, her clothes, everything. Gone. Out of his life for good."

"You paint a pretty brutal picture," I say.

"Wait. It gets worse," he says, tapping out another cigarette and lighting it with the remains of the first one. "It was past ten, maybe even ten-thirty when she comes knocking on my door. As soon as I see it's her, I tell her to go away but she starts crying and tells me Buddy hit her, not once but several times. I'm a sucker for tears. I let her in. Big mistake. She starts in again, about how much she loves me and there's never really been anyone else. She wants me to run away with her, start a new life somewhere. Bullshit. All bullshit. I tell her no and tell her to get out. By now she's shaking all over, tears running down her face. She says she needs to take a pill and goes in the kitchen to get a glass of water. When she comes back she's calmer. Now she apologizes, says she understands, just wants to get her things and she'll leave.

"Get her things? What things?" I ask.

"A suitcase full of old clothes. Stuff she wore when she was skinny. Too good to throw away, she told me. Every unit has a basement storage area so that's where I was keeping it for her."

"Why didn't she keep it at her house?"

"Search me," Seth says. "Why did Heather do anything? It was easier to go along than argue with her. Anyway, we go down into the basement to my storage space. I keep my own empty suitcases there along with my bicycle which I no longer ride. an old coffee table and three or four cartons of books I don't have room for here in the apartment. Anyway I wade in to get this little green suitcase of hers and then I hear a noise behind me and I look back and there she is, right behind me, the knife in her hand raised high above her head and a look in her eyes I can't begin to describe.

She's like something out of Dante's 'Inferno" and as she slashes the knife down she screams,"You bastard!" I duck and she misses me by an inch and I grab her wrist and we struggle for control of the knife. I'm telling you, she fought like a banshee. Spitting in my face, trying to bite me, all the while cursing me out, undiluted hatred, that's what it was. And then we stumbled over the bike and we both went down and I heard her gasp and then go limp and when I was able to get to my feet, she was just lying there, eyes wide open, the knife plunged into her chest and blood everywhere."

"Self defense," I say.

"Maybe. I guess so. If I'd been thinking straight I'd have realized it right away but I think I was in shock. I'd been so angry, so fed up with her that a piece of me had wanted her dead and there I was, confused and riddled with doubt. I sat down on a nearby steamer trunk and just stared at her body. There was no question she was dead. Those wide open blank eyes seeing nothing. Her white cashmere sweater stained scarlet with her blood. I knew I had to do something but I didn't know what."

His voice is starting to catch and his eyes are moist and he is undergoing the torture of the damned reliving those minutes when his life suddenly careened out of control.

"That's when I got the idea of taking her body over to her office and making it look like that's where she was killed."

"Pretty difficult thing to accomplish by yourself, Seth," I say.

He glares at me angrily.

"Not hard at all. Just had to get her into my car and get her over there. That time of night there was nobody around. I had her keys to get into the building and into the office."

"No problem handling the body?"

"I told you no. She didn't weigh much. No, no problem."

"Awkward, though."

"Yeah, I suppose."

"What did you wrap her in?"

"Wrap her in? What for?"

"To transport her. A sheet or a blanket? Something like that?"

Again he flares impatiently.

"What the hell difference does it make? I told you I killed her. How about if we just get the cops in here and get this over with?"

I stare at him. He's lying and there's a look of desperation about him.

The phone rings, the sharp jangle cutting through the silence like a razor. We are both momentarily startled. Seth looks over at the phone which hangs from the kitchen wall. It rings again. Seth takes a furtive glance at his watch.

"Aren't you going to answer it?" I ask.

"No. Let it ring," he says.

I start to get to my feet.

"I'll get it," I say.

"No!" Seth says sharply. "I'll get rid of them."

He goes to the phone and lifts the receiver.

"Hello... Oh, yeah, hi... Yeah, I just realized. I fell asleep... No, not a good idea. Let's skip tonight, We'll make it tomorrow morning. Nine o'clock...No,nothing's wrong. Why should anything be wrong?... I told you, I overslept...Tomorrow, Buddy. Forget this evening. I'll see you around nine," With that he hangs up. "I was supposed to be at his place twenty minutes ago to work on the script."

"Does he know?"

"Know what?"

"That you killed his wife?"

"No. Of course not. How could he know?"

"You could have told him."

"Well, I didn't."

At that moment, the apartment door bell rings. I get to my feet. "Who's that?" Seth asks.

"The police," I tell him. I start for the door but first I pick up the knife from the kitchen table. I've learned that Seth is not homicidal. I'm not quite sure whether he's suicidal.

i open the door. Brubaker and a uniformed officer named Henry step inside.

"You get it?" I ask.

"Every word," he replies. "Where is he?"

"The kitchen," I say.

He nods, eying the kitchen knife.

"Cute," he says.

Seth is sitting at the kitchen table, head in his hands. He looks up when Brubaker enters the room. His eyes are red. He's been crying.

"Are you all right, Mr. Donnelley?" Brubaker asks. Seth nods. "Your conversation with Mr. Bernardi, it was recorded. Do you understand?" He nods again. "The place where you and the victim struggled. Could you show us where that was?"

"Sure," he says and gets up from the table. He leads Brubaker and me out of the apartment. Officer Henry stays behind. We go down the hallway to a set of stairs that leads to the lower level. Seth flips the switch at the top of the steps and a grid of fluorescent lights illuminates the basement. We descend to the basement floor and Seth turns right and leads us to the far side of the huge room where there are several dozen partitioned areas, each one marked with an apartment number. We stop in front of 2D. I look down at the floor. It looks reasonably clean but you can still see where the blood had pooled and where Seth had apparently tried to eradicate all traces of it. Brubaker has seen it too. He pulls his radio from his pocket.

"Henry?"

"Here, Sarge," comes a crackling voice from Brubaker's two-way.

"Roust the lab guys. Get 'em over here. We need everybody. And send another squad car."

"Yes, sir." Henry crackles out.

"I tried to clean things up," Seth says,

"I can see that," Brubaker replies. "Okay, now, Mr. Donnelley, show me how it happened."

Seth mimes the action, ending up on the floor atop Heather. When he stood up, he reiterates, she was lying there wide-eyed, the knife protruding from her chest. Blood was everywhere. He swears again that it was an accident and all the while Seth is recreating the death scene I have my eye on that little green leather suitcase of Heather's. I have a suspicion it may contain a great deal more than ill-fitting clothes.

I suggest to Brubaker that he confiscate the suitcase and for a moment he doesn't get it. When I remind him that it belonged to Heather, the light dawns but he says he can't touch it until the photographer records the scene and the print guy dusts for prints. Again he takes out his radio and this time orders Henry down here to babysit the crime scene until forensics arrives. We head back upstairs, passing Henry on the way.

Then, as we step into the corridor, the elevator doors open and Buddy Lovejoy emerges. He looks at us with a puzzled expression.

"What the hell's going on here?" he asks.

Before either Brubaker or I can respond, a look passes between he and Seth who speaks up quickly.

"It's okay, Buddy. I told them everything that happened between me and Heather. No reason for you to get involved,"

Brubaker and I share a knowing look. But of course by now we have figured out that Buddy IS involved, right up to his silly-looking comb over.

CHAPTER TWENTY-ONE

"I was walking in the door when the phone rang. When I answered it Seth was on the other end of the line," Buddy says.

"Stop it, Buddy," Seth says anxiously. "I don't need you to lie for me."

Buddy's leaning forward in an easy chair, calm and thoughtful. Seth is sitting on the sofa next to Brubaker. I'm standing over by the fireplace while Officer Henry is watchful by the door.

"Let him talk, Mr. Donnelley," Brubaker says.

"He's lying. He doesn't know what he's talking about."

"Look, either you shut up or we take you outside and throw you in the back of a squad car while we get Mr. Lovejoy's statement. Now which is it?"

Seth starts to say something, then just looks away.

"Go on, Mr. Lovejoy," Brubaker says.

Buddy nods, lighting up a cigarette.

"Like I said, it was Seth on the phone and right away I knew he was upset. He told me what happened and he was choking back tears. I knew he was terrified. I told him to sit tight, do nothing, that I'd be there in twenty minutes. When I arrived he was sitting on the bottom step of the staircase just staring straight ahead. I could see Heather's body over by the storage area. Even at that distance, she was a gory sight. I walked over and looked around and I got a chill, the way her eyes were wide open staring into nothingness. Of course I believed him. It was self-defense. It was also an accident but he'd told me about the fight at the motel parking lot. When you threaten to kill someone, even if it's meaningless, and then that person ends up dead at your hands, well, by me you've got a major problem."

He looks at Brubaker, then over at me.

"No witnesses to the truth, forensics that point directly to a violent murder, what would you do, Mr. Bernardi?"

The question's rhetorical. He doesn't really expect an answer, so I don't voice one.

"Seth wanted to call the police," Buddy continues. "I wouldn't let him. No offense, Sergeant, but the system is rigid and lacking in curiosity. An overworked police force looking for an easy collar, a zealous district attorney who cares only about his conviction record and Seth could end up doing life at San Quentin."

"I could take offense at that," Brubaker says.

"Understood," Buddy says, "but you know the statistics as well as I do. Miscarriages of justice happen all the time. I was determined Seth was not going to be one of them. So we wrapped her in a sheet and after I pulled up to the rear door by the dumpsters, we loaded her into my trunk and drove to her office. It was just past two in the morning. There was no one around. We used her key to get her into the office and placed her body behind her desk. Then I typed that note that pointed the finger at someone involved with the studio."

He looks over at me.

"It could have referred to a dozen different people, Mr. Bernardi," he says. "I'm sorry the police fixated on your friend."

I shrug noncommittally.

"Looking back, I realize we did a sloppy job. A rookie just out of the academy could have figured out the scene was staged but we had to work fast. We went back to the basement and tried to clean up. Same thing. Sloppy job. Not enough time. We had to hope nobody came poking around the basement any time soon."

He falls silent, taking a drag on his cigarette.

"Is that it?" Brubaker asks.

"Pretty much. For months, maybe as far back as Northwestern, Heather tried to break us up. Crazy bitch. As if she could. When we were like six or seven, me and Seth were out sledding. Seth lost control and fell off his sled and fell, spraining his ankle. I put him on his sled and tugged him two miles to the hospital. In junior high this guy named Rolf tried beating me up at the bus stop. The next morning Seth came with me, blackened the guy's eye and knocked out two of his teeth. It was like that ever since I can remember. Oh, she hated it, the way we stuck together. And worse, we both had spurned her and her ego couldn't handle it. It would be ironic if she accomplished in death what she couldn't do in life."

"That's not up to me, Mr. Lovejoy," Brubaker says. "The D.A. will have something to say about it, maybe a jury if it goes that far. Meanwhile, you're both under arrest. For the time being the charges are tampering with a crime scene and lying to an officer of the law. On your feet."

An hour later we're at the Hollywood Division, watching as Buddy and Seth go through booking. As soon as they are processed they'll be transported to the county jail where they will spend the night before appearing in court early in the morning. If they haven't retained counsel, a Public Defender will represent them at their bail hearing. Since the charges on which they're being held are pretty low level, it's likely they'll be on the street by noon. I don't figure either one of them for a flight risk and if they have any brains they'll find themselves a top criminal attorney immediately.

I check my watch. Ten forty-five. I should be getting home. Bunny doesn't exactly worry about me but she feels more secure knowing where I am. I'm about to head out when one of the lab guys enters the booking facility carrying the green leather suitcase and brings it to Brubaker.

"You wanted this, Sarge?" he says.

"Yeah, thanks, Pete," Brubaker says, taking it from him. "You get anything?"

"Nope. Lots of dust, no prints."

"Did you check the contents?"

"It's locked. No key."

"Okay, thanks."

As the lab guy walks away, Brubaker looks at me with a half smile on his face.

"Shall we take this to my office?" he asks.

"Let's," I reply.

With the suitcase sitting atop his desk, Brubaker rummages around in one of his desk drawers and extracts a pair of scissors. He jams them into one of the two locks and pries it open, then repeats the process with its counterpart. When he flips open the lid, he finds the suitcase stuffed with women's clothes: dresses, sweaters, skirts and what the Victorians used to call 'unmentionables'. We're momentarily disappointed that we find nothing else but Brubaker is not so easily thwarted. He starts to run his hand around the perimeter of the suitcase interior and after a few seconds, his hand freezes in place. He looks at me with a knowing grin and once again applying the scissors, cuts away the fabric lining. Tucked away out of sight he locates a zippered leather pouch which he pulls out into the open. He dumps the suitcase onto the floor, then unzips the pouch and pours its contents onto his desk.

Several dozen glittery diamonds stare up at us from Brubaker's blotter pad. I don't need an appraiser to tell me these are top grade. I look across the desk at the sergeant.

"What do you think these are worth, Sarge? Around nine million?" I ask.

"Give or take a buck or two," Brubaker responds with a smile.

"Travis Wright isn't going to be happy about this," I say.

"I'm sure he won't."

"By the way, Sarge," I ask, "where is Wright these days?"

"San Diego. The SDPD came and got him yesterday. When they get through processing him for parole violations, he'll be headed back to the state prison at Tehachapi to finish out his sentence."

"So close and yet so far," I wax philosophical. "So what happens to the diamonds?"

"Got no idea," Brubaker says. "I'm going to hand them over to the D.A. I got a feeling he's going to ship them down to the D.A. in San Diego. Either way, they're not our problem." He furrows his brow. "You know, Joe, you look like like hell. Why don't you go home and get some sleep?"

I have to smile. It's the first time he's called me by my first name. Brubaker seems to be defrosting.

"Thanks, Willie, I believe I will," I say.

Glowering, he shakes his head, waving me away, but there's a smile on his lips.

Despite Bunny's best efforts to the contrary I am determined to sleep Sunday away. Unbeknownst to me, she has invited Dex and Cissy over for Sunday supper. I am grateful they can't make it. I accept Dex's fulsome gratitude for all my help and his sincere regret that he has to turn down our gracious invitation but Cissy has run down a propmaster who worked for Mack Sennett for almost a dozen years. He's 89 years old, lives in Barstow and Cissy wants to pump him for everything he knows before he flies off to that big drive-in theater in the sky. If I thought that would free me up for hammock time on the back patio, I was severely mistaken. Bunny and Yvette manage to finagle me into an excursion to the Malibu

Pier which I am sure I will enjoy once I get there. Meanwhile these old bones think wistfully about my hammock, a good book, and the one cold Coors I allow myself each evening with Bunny's blessing.

On Monday morning, I am up early to drive to Paramount for my farewell to the gang and my welcome back to Lila. As advertised she is hobbling around on crutches and making a good job of it. I borrow a desk and a phone in the production office and make my obligatory call to Louella Parsons. A promise is a promise. I tell her that the police are investigating the possibility of accidental death and there are two individuals involved although I am not at liberty to give their names. I pass along Brubaker's name and phone number. He won't be happy to get her call but like any good publicity guy, I keep my word no matter what. Now Louella is Willie's problem.

I amble down to the set on Stage 7, say my goodbyes to Frank Capra and Peter Falk and get a big hug from Bette Davis. Even Glenn Ford shakes my hand and wishes me well. After that, I have only one more thing on my plate.

I find Noel Peabody, the manager of studio operations, on the phone in the security office. To date he has found no one on staff willing to step into Al Rhinehalter's shoes. Amend that. He has found no one who actually wants to work for Noel Peabody. The guy on the other end of the line fits that category and although Peabody is throwing around some pretty fancy numbers for a security chief, he's getting nowhere. Finally he hangs up in disgust which is when he notices me standing in his open doorway.

"I thought you were gone," Peabody says.

"Not yet gone, not yet forgotten," I reply cheerily.

"Well, I'm sorry but I have no time for you right now, Mr. Bernardi."

"Oh, I understand. It must be difficult finding someone to replace a man of the caliber of Al Rhinehalter."

He glares at me silently and then consults a clipboard on his desk. He starts to dial a number.

"I just stopped by to give you a heads up," I say.

He freezes in mid-dial.

"About what?"

"You know that I've been working with the police on the Heather Leeds murder."

"I'd heard that," he says.

Did I say that I do not lie and that I keep my word no matter what? Professionally I am a model of honesty and decorum but Noel Peabody is outside the boundaries of my profession. Happily so.

"Were you aware that Heather Leeds kept a diary?" I ask, knowing that almost certainly she did not.

"What's that to me?" Peabody asks.

"Well, the police have found at least a dozen entries describing her efforts to cause trouble at the studio, mostly aimed at getting Chick MacGruder, Glenn Ford's publicity guy, booted off the lot. She felt she could make accusations against MacGruder and Al Rhinehalter and anyone else she chose because the guy who ran studio operations was a gutless weasel who would do anything just to keep the peace including firing a valuable employee for absolutely no good reason. Her words, not mine, but I believe she was talking about you, Noel."

"I did nothing wrong," Peabody fumes.

"Well, that's good to hear. You can tell it to Al Rhinehalter's lawyer who should be coming by any time this morning. By the way, did you know that because you fired him, Al's wife left him taking his two kids with her. "

"No, I didn't know," Peabody says, his skin fading from apoplectic pink to sheet white.

"She's also threatening divorce which is why Al's lawyer couldn't wait to take his case. I know the guy and he's a greedy shark. But maybe the studio will back you up. I can't think why but there might be a reason. Do you have any close relatives in top management?"

"I was just doing my job," Peabody whines.

"And badly," I say. "I suppose maybe if you apologized—"

"I could do that."

"—and offered him his job back—"

"That,too."

"— at the kind of money you were offering on the phone when I walked in."

"Of course."

"Why don't you give him a call while I'm here. I might even be able to head off his lawyer before he gets to you."

"Yes. A good thought, Mr. Bernardi."

He refers to a studio directory and quickly dials a number. I busy myself checking out the fire and safety regulations posted on a nearby wall. Before he's connected, I turn to him.

"And one other thing. You might ask him for a phone number where you can reach his wife and explain that the whole misunderstanding was based on a screw up on your part."

"Right. I'll do that," he says and then into the phone, ebulliently, "Al, Noel Peabody here. Glad I caught you in."

Pleased with myself, I slip out the door into the crisp morning air, my good deed for the day over and done with. Now it's back to the office and another go round with Bertha who is determined to ship me east for the pool parlor movie. I start to cross the street to the spot where my car is parked when I find a familiar figure walking toward me.

"Joe!" he calls out.

"Mike!" I respond and we greet each other warmly. Myron McCormack is one of those actors who is always working, everyone knows his face and no one knows his name. I met him several years ago on the set of "No Time for Sergeants". He played the chief sergeant that Andy Griffith had no time for.

"What have you been doing with yourself?" I ask.

"Just did a few days on a shoot in New York. Paul Newman's new picture."

"The Hustler," I say.

"Right."

"How is it?"

"It's going to be great but I am sure as hell glad to be out of New York."

"What's the problem?"

"Snow, ice, sleet, 20 degree temperatures and there was a huge storm heading in when I was heading out. They're predicting eight to twelve inches by tomorrow morning. Well, nice seeing you, Joe." And with a wave he walks off.

I watch him go. There are some who consider New York City a winter wonderland. I am not one of them. When snow hits, it becomes grey, grim, cold and nasty. The Indians were right to sell it for twenty four dollars.

My thoughts turn to my old friend, Lila James, hobbling around on those crutches, without an assistant to help lighten her burden in publicizing this movie. Well, I'm no Heather Leeds but nothing says I can't help out a little for an old buddy for a day or two or eight or maybe even twenty.

I start to retrace my steps to Stage 7 where Frank Capra, headaches and all, continues to referee the battle of the sexes.

The End

AUTHOR'S NOTE

"A Pocketful of Miracles" was not the rousing success everyone had hoped for. Had the stars aligned perfectly, it might have been. The sneak previews were fabulous. Viewers comments were nearly one hundred percent favorable but something happened between previews and release. The film opened in over six hundred theaters simultaneously over the Christmas holiday and a month later it was nothing but a memory. Capra felt that in many ways this version of the Apple Annie story was superior to 'Lady for a Day' but for the most part the critics disagreed as did the moviegoing public. It proved to be Capra's last film and one of only three that did not show a profit. It was Ann-Margaret's first film appearance and Thomas Mitchell's last. Following this film, Mitchell appeared on stage as a scruffy police lieutenant named Columbo, a role later transferred to television by playwrights Richard Levinson and William Link and made famous by Mitchell's co-star, Peter Falk. As for Falk, for the second year in a row he was nominated for Best Supporting Actor by the Academy and for the second time, he lost. Several sources were utilized in researching the making of "Pocketful of Miracles" but by far, the most valuable was "The Name Above the Title", Frank Capra's captivating autobiography, must reading for anyone interested in the history of American filmmaking. As for this volume in the Hollywood Murder Mysteries series, the usual caveats apply. This is a work of fiction and incidents and dialogue involving real life individuals are all products of the author's imagination and nothing written here is intended to demean or disparage.

ABOUT THE AUTHOR

Peter S. Fischer is a former television writer-producer who currently lives in the Monterey Bay area of Central California. He is a co-creator of "Murder, She Wrote" for which he wrote over 40 scripts. Among his other credits are a dozen "Columbo" episodes and a season helming "Ellery Queen." He has also written and produced several TV mini-series and Movies of the Week. In 1985 he was awarded an Edgar by the Mystery Writers of America. In addition to four EMMY nominations, two Golden Globe Awards for Best TV series, and an Anthony Award from the Boucheron, he has received the IBPA award for the Best Mystery Novel of the Year, a Bronze Medal from the Independent Publishers Association and an Honorable Mention from the San Francisco Festival for his first novel.

THE HOLLYWOOD MURDER MYSTERIES

www.petersfischer.com

PRAISE FOR THE HOLLYWOOD MURDER MYSTERIES

Jezebel in Blue Satin

In this stylish homage to the detective novels of Hollywood's Golden Age, a press agent stumbles across a starlet's dead body and into the seamy world of scheming players and morally bankrupt movie moguls.....An enjoyable fast-paced whodunit from opening act to final curtain.

—Kirkus Reviews

Fans of golden era Hollywood, snappy patter and Raymond Chandler will find much to like in Peter Fischer's murder mystery series, all centered on old school studio flak, Joe Bernardi, a happy-go-lucky war veteran who finds himself immersed in tough situations.....The series fills a niche that's been superseded by explosions and violence in too much of popular culture and even though jt's a world where men are men and women are dames, its glimpses at an era where the facade of glamour and sophistication hid an uglier truth are still fun to revisit.

—2012 San Francisco Book Festival, Honorable Mention

Jezebel in Blue Satin, set in 1947, finds movie studio publicist Joe Bernardi slumming it at a third rate motion picture house running on large egos and little talent. When the ingenue from the film referenced in the title winds up dead, can Joe uncover the killer before he loses his own life? Fischer makes an effortless transition from TV mystery to page turner, breathing new life into the film noir hard boiled detective tropes. Although not a professional sleuth, Joe's evolution from everyman into amateur private eye makes sense; any bad publicity can cost him his job so he has to get to the bottom of things.

—ForeWord Review

We Don't Need No Stinking Badges

A thrilling mystery packed with Hollywood glamour, intrigue and murder, set in 1948 Mexico.....Although the story features many famous faces (Humphrey Bogart, director John Huston, actor Walter Huston and novelist B. Traven, to name a few), the plot smartly focuses on those behind the scenes. The big names aren't used as gimmicks—they're merely planets for the story to rotate around. Joe Bernardi is the star of the show and this fictional tale in a real life setting (the actual set of 'Treasure of the Sierra Madre' was also fraught with problems) works well in Fischer's sure hands....A smart clever Mexican mystery.

– Kirkus Reviews

A former TV writer continues his old-time Hollywood mystery series, seamlessly interweaving fact and fiction in this drama that goes beyond the genre's cliches. "We Don't Need No Stinking Badges" again transports readers to post WWII Tinseltown inhabited by cinema publicist Joe Bernardi... Strong characterization propels this book. Toward the end the crosses and double-crosses become confusing, as seemingly inconsequential things such as a dead woman who was only mentioned in passing in the beginning now become matters on which the whole plot turns (but) such minor hiccups should not deter mystery lovers, Hollywood buffs or anyone who adores a good yarn.

– ForeWord Review

Peter S. Fischer has done it again—he has put me in a time machine and landed me in 1948. He has written a fast paced murder mystery that will have you up into the wee hours reading. If you love old movies, then this is the book for you.

– My Shelf. Com

This is a complex, well-crafted whodunit all on its own. There's plenty of action and adventure woven around the mystery and the characters are fully fashioned. The addition of the period piece of the 1940's filmmaking and the inclusion of big name stars as supporting characters is the whipped cream and cherry on top. It all comes together to make an engaging and fun read.

– Nyssa, Amazon Customer Review

Love Has Nothing to Do With It

Fischer's experience shows in 'Love Has Nothing To Do With It', an homage to film noir and the hard-boiled detective novel. The story is complicated... but Fischer never loses the thread. The story is intricate enough to be intriguing but not baffling....Joe Bernardi's swagger is authentic and entertaining. Overall he is a likable sleuth with the dogged determination to uncover the truth.... While the outcome of the murder is an unknown until the final pages of the current title, we do know that Joe Bernardi will survive at least until 1950, when further adventures await him in the forthcoming 'Everybody Wants an Oscar'.

—Clarion Review

A stylized, suspenseful Hollywood whodunit set in 1949....Goes down smooth for murder-mystery fans and Old Hollywood junkies.

—Kirkus Review

The Hollywood Murder Mysteries just might make a great Hallmark series. Let's give this book: The envelope please: FIVE GOLDEN OSCARS.

—Samfreene, Amazon Customer Review

The writing is fantastic and, for me, the topic was a true escape into our past entertainment world. Expect it to be quite different from today's! But that's why readers will enjoy visiting Hollywood as it was in the past. A marvelous concept that hopefully will continue up into the 60s and beyond. Loved it!

—GABixlerReviews

The Unkindness of Strangers

*Winner of the Benjamin Franklin Award
for Best Mystery Book of 2012
by the Independent Book Publisher's Association.*

Book One—1947
JEZEBEL IN BLUE SATIN

WWII is over and Joe Bernardi has just returned home after three years as a war correspondent in Europe. Married in the heat of passion three weeks before he shipped out, he has come home to find his wife Lydia a complete stranger. It's not long before Lydia is off to Reno for a quickie divorce which Joe won't accept. Meanwhile he's been hired as a publicist by third rate movie studio, Continental Pictures. One night he enters a darkened sound stage only to discover the dead body of ambitious, would-be actress Maggie Baumann. When the police investigate, they immediately zero in on Joe as the perp. Short on evidence they attempt to frame him and almost succeed. Who really killed Maggie? Was it the over-the-hill actress trying for a comeback? Or the talentless director with delusions of grandeur? Or maybe it was the hapless leading man whose career is headed nowhere now that the "real stars" are coming back from the war. There is no shortage of suspects as the story speeds along to its exciting and unexpected conclusion.

Book Two—1948
WE DON'T NEED NO STINKING BADGES

Joe Bernardi is the new guy in Warner Brothers' Press Department so it's no surprise when Joe is given the unenviable task of flying to Tampico, Mexico, to bail Humphrey Bogart out of jail without the world learning about it. When he arrives he discovers that Bogie isn't the problem. So-called accidents are occurring daily on

Available in paperback or Kindle editions from Amazon.com

the set, slowing down the filming of "The Treasure of the Sierra Madre" and putting tempers on edge. Everyone knows who's behind the sabotage. It's the local Jefe who has a finger in every illegal pie. But suddenly the intrigue widens and the murder of one of the actors throws the company into turmoil. Day by day, Joe finds himself drawn into a dangerous web of deceit, dupliciity and blackmail that nearly costs him his life.

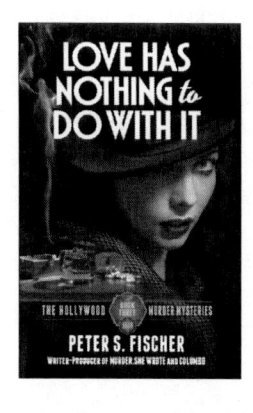

Book Three—1949
LOVE HAS NOTHING TO DO WITH IT

Joe Bernardi's ex-wife Lydia is in big, big trouble. On a Sunday evening around midnight she is seen running from the plush offices of her one- time lover, Tyler Banks. She disappears into the night leaving Banks behind, dead on the carpet with a bullet in his head. Convinced that she is innocent, Joe enlists the help of his pal, lawyer Ray Giordano, and bail bondsman Mick Clausen, to prove Lydia's innocence, even as his assignment to publicize Jimmy Cagney's comeback movie for Warner's threatens to take up all of his time. Who really pulled the trigger that night? Was it the millionaire whose influence reached into City Hall? Or the not so grieving widow finally freed from a loveless marriage. Maybe it was the partner who wanted the business all to himself as well as the new widow. And what about the mysterious envelope, the one that disappeared and everyone claims never existed? Is it the key to the killer's identity and what is the secret that has been kept hidden for the past forty years?

Available in paperback or Kindle editions from Amazon.com

Book Four—1950
EVERYBODY WANTS AN OSCAR

After six long years Joe Bernardi's novel is at last finished and has been shipped to a publisher. But even as he awaits news, fingers crossed for luck, things are heating up at the studio. Soon production will begin on Tennessee Williams' "The Glass Menagerie" and Jane Wyman has her sights set on a second consecutive Academy Award. Jack Warner has just signed Gertrude Lawrence for the pivotal role of Amanda and is positive that the Oscar will go to Gertie. And meanwhile Eleanor Parker, who has gotten rave reviews for a prison picture called "Caged" is sure that 1950 is her year to take home the trophy. Faced with three very talented ladies all vying for his best efforts, Joe is resigned to performing a monumental juggling act. Thank God he has nothing else to worry about or at least that was the case until his agent informed him that a screenplay is floating around Hollywood that is a dead ringer for his newly completed novel. Will the ladies be forced to take a back seat as Joe goes after the thief that has stolen his work, his good name and six years of his life?

Book Five—1951
THE UNKINDNESS OF STRANGERS

Warner Brothers is getting it from all sides and Joe Bernardi seems to be everybody's favorite target. "A Streetcar Named Desire" is unproducible, they say. Too violent, too seedy, too sexy, too controversial and what's worse, it's being directed by that well-known pinko, Elia Kazan. To make matters worse, the country's number one

Available in paperback or Kindle editions from Amazon.com

hate monger, newspaper columnist Bryce Tremayne, is coming after Kazan with a vengeance and nothing Joe can do or say will stop him. A vicious expose column is set to run in every Hearst paper in the nation on the upcoming Sunday but a funny thing happens Friday night. Tremayne is found in a compromising condition behind the wheel of his car, a bullet hole between his eyes. Come Sunday and the scurrilous attack on Kazan does not appear. Rumors fly. Kazan is suspected but he's not the only one with a motive. Consider:

    Elvira Tremayne, the unloved widow. Did Tremayne slug her one time too many?

    Hubbell Cox, the flunky whose homosexuality made him a target of derision.

    Willie Babbitt, the muscle. He does what he's told and what he's told to do is often unpleasant.

    Jenny Coughlin, Tremayne's private secretary. But how private and what was her secret agenda?

    Jed Tompkins, Elvira's father, a rich Texas cattle baron who had only contempt for his son-in-law.

    Boyd Larabee, the bookkeeper, hired by Tompkins to win Cox's confidence and report back anything he's learned.

    Annie Petrakis, studio makeup artist. Tremayne destroyed her lover. Has she returned the favor?

Book Six—1952
NICE GUYS FINISH DEAD

Ned Sharkey is a fugitive from mob revenge. For six years he's been successfully hiding out in the Los Angeles area while a $100,000 contract for his demise hangs over his head. But when Warner Brothers begins filming "The Winning Team", the story of Grover Cleveland Alexander, Ned can't resist showing up at the ballpark

Available in paperback or Kindle editions from Amazon.com

to reunite with his old pals from the Chicago Cubs of the early 40's who have cameo roles in the film. Big mistake. When Joe Bernardi, Warner Brothers publicity guy, inadvertently sends a press release and a photo of Ned to the Chicago papers, mysterious people from the Windy City suddenly appear and a day later at break of dawn, Ned's body is found sprawled atop the pitcher's mound. It appears that someone is a hundred thousand dollars richer. Or maybe not. Who is the 22 year old kid posing as a 50 year old former hockey star? And what about Gordo Gagliano, a mountain of a man, who is out to find Ned no matter who he has to hurt to succeed? And why did baggy pants comic Fats McCoy jump Ned and try to kill him in the pool parlor? It sure wasn't about money. Joe, riddled with guilt because the photo he sent to the newspapers may have led to Ned's death, finds himself embroiled in a dangerous game of who-dun-it that leads from L. A.'s Wrigley Field to an upscale sports bar in Altadena to the posh mansions of Pasadena and finally to the swank clubhouse of Santa Anita racetrack.

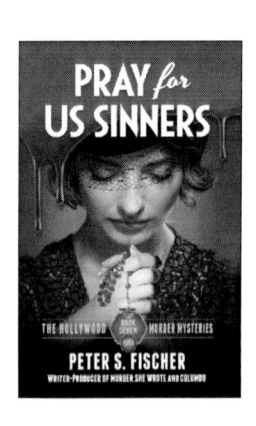

Book Seven—1953
PRAY FOR US SINNERS

Joe finds himself in Quebec but it's no vacation. Alfred Hitchcock is shooting a suspenseful thriller called "I Confess" and Montgomery Clift is playing a priest accused of murder. A marriage made in heaven? Hardly. They have been at loggerheads since Day One and to make matters worse their feud is spilling out into the newspapers. When vivacious Jeanne d'Arcy, the director of the Quebec Film Commisssion volunteers to help calm the troubled waters, Joe thinks his troubles are over but that was before Jeanne got into a violent spat with a former lover and suddenly found herself under arrest on a charge of first degree murder. Guilty or

Available in paperback or Kindle editions from Amazon.com

not guilty? Half the clues say she did it, the other half say she is being brilliantly framed. But by who? Fingers point to the crooked Gonsalvo brothers who have ties to the Buffalo mafia family and when Joe gets too close to the truth, someone tries to shut him up. . . permanently. With the Archbishop threatening to shut down the production in the wake of the scandal, Joe finds himself torn between two loyalties.

Book Eight—1954
HAS ANYBODY HERE SEEN WYCKHAM?

Everything was going smoothly on the set of "The High and the Mighty" until the cast and crew returned from lunch. With one exception. Wiley Wyckham, the bit player sitting in seat 24A on the airliner mockup, is among the missing, and without Wyckham sitting in place, director William Wellman cannot continue filming. A studio wide search is instituted. No Wyckham. A lookalike is hired that night, filming resumes the next day and still no Wyckham. Except that by this time, it's been discovered that Wyckham, a British actor, isn't really Wyckham at all but an imposter who may very well be an agent for the Russian government, The local police call in the FBI. The FBI calls in British counterintelligence. A manhunt for the missing actor ensues and Joe Bernardi, the picture's publicist, is right in the middle of the intrigue. Everyone's upset, especially John Wayne who is furious to learn that a possible Commie spy has been working in a picture he's producing and starring in. And then they find him . It's the dead of night on the Warner Brothers backlot and Wyckham is discovered hanging by his feet from a streetlamp, his body bloodied and tortured and very much dead. and pinned to his shirt is a piece of paper with the inscription "Sic Semper Proditor". (Thus to all traitors). Who was this man who had been posing as an obscure British actor? How did he smuggle

Available in paperback or Kindle editions from Amazon.com

himself into the country and what has he been up to? Has he been blackmailing an important higher-up in the film business and did the victim suddenly turn on him? Is the MI6 agent from London really who he says he is and what about the reporter from the London Daily Mail who seems to know all the right questions to ask as well all the right answers.

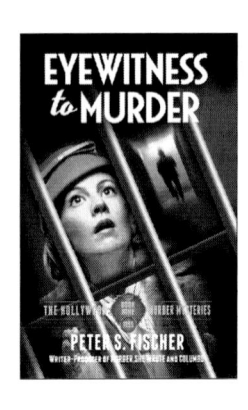

Book Nine—1955
EYEWITNESS TO MURDER

Go to New York? Not on your life. It's a lousy idea for a movie. A two year old black and white television drama? It hasn't got a prayer. This is the age of CinemaScope and VistaVision and stereophonic sound and yes, even 3-D. Burt Lancaster and Harold Hecht must be out of their minds to think they can make a hit movie out of "Marty". But then Joe Bernardi gets word that the love of his life, Bunny Lesher, is in New York and in trouble and so Joe changes his mind. He flies east to talk with the movie company and also to find Bunny and dig her out of whatever jam she's in. He finds that "Marty" is doing just fine but Bunny's jam is a lot bigger than he bargained for. She's being held by the police as an eyewitness to a brutal murder of a close friend in a lower Manhattan police station. Only a jammed pistol saved Bunny from being the killer's second victim and now she's in mortal danger because she knows what the man looks like and he's dead set on shutting her up. Permanently. Crooked lawyers, sleazy con artists and scheming businessmen cross Joe's path, determined to keep him from the truth and when the trail leads to the sports car racing circuit at Lime Rock in Connecticut, it's Joe who becomes the killer's prime target.

Available in paperback or Kindle editions from Amazon.com

Book Ten—1956
A DEADLY SHOOT IN TEXAS

Joe Bernardi's in Marfa, Texas, and he's not happy. The tarantulas are big enough to carry off the cattle , the wind's strong enough to blow Marfa into New Mexico, and the temperature would make the Congo seem chilly. A few miles out of town Warner Brothers is shooting Edna Ferber's "Giant" with a cast that includes Rock Hudson, Elizabeth Taylor and James Dean and Jack Warner is paying through the nose for Joe's expertise as a publicist. After two days in Marfa Joe finds himself in a lonely cantina around midnight, tossing back a few cold ones, and being seduced by a gorgeous student young enough to be his daughter. The flirtation goes nowhere but the next morning little Miss Coed is found dead . And there's a problem. The coroner says she died between eight and nine o'clock. Not so fast, says Joe, who saw her alive as late as one a.m. When he points this out to the County Sheriff, all hell breaks loose and Joe becomes the target of some pretty ornery people. Like the Coroner and the Sheriff as well as the most powerful rancher in the county, his arrogant no-good son and his two flunkies, a crooked lawyer and a grieving father looking for justice or revenge, either one will do. Will Joe expose the murderer before the murderer turns Joe into Texas road kill? Tune in.

Available in paperback or Kindle editions from Amazon.com

Book Eleven—1957
EVERYBODY LET'S ROCK

Big trouble is threatening the career of one of the country's hottest new teen idols and Joe Bernardi has been tapped to get to the bottom of it. Call it blackmail or call it extortion, a young woman claims that a nineteen year old Elvis Presley impregnated her and then helped arrange an abortion. There's a letter and a photo to back up her claim. Nonsense, says Colonel Tom Parker, Elvis's manager and mentor. It's a damned lie. Joe is not so sure but Parker is adamant. The accusation is a totally bogus and somebody's got to prove it. But no police can be involved and no lawyers. Just a whiff of scandal and the young man's future will be destroyed, even though he's in the midst of filming a movie that could turn him into a bona fide film star. Joe heads off to Memphis under the guise of promoting Elvis's new film and finds himself mired in a web of deceit and danger. Trusted by no one he searches in vain for the woman behind the letter, crossing paths with Sam Philips of Sun Records, a vindictive alcoholic newspaper reporter, a disgraced doctor with a seedy past, and a desperate con artist determined to keep Joe from learning the truth.

Available in paperback or Kindle editions from Amazon.com

Book Twelve—1958
A TOUCH OF HOMICIDE

It takes a lot to impress Joe Bernardi. He likes his job and the people he deals with but nobody is really special. Nobody, that is, except for Orson Welles, and when Avery Sterling, a bottom feeding excuse for a producer, asks Joe's help in saving Welles from an industry-wide smear campaign, Joe jumps in, heedless that the pool he has just plunged into is as dry as a vermouthless martini. A couple of days later, Sterling is found dead in his office and the police immediately zero in on two suspects—Joe who has an alibi and Welles who does not. Not to worry, there are plenty of clues at the crime scene including a blood stained monogrammed handkerchief, a rejected screenplay, a pair of black-rimmed reading glasses, a distinctive gold earring and petals from a white carnation. What's more, no less than four people threatened to kill him in front of witnesses. A case so simple a two-year old could solve it but the cop on the case is a dimwit whose uncle is on the staff of the police commissioner. Will Joe and Orson solve the case before one of them gets arrested for murder? Will an out-of-town hitman kill one or both of them? Worst of all, will Orson leave town leaving Joe holding the proverbial bag?

Available in paperback or Kindle editions from Amazon.com

Book Thirteen—1959
SOME LIKE 'EM DEAD

After thirteen years, the great chase is over and Joe Bernardi is marrying Bunny Lesher. After a brief weekend honeymoon, it'll be back to work for them both; Bunny at the Valley News where she has just been named Assistant Editor and Joe publicizing Billy Wilder's new movie, Some Like It Hot about two musicians hiding out from the mob in an all-girl band. It boasts a great script and a stellar cast that includes Tony Curtis, Jack Lemmon and Marilyn Monroe, so what could go wrong? Plenty and it starts with Shirley Davenport, Bunny's protege at the News, who has been assigned to the entertainment pages. To placate Bunny and against his better judgement Joe gives Shirley a press credential for the shoot and from the start, she is a destructive force, alienating cast and crew, including Billy Wilder, who does not suffer fools easily. Someone must have become really fed up with her because one misty morning a few hundred yards down the beach from the famed Hotel Del Coronado, Shirley's lifeless body, her head bashed in with a blunt instrument, is discovered by joggers. This after she'd been seen lunching with George Raft; hobnobbing with up and coming actor, Vic Steele; angrily ignoring fellow journalist Hank Kendall; exchanging jealous looks with hair stylist Evie MacPherson; and making a general nuisance of herself everywhere she turned. United Artists is aghast and so is Joe This murder has to be solved and removed from the front pages of America's newspapers as soon as possible or when it's released, this picture will be known as 'the murder movie', hardly a selling point for a rollicking comedy.

Available in paperback or Kindle editions from Amazon.com

Book Fourteen—1960
DEAD MEN PAY NO DEBTS

Among the hard and fast rules in Joe Bernardi's life is this one: Do not, under any circumstances, travel east during the winter months. In this way one avoids dealing with snow, ice, sleet, frostbite and pneumonia. Unfortunately he has had to break this rule and having done so, is paying the price. His novel 'A Family of Strangers' has been optioned for a major motion picture and he needs to fly east in January to meet with the talented director who has taken the option. Stuart Rosenberg, in the midst of directing "Murder Inc." an expose of the 1930's gang of killers for hire, has insisted Joe write the screenplay and he needs several days to guide Joe in the right direction. Reluctantly Joe agrees, a decision which he will quickly rue when he finds himself up to his belly button with drug dealers, loan sharks, Mafia hit men, wannabe Broadway stars and an up and coming New York actor named Peter Falk who may be on the verge of stardom. Someone has beaten drug dealer Gino Finucci to death and left his body in the basement of The Mudhole, an off-off-Broadway theater which is home to Amythyst Breen, a one time darling of Broadway struggling to find her way back to the top and also Jonathan Harker, slimy and ambitious, an actor caught in the grip of drug addiction even as he struggles to get that one lucky break that will propel him to stardom. Even as Joe fights to remain above the fray, he can feel himself being inexorably drawn into the intrigue of underworld vendettas culminating in a face to face confrontation with Carlo Gambino, the boss of bosses, and the most powerful Mafia chieftain in New York City.

Available in paperback or Kindle editions from Amazon.com

Book Fifteen—1961
APPLE ANNIE AND THE DUDE

Joe Bernardi is a sucker for a sad story and especially when it comes from an old pal like Lila James who, after years of trying, has landed a plum assignment as a movie publicist. Frank Capra has okayed her for his newest film, A Pocketful of Miracles, now shooting on the Paramount lot. Get this right and her little company has a big future which is when God intervenes by inflicting her with a broken leg which will put her out of commission for at least a couple of weeks. Enter Joe as Sir Galahad to save the day and fill in. A simple favor, you say? Not so fast. First he'll have to deal with Heather Leeds, Lila's assistant, an ambitious tart in the mold of Eve Harrington, a devious cupcake who makes enemies the way Betty Crocker makes biscuits. Making his job even more difficult are the on-set feuds between Bette Davis and Glenn Ford with Capra getting migraines trying to referee. And then the fun really starts as a mysterious woman named Claire Philby from Northwestern University shows up to give Heather an award and maybe something else she never bargained for. Who killed Heather Leeds? Was it Philby or maybe Heather's husband Buddy Lovejoy, a struggling television writer, or perhaps even his writing partner, Seth Donnelley. And what about Heather's ex-husband Travis Wright who was just released from prison and claims Heather owes him $9,000,000 which he left in her care? Of more concern to Joe is the shadow of suspicion that has fallen on Dexter Craven, an old friend from the Warner Bros. days. Good old Lila, she's lying peacefully in a hospital bed while Joe deals with a nest of vipers, one of which is a cold blooded killer, and a movie in the making which is being tattered by conflicting egos. It's enough to make a man long for happier days when he was slogging through muddy France at the tail-end of World War II.

Available in paperback or Kindle editions from Amazon.com

Book Sixteen—1962
'TILL DEATH US DO PART

Who would want to kill a sweet old guy like Mike O'Malley, the prop master on Universal's "To Kill a Mockingbird"? Nobody, but dead he is, the victim of a hit and run that looks more like deliberate murder than accidental death. More likely the killer was after Mike's grandson Rory who had earned the enmity of Hank Greb, a burly mean-spirited teamster as well as Wayne Daniels, a wannabe actor, who claims erroneously that Rory's carelessness caused his face to be disfigured. Is this any of Joe Bernardi's business? Not really but when he showed up on the Mockingbird set as a favor to his hospitalized partner, Bertha Bowles, to woo newcomer William Windom to join the Bowles & Bernardi management firm, Joe was sucked into the situation right up to his tonsils, something he had little time for since his first priority was handling publicity for 'Lilies of the Field', a Sidney Poitier film, shooting in Tucson. Meanwhile Joe, who longs to write a second novel, has become increasingly bored with working at movie promotion and publicity. A twist of fate finds him befriended by Truman Capote and by Harper Lee who, like Joe, is trying to find that elusive second novel. Both are huge admirers of Joe's highly praised first novel and vow to help Joe get it made as a motion picture, even as Joe tries to expose the truth about Mike O'Malleys' death.

Available in paperback or Kindle editions from Amazon.com

Book Seventeen—1963
CUE THE CROWS

How do you make a movie when the star of your dreams, eager to sign, is suddenly faced with a murder charge and could spend the rest of his life cooped up in San Quentin? Joe Bernardi, author, screenwriter and possibly a co-producer, has traveled north along the California coastline to Bodega Bay to hobnob with Rod Taylor who is filming Alfred Hitchcock's thriller, 'The Birds'. Rod is on the verge of signing the contract when a funny thing happens. The body of a young attractive redhead named Amanda Broome is found dead in the trunk of his Corvette. Taylor screams frame-up, even though Amanda has been stalking him for weeks and they had a violent and very public argument only hours before her body was discovered. Further filming of 'The Birds' is in jeopardy and so is the filming of Joe's movie based on his best-selling book. Looming large in the midst of this is Henrietta Boyle, a county attorney with gubernatorial ambitions and what better way to grease the path to the State House than to convict a famous movie star of homicide. But who else might have an interest in seeing Amanda dead? Perhaps her aunt, executrix of a trust fund which would have made Amanda a millionairess in a few short weeks. A definite possibility . Determined to prove Taylor innocent, Joe follows a trail that leads from a teen hangout in Palo Alto to the halls of academia to a posh country club where a triple A credit rating is the first requirement for membership. When a mysterious car tries to run Joe off the road into a deep and deadly crevasse in the hills above the Bay, he knows he's getting close to the truth but will the truth be revealed before Joe becomes buzzard bait?

Available in paperback or Kindle editions from Amazon.com

FUTURE TITLES IN THE SERIES:

Murder Aboard the Highland Rose
Ashes to Ashes
The Case of the Shaggy Stalker

Made in United States
North Haven, CT
07 March 2024

49634938R00145